DEBBIE MACOMBER

Orchard Valley Grooms

MIRA

ISBN-13: 978-0-7783-3020-2

Recycling programs for this product may not exist in your area.

Orchard Valley Grooms

Copyright © 2010 by Harlequin Books S.A.

The publisher acknowledges the copyright holder of the individual works as follows:

Valerie
Copyright © 1992 by Debbie Macomber

Stephanie
Copyright © 1992 by Debbie Macomber

For questions and comments about the quality of this book, please contact us at CustomerService@Harlequin.com.

www.MIRABooks.com

Printed in U.S.A.

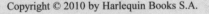

Midnight Sons

Alaska Skies
  (*Brides for Brothers* and
  The Marriage Risk)
Alaska Nights
  (*Daddy's Little Helper* and
  Because of the Baby)
Alaska Home
  (*Falling for Him,*
  Ending in Marriage and
  Midnight Sons and Daughters)

This Matter of Marriage
Montana
Thursdays at Eight
Between Friends
Changing Habits
Married in Seattle
  (*First Comes Marriage* and
  Wanted: Perfect Partner)
Right Next Door
  (*Father's Day* and
  The Courtship of Carol Sommars)
Wyoming Brides
  (*Denim and Diamonds* and
  The Wyoming Kid)
Fairy Tale Weddings
  (*Cindy and the Prince* and
  Some Kind of Wonderful)
The Man You'll Marry
  (*The First Man You Meet* and
  The Man You'll Marry)
Orchard Valley Grooms
  (*Valerie* and *Stephanie*)
Orchard Valley Brides
  (*Norah* and *Lone Star Lovin'*)
The Sooner the Better
An Engagement in Seattle
  (*Groom Wanted* and
  Bride Wanted)
Out of the Rain
  (*Marriage Wanted* and
  Laughter in the Rain)
Learning to Love
  (*Sugar and Spice* and *Love by Degree*)

You...Again
  (*Baby Blessed* and
  Yesterday Once More)
The Unexpected Husband
  (*Jury of His Peers* and
  Any Sunday)
Three Brides, No Groom
Love in Plain Sight
  (*Love 'n' Marriage* and
  Almost an Angel)
I Left My Heart
  (*A Friend or Two* and
  No Competition)
Marriage Between Friends
  (*White Lace and Promises* and
  Friends—And Then Some)
A Man's Heart
  (*The Way to a Man's Heart*
  and *Hasty Wedding*)
North to Alaska
  (*That Wintry Feeling* and
  Borrowed Dreams)
On a Clear Day
  (*Starlight* and
  Promise Me Forever)
To Love and Protect
  (*Shadow Chasing* and
  For All My Tomorrows)
Home in Seattle
  (*The Playboy and the Widow*
  and *Fallen Angel*)
Together Again
  (*The Trouble with Caasi* and
  Reflections of Yesterday)
The Reluctant Groom
  (*All Things Considered*
  and *Almost Paradise*)
A Real Prince
  (*The Bachelor Prince*
  and *Yesterday's Hero*)
Private Paradise
  (in *That Summer Place*)

Debbie Macomber's
  Cedar Cove Cookbook
Debbie Macomber's
  Christmas Cookbook

CONTENTS

VALERIE

To all the Seahawks 12s

One

"Norah? Is that you?" Valerie Bloomfield's voice rose expectantly. She'd been trying to reach her sister for the past hour with no success.

"Valerie, where are you?"

"I'm on a layover in Chicago." She glanced around the departure lounge and surveyed the other passengers. "How's Dad?"

Norah hesitated, and that slight pause sent Valerie's worry escalating into panic. "Norah..." she began.

"He's doing as well as can be expected."

"Did you tell him I'm on my way?" Valerie had been in the middle of a business meeting in New York when she received the message. Her youngest sister had called the Houston office, and they'd passed on the news of her father's heart attack. Valerie had left immediately, catching the first available flight. Unfortunately that meant going to Oregon via Chicago.

"Dad knows you're coming."

"Were you able to get hold of Steff?"

Norah's sigh signaled her frustration. "Yes, but it took forever and my Italian is nonexistent. She's planning to catch whatever she can out of Rome, but she has to get there first—she's in some little village right now. It might take her a couple of days. The connection was bad and I couldn't understand everything she said. Apparently there's some sort of transportation strike. But she's doing her best...."

Valerie's sympathies went out to Stephanie, the middle Bloomfield sister. She must be frantic, stuck halfway across the world and desperate to find a way home.

"When will you get here?" Norah asked anxiously.

"The plane's scheduled to land at six-ten."

"Do you want me to meet you? I could—"

"No," Valerie interrupted. She didn't think it was a good idea for Norah to leave their father. "I've already ordered a car. It shouldn't take me more than forty minutes once I land, so don't worry about me."

"But the hospital's an hour's drive from the airport. You shouldn't even try to make it in less."

It generally did take an hour, but Valerie had every intention of getting there a lot sooner. "I should be at the hospital somewhere around seven," she said evasively.

"I'll see you then." Norah sounded resigned.

"Don't worry, kid, everything's going to be all right."

"Just be careful, will you?" Norah pleaded. "You being in an accident won't help Dad any."

"I'll be careful," Valerie promised, smiling at her sister's words. Trust Norah to take the practical approach. After a brief farewell, Valerie closed her cell phone and slipped it into her purse.

Half an hour later, she boarded her plane. She'd only brought a carry-on bag, unwilling to waste precious time waiting for luggage to be unloaded. Shutting her eyes, she leaned back in her seat as the plane taxied down the runway.

Her father was dying. Her dear father… His hold on life was precarious, and the burning need to get to him as quickly as possible drove her like nothing she'd ever experienced.

She was exhausted but sleep was out of the question. Valerie bent down for her purse, rummaging through it until she found the antacid tablets. She popped one in her mouth and chewed it with a vengeance.

No sooner had she swallowed the chalky tablet than she reached for a roll of the hard candies she always had with her. Four years earlier she'd quit smoking, and sucking on hard candy had helped her through the worst of the nicotine withdrawal. If she'd ever needed a cigarette, it was now. Her nerves were stretched to the breaking point.

Please, she prayed, not her father, too. Valerie was only beginning to come to grips with her mother's death. Grace Bloomfield had died of cancer almost four years ago, and the grief had shaken Valerie's well-ordered life. She'd buried her anguish in work; the biggest strides in her career with CHIPS, a Texas-based computer software company, had come in the past few years. She'd quickly climbed up the corporate ladder, until she was the youngest executive on the management team.

Her father had reacted similarly to Grace's death. Working too many hours, driving himself too hard. Norah had tried to tell her, but Valerie hadn't paid attention. She should've done something, anything, to get their father to slow down, to relax and enjoy life. He should have retired years before; he could be traveling, seeing exotic places, meeting with old friends and making new ones. In the years since her mother's death, Valerie had convinced her father to leave Orchard Valley only once and that had been a two-week trip to Italy to visit Steffie.

And now he was fighting for his life in a hospital.

Valerie hadn't said anything to him because...well, because they were so much alike. David Bloomfield was working out his grief the same way she was. Valerie couldn't very well criticize him for something she was doing herself.

Before she knew it, she'd chomped her way through two rolls of candy and another of antacid tablets.

When the plane landed, Valerie was the first one off, scurrying with her bag down the concourse to the rental car agency. Within fifteen minutes, she was on the freeway heading east toward Orchard Valley.

Heading toward home.

Norah was right; it took Valerie longer than forty minutes to reach Orchard Valley Hospital. She got there in forty-five. She took the first available parking space, unconcerned about whether the rental car would be towed. What did concern her was seeing her father.

Norah was standing in the hospital lobby when Valerie walked through the double glass doors. Her sister, looking drawn and pale, was visibly relieved by her presence. "Oh, Valerie," she said, covering her mouth with one hand. "Oh, Valerie… I'm so glad you're here."

"Dad?" Valerie's throat closed up. If her cantankerous father had had the audacity to die before she arrived, she'd never forgive him. The thought made her realize how much this ordeal had drained her.

"He's resting comfortably…for now."

Valerie hugged her sister. Norah looked dreadful, her stylish shoulder-length blond hair brushed away from her face as if her hands had swept it behind her ears countless times. Her blue eyes, normally so clear and bright, were red-rimmed from tears and lack of sleep.

Valerie hadn't had much rest herself, but she was still running on adrenaline. She wouldn't collapse until after she'd had a chance to see her father.

"What exactly happened?" she asked as they hurried to the elevator. Their shoes made a sharp, clicking sound against the polished linoleum floor, a sound that reminded Valerie of similar visits a few years ago, when her mother was dying. She remembered similar nighttime walks down these silent corridors. She hadn't been to this hospital since. The memories overwhelmed her now, tearing at the facade of her poise.

"After dinner last night, Dad went out onto the porch," Norah began, her voice quavering.

As far back as Valerie could remember, after the evening meal her parents had adjourned for coffee to the sweeping front porch of their large colonial home. They'd sat together on the old wicker chairs, some-times holding hands and whispering like teenagers. Valerie was never sure what they discussed, but she'd learned early on not to interrupt them. In the winters, they'd sat in front of the basalt fireplace in her father's den, but during spring, summer and the early part of autumn, it was the porch.

"I should've known something was wrong," Norah continued. "Dad hasn't sat on the porch much since Mom's been gone. After dinner he goes right into his office and does his bookkeeping."

The guilt Valerie experienced was crushing. Norah had repeatedly told her how hard their father was work-ing. She should have listened, should have demanded he hire an assistant, take a vacation, *something*. As the oldest, she felt responsible.

His heart was weak and had been since a bout of rheumatic fever in his thirties. By all accounts he should've died then, but a young nurse's devotion had pulled him through. The nurse was Grace Johnson, who'd become David's wife, and Valerie, Stephanie and Norah's mother.

"I brought him a cup of coffee," Norah went on, "and he looked up at me and smiled. He…he seemed to think I was Mom."

"Was he in terrible pain?"

Norah bit her lower lip. "Yes, he must have been. He was so pale… Only he was too proud to admit it.

I asked him what was wrong, but he wouldn't answer. He just kept saying he was ready."

"Ready for what?"

Norah glanced away. "Ready to die."

"Die!" Valerie cried. "That's ridiculous! If there was ever a man who had something to live for, it's Dad. Good grief, he's worked hard all his life! Now, it's time to reap the fruits of his labors, to enjoy his family, to travel, to—"

"You don't need to convince me," Norah said quietly as they reached the third floor and stepped out of the elevator. The Coronary Care nurses' station was directly in front of them. Norah walked to the counter.

"Betty, would you tell Dr. Winston my sister's arrived?"

"Right away," the other woman replied. She appeared to be gentle, compassionate—and practical. No-nonsense. Valerie recognized those traits because Betty shared them with Norah. And with their mother…

Valerie had to suppress a sudden smile at the memory of her youngest sister lining up dolls in her bed and sticking thermometers in their mouths. She'd fussed over them like an anxious mother, bandaging their limbs and offering comfort and reassurance.

Norah came by this temperament naturally, Valerie supposed, since their mother had been the same. Although she'd given up her hospital job when she married David Bloomfield, Grace continued to nurture those around her. It had been her gift. It was Norah's gift, too.

"Who's Dr. Winston?" Valerie asked. She'd never

heard of him before; he must be a recent addition to the hospital staff. But the last thing their father needed at a time like this was some hayseed family practitioner. He should be in a major hospital with the best heart surgeon available!

"Dr. Winston's been wonderful," Norah returned, her eyes lighting up briefly. "If it hadn't been for Colby, we would've lost Dad in the first twelve hours."

"Colby?" The doctor was named after a cheese? This didn't sound promising.

"I don't know what I would've done without him," Norah said. "I wasn't sure what to do at first. I could tell Dad was in a lot of pain, but I knew he'd object if I called for an aid car. He'd argue with me and that would've made matters even worse if it was his heart like I suspected."

"So you phoned Dr. Winston?"

"Yes. Luckily I was able to get hold of him, and he drove out, pretending to drop in out of the blue. He knew the minute he saw Dad that it was a heart attack. He immediately gave him a couple of aspirin. Then he sat down on the porch and had a cup of coffee with him."

"He drank coffee while our father was having a *heart attack?*" Valerie wasn't finding this doctor too impressive.

"I believe it was what saved Dad's life," Norah said, her eyes flashing a protest. "Dr. Winston convinced Dad to go to the hospital voluntarily. It wasn't until he'd been admitted that he suffered the worst of the attack. If he'd been at home arguing, no one could've done anything to save him."

"Oh." That took some of the heat out of Valerie's argument. She suspected she was looking for someone to blame—in an attempt to ease her own guilt for having ignored Norah's concerns about their father.

The door Betty had walked through opened, and a tall dark-haired man came toward them, his expression serious. Valerie couldn't help noticing how attractive he was. In fact, the man had movie-star good looks, but good looks with nothing soft or insipid about them.

"Hello," he said, his voice deep and resonant. "I'm Dr. Winston." He held out his hand.

"Valerie Bloomfield," she responded briskly, placing her hand in his. She'd always been taught that it was impolite to stare, but she couldn't stop herself. Her father's physician didn't look much older than her own thirty-one years. "Excuse me," she said, not glancing at Norah, who would, she suspected, immediately leap to Dr. Winston's defense. "I don't mean to be rude— but how old are you?"

"Valerie," Norah groaned under her breath.

"I just want to know how long he's been practicing medicine. Good grief, Norah, this is our *father*."

"It's quite all right," Dr. Winston said, smiling at Norah. "If David was my father I'd have a few questions myself. I'm thirty-six."

Valerie found it hard to believe, but she couldn't very well insist on seeing his birth certificate. Besides, her thoughts were muddled and she was exhausted.

Now wasn't the time to question his qualifications. "How's my father?" she asked instead.

"He's resting."

"When will I be able to see him?"

"I'd rather you didn't go in right away."

"What do you mean?" Valerie snapped. "I've flown across the country to be with my father. He needs me! Why shouldn't I be able to go to him?"

"It's not a good idea just now. He's sleeping for the first time in nearly twenty hours and I don't want anything to disturb him."

"I think you should wait," Norah seconded, as if she feared Valerie might be on the verge of making a scene.

Valerie sighed; her sister was right. "Of course I'll wait. It's just that I'm anxious."

"I understand," Dr. Winston said. But he spoke without emotion. He led them to a room not far from the nurses' station. Two well-worn couches faced each other, and several outdated magazines littered the coffee table that stood between them. There was a coffeepot in one corner, with powdered creamer and an ample supply of disposable cups.

Norah sat first, raising both hands to her mouth in an effort to hide a yawn.

"How long have you been here?" Valerie asked, realizing even before she asked that Norah had stayed at the hospital all night. Her youngest sister was exhausted. "Listen, kid, you go on home and get some sleep. I'll hold down the fort for a while."

Norah grinned sheepishly. "I used to hate it when you called me kid, but I don't anymore."

"Why not?" Valerie asked softly, resisting the urge to brush a stray curl from her sister's forehead. She wasn't the maternal type, but she felt protective toward Norah, wanting to ease her burden.

"You can call me kid anytime you like because that's exactly the way I feel, like a child whose world's been turned upside down. I'm scared, Val, really scared. We almost lost him—we still could."

Valerie nodded, hugging her briefly. Norah had suffered through the worst of the nightmare alone, not knowing from one minute to the next if their father was going to live or die.

"Valerie's right," Dr. Winston added. "There's nothing you can do here. Go home and rest. I promise I'll call you if there's any change."

"Okay." Norah rubbed her eyes. "I'll take a shower and try to sleep for a couple of hours. That's all I need. Two, maybe three hours."

Valerie wondered if Norah was too tired to drive; Dr. Winston must have had the same concern.

"We'll phone for a cab from the nurses' station. I don't want you driving like this." He placed his arm around Norah's shoulders, apparently intending to walk her to the elevator. As they left, he turned to Valerie. "I'll be back in a few minutes."

While he was away, Valerie poured herself a cup of coffee. The pot had obviously been sitting there for hours; the coffee was black and thick and strong, just the way she needed it.

The urge for a cigarette was nearly overwhelming, so when Dr. Winston returned to the room she looked up at him and automatically asked, "Do you have any hard candy?"

"I beg your pardon?"

"Mints, anything like that." She was pacing the room, holding her coffee cup in both hands.

"I'm afraid not. Would you like me to see if I could get you some?"

Valerie dismissed his offer with a shake of her head. He was polite to a fault. The first thing she'd done had been to insult him, question his competence, and he'd taken it all in stride.

"Please, tell me about my father."

They sat, and for the next fifteen minutes, Dr. Winston explained what had happened to her father's heart. He did his best to describe it in layman's terms, but much of what he said was beyond Valerie's comprehension. She'd never been comfortable with medical matters. Her mother and Norah had always dealt with those. For her part, Valerie hated anything to do with hospitals or doctors. She detested being sick herself, and knew her father felt the same way.

"There's one underlying problem that needs to be dealt with, however."

"Yes?" Valerie asked, hating the way her voice betrayed her fear. Any show of weakness distressed her. If she'd ever needed to be strong, it was now, for everyone's sake, including her own. She was the oldest, and the others would rely on her.

"Your father's lost his will to live."

"That's ridiculous," she said, battling the urge to

argue with him. "My father's life is brimming over, it's so full. Why, he's—"

"Lost without your mother," Dr. Winston finished simply.

Valerie bolted to her feet and resumed pacing. What Dr. Winston said was absolutely true; she had to admit it. Her father had been crushed under the load of grief, and while Valerie and her two sisters struggled to regain their own balance, their father had been slowly destroyed by his loss.

"What can we do?" she asked, trying to swallow her fears and her guilt.

"Support him, give him your love. The only thing keeping him alive now is his desire to see all three of his daughters before he dies."

"But... Okay, then don't let him know I'm here." It was the obvious solution. And if that was what it took to keep him alive, she was willing to play a little game of hide-and-seek. Norah could make up a series of excuses. No, forget Norah, Valerie mused bleakly. Her youngest sister couldn't tell a lie without blushing.

"How well do you lie?" she asked, thinking fast.

Dr. Winston blinked. "I beg your pardon?"

"We can't let my father know I've arrived. And that means lying to him."

"Miss Bloomfield—"

"Ms."

"Whatever," he said, sounding impatient with her for the first time. "We aren't going to be able to fool your father. Norah talked to him shortly after you phoned from...where was it? Chicago? He knows you caught a flight out of New York. No one's going to make him believe something more important came up that's kept you from him."

"Steffie!" Valerie cried. "When Norah spoke to her, she said there was a transportation strike."

"Yes, but these are only stopgap measures. Your father feels there's nothing left to live for. He talks about your mother constantly, almost as though he's waiting to join her. We need something concrete that'll give him the will to fight, to hold on to life."

Again Valerie knew the doctor was right, but her confused brain was having trouble assimilating the most basic details, let alone a situation as complex as this.

"He's all we have," she whispered despondently. "Surely he realizes that."

"Yes, but at the same time, he believes you have one another."

"We have nothing in common," Valerie told him. "Steffie's a crazy woman who flies off to Europe to study the Italian Renaissance, and Norah's main goal in life is to become another Clara Barton. We don't even *look* alike." Valerie was grasping at weak excuses, and she knew it. Anything she could think of to enlist Dr. Winston's help in keeping her father alive...

"That has nothing to do with me, Valerie," he told her gently. "However, I'll do everything I can to see that your father regains his health and lives to a ripe old age."

Blinking away tears, Valerie nodded, reminding herself once again that she was the oldest of David

Bloomfield's daughters. In a crisis everyone looked to her; she was the one who needed a cool, decisive head, who couldn't let her emotions dictate her reactions.

But it was different this time.

The man in that hospital bed, barely holding on to life, was her father, the man she idolized and loved beyond reason. Her emotions were so close to the surface that the force of them frightened her.

"I'd—I'd like to see him as soon as possible. Please." She'd grovel if necessary. She *had* to be with her father. "I won't make the least bit of noise, I promise." She certainly didn't want to disturb his rest. Somehow, though, she had to reassure herself that he was still alive. She'd never been more frightened.

Dr. Winston hesitated. "Wait here, I'll go and check on him."

He returned a few minutes later. "David's awake and asking for you."

Valerie was so eager that she nearly vaulted out of the room, but Dr. Winston stopped her. "Before you go to your father, let me prepare you for what you're going to see." He spent the next five minutes explaining the different medical devices used to monitor his patient's heart. He explained how the small electrodes on her father's chest detected the electrical impulses that signal the heart's activity. He warned her about the tubes going in and out of his body.

But nothing he said could have prepared Valerie for what she saw. Her father was connected to a frightening number of tubes, machines and devices. His face was ashen, so pale and bloodless that his skin seemed iridescent. His eyes, which had always sparked with vitality, revealed no emotion, only a weariness that was soul-deep.

"Oh, Daddy," Valerie whispered, fighting tears. She locked her fingers around his hand, careful not to disturb the intravenous needle.

"Valerie…so pleased you're here…at last."

"Where else would I be?" she asked, managing a smile. With the back of her other hand, she brushed a tear from her cheek.

"She's beautiful, isn't she?" her father said, apparently talking to Dr. Winston, who hovered in the doorway. "Only…what did you do to your hair?"

"Do you like it?" Valerie asked, rallying somewhat, surprised he'd even noticed that she'd changed the style. "I had it cut." The new look was short and tousled.

"She's got the temper to go with that red hair, you know."

Her father was speaking to Colby Winston again.

"My hair isn't even close to being red," she argued, annoyed by the doctor's effort not to grin. "It's auburn."

"Looks like you haven't combed it in a month," her father mumbled.

"Dad, I'll have you know I paid good money for this."

"In that case, you should demand a refund." His voice was weak, and speaking had clearly depleted him of what little energy he possessed.

"Dad," Valerie said, trying to disguise her concern.

"Instead of complaining about my hair, you should rest."

He didn't respond, merely closed his eyes and sighed audibly.

"I'm going to leave you for a little while," Valerie said. "But I'll be right outside, so if you want to tell me how much you like my hair and beg my forgiveness, then all you need to do is ring for the nurse." Dr. Winston had told her earlier that she'd be allowed to visit her father five minutes out of every hour, depending on how well he was doing.

David's smile was barely discernible.

"Rest now, Daddy. I'm here."

Dr. Winston's hand was at her elbow directing her out of the glass-enclosed cubicle.

"Doc?" Her father's voice had a sense of urgency.

"What is it, David?"

"She's the one I was telling you about. You remember what I said, don't you?"

"Yes. Now don't you worry about a thing."

"Her hair doesn't usually look like a rag doll's."

"Daddy!" Valerie had no idea what was taking place between the two men but she wasn't going to stand idly by and let them insult her.

"This way," Colby Winston said, leading her from the Coronary Care Unit.

"What was *that* all about?" Valerie asked the instant they were out of earshot.

"I'm not sure I know what you mean," he said without meeting her eyes.

Valerie wasn't fooled. There was definitely something going on, and she wanted to know what. She'd been in business far too long to allow questionable remarks to slip past her unchallenged.

"What did Dad mean, I'm 'the one'?"

Dr. Winston still refused to look at her. "While we—your father and I—were talking earlier, he voiced a few concerns about his daughters."

"Yes?" Valerie said. Making an effort to appear nonchalant and relaxed, she walked over to the coffeepot and lifted it to him in silent invitation.

Dr. Winston shook his head and Valerie refilled her own paper cup. "So, what did Dad have to say about us girls?" she asked.

"He's very proud of all three of you."

"Naturally. We're his children. What I'd like to know is what he meant when he said I was 'the one.'"

"Yes, well…" He walked away from her and stood gazing out the window into the night sky.

"Come on, Dr. Winston, I'm a mature woman and this is my father. I'm sure if I insisted he'd tell me." They both knew that coercing her father was out of the question; nevertheless, it was an effective ploy. Dr. Winston went to the coffeepot and filled a cup, even though he'd declined one moments earlier.

"It seems he's the most worried about you."

"Me?" Valerie blurted. Of the three girls, she was the most financially secure. She was established in an excellent career and living on her own. For heaven's sake, she was the only one with investments! "That makes no sense at all."

"Yes, well…"

"Why is he worried about me? Furthermore, why didn't he talk to *me* instead of discussing it with you?"

"There are any number of reasons—"

"Just tell me what he said," Valerie interrupted impatiently.

"Your father seems to think—"

"Yes?" she prompted.

"That you should be married."

Valerie couldn't restrain her laughter. It shot out of her, like bubbles from a champagne bottle.

"In fact," Colby continued grimly, "your father seems to think you should be married to me."

Two

"Married to you?" Valerie echoed, her laughter fading. Dr. Colby Winston! She'd never heard anything so preposterous. She had no intention of marrying *anyone* within the foreseeable future. There was simply no room for a man in her life. She wasn't a romantic; even when she was younger and in college, she hadn't dated much. Her father knew all that, and he'd never seemed particularly worried about it. This latest revelation shocked her nearly as much as Norah's call.

"I see no reason to be too concerned," Colby said, his voice compassionate as though he understood that his announcement had unsettled her. She was usually more proficient at controlling her emotions.

"This sort of delusion isn't unheard of in heart patients," he went on. "As I said, I certainly don't think you have anything to worry about."

"You mean your patients generally try to marry you off?"

"No." He smoothed his tie as if he needed something

to do. "Your father fully expects to die. It's what he wants, but he'd feel better about leaving the three of you behind if at least one of you was married. Your father and I are friends, and I guess it's only natural that he'd attempt to match me up with one of his daughters."

"It should've been Norah. She seems more your type."

His smile was fleeting. "Perhaps, but it's your name he repeatedly mentions."

"Then apparently I'm the one," Valerie said, not realizing what she was saying until the words had left her mouth. "I mean—" She stopped abruptly.

"I know exactly what you mean," Colby assured her. "But I'm sure we don't have to take any of this seriously."

"Oh, I agree. That would be foolish in the extreme."

"Maybe your father feels you should marry first because you're the oldest," Colby ventured.

"Maybe," Valerie agreed. But something inside her suggested that wasn't the sole reason. She tucked her arms around her waist and inhaled deeply, hoping to breathe in a bit of calm and sense.

"I wouldn't have said anything," Colby said, "but I thought it was best to air this. If he mentions marriage again, my feeling is we should go along with him, at least for now."

"Go along with him? You've got to be kidding." Valerie could hardly believe her ears.

Colby shrugged. "You know your father better than I do," he muttered. "He's as stubborn as they come. Don't lie, but if he brings up the subject of…marriage, take the route of least resistance, then try to channel the conversation in a different direction."

"I'm not going to give my father any false hope. Or you either." She added the last part coyly and was rewarded when she saw him swallow tightly. An angry spark momentarily leaped into his dark eyes, but was soon quelled.

Sitting down, Valerie rummaged through her purse for a roll of antacid tablets. Her stomach ached and she was weary to her very bones.

Colby ignored her, although he made no move to go. The preoccupied look on his face suggested that he had something else to say; he seemed to be searching for words.

Valerie considered what Colby had told her. If she ever decided to marry—*if*—she'd settle down with someone who had the same drive, the same will to succeed, as she did. A man who knew where he was going, who'd set his sights high. Not some well-meaning small-town doctor.

She'd marry a man like Rowdy Cassidy.

The name sprang into her mind with a suddenness that shocked her.

Until that moment, Valerie didn't fully grasp how much she admired her employer. Rowdy had started his computer software business out of a friend's garage fifteen years earlier. He'd built the company into one of the most successful in the country. Although he'd earned more money than he could possibly spend in a lifetime, he continued to work ten- and twelve-hour days, demanding as much of his staff as he did of himself.

"It might, uh, help matters if you were involved with someone," Colby said in a casual voice. Valerie found his nonchalant tone a bit exaggerated, which for some reason made her suspect that he *wasn't* "involved with someone."

"I'm not in a relationship at the moment, but I might be soon," she told him. Valerie and Rowdy—a couple. Odd that she'd never thought of him in romantic terms before. He'd be the perfect husband for her. She liked him and respected him, as a man and a professional. Rowdy had handpicked her for his management team because he believed in her abilities.

In retrospect, she realized Rowdy had sought out her company on several occasions. But she'd been so absorbed in proving herself worthy of his faith that she hadn't guessed he might have any personal feelings for her.

For months she'd been blind to what was right in front of her. Not that she was entirely to blame, though. Rowdy wasn't exactly a heartthrob kind of guy. Oh, he was handsome enough, with his rugged cowboy looks, but his brusque, outspoken manner didn't encourage romantic aspirations. As far as she knew, he'd never dated anyone seriously, at least not in the years she'd worked for him.

For that matter, Valerie wasn't any expert on falling in love, either. She'd dismissed the possibility of romance in her own life; it was fine for her sisters and schoolfriends, but not for her. There'd always been too much she wanted to do, too much to strive for. Too much to achieve before settling down in a permanent relationship.

"I'm afraid I don't understand," Colby said, breaking into her thoughts. At her blank look, he elaborated. "You said you weren't involved with someone *yet,* but you will be soon. I may be overstepping my bounds here, but I wouldn't advise you to invent a phony relationship. Your father would see through that in a minute."

"I agree. I wouldn't even attempt anything so foolish. But there's a man I work with, and, well, it seems natural for the two of us to…get involved."

Dr. Winston looked so relieved that she might've been offended if she hadn't been warmed by the newly risen hope of a romance with Rowdy Cassidy.

"I've given your father something to help him rest," Colby went on. "He should sleep through the night without a problem, so if you want to drive home and join your sister—"

"No," Valerie interrupted quickly. "I won't leave Dad. I understand that I can't see him yet, but I want to be here…in case anything happens. It's important to me."

"That's fine."

Valerie was grateful. "Thank you."

He nodded, then yawned, revealing for the first time his own fatigue. "I've left orders that I'm to be contacted the minute there's any change in his condition."

"I can't thank you enough for everything you've done."

"No thanks necessary. I'll talk to you in the morning."

Valerie smiled and sat down to leaf through a six-month-old news magazine. She'd just finished reading the letters to the editor when the nurse appeared, carrying a pillow and a blanket.

"Dr. Winston thought you might need these," she said, setting the bundle down next to Valerie.

It was a thoughtful thing to do, she mused later as she rested her head against the pillow and tucked the thin blanket around her shoulders. She felt a twinge of guilt, especially since she'd already decided to call in the country's top heart surgeon first thing in the morning.

By noon, it was unlikely that her father would still be a patient of Dr. Colby Winston's.

He liked her, Colby realized. He'd been prepared not to. Valerie Bloomfield was everything her father had claimed. Professional, astute and lovely. But when it came to relationships, she was precisely the type of woman Colby made a point of avoiding.

He liked his women soft and feminine. He was looking for a wife, and David Bloomfield had somehow intuited that, or he wouldn't have dragged his eldest daughter into almost every conversation. But Colby didn't have a business executive in mind. He needed a helpmate, a woman who understood the never-ending demands of a doctor's work. A woman who'd understand the long hours, the emotional stress, the intrusions into his private life.

What he didn't need was a career-obsessed executive. Perhaps he was outdated in his thinking. He certainly acknowledged that a woman had every right to pursue her own profession, to choose her own calling in life, but Colby was looking for a woman who'd make that calling *him*. Well, not just him but *them*—their marriage, their family, their home.

He had to admit it sounded selfish and egocentric to expect his wife to wrap her life around his. Nevertheless that was exactly what he wanted.

His own career was all-consuming; there weren't enough hours in the day to do everything that needed to be done. When he got home at night he wanted someone there to greet him, to offer comfort, serenity.

Sherry Waterman fit the bill perfectly. They'd been dating off and on for almost a year. Lately, it seemed, more off than on. Colby wasn't sure why he'd allowed his relationship with Sherry to taper off. He hadn't talked to her in nearly two weeks now—maybe longer. But he knew she'd be an ideal wife for him, and for that matter so would Norah Bloomfield. Yet he couldn't picture spending the rest of his life with either of them.

If he was going to analyze his lack of interest in both Sherry and Norah, then he might as well examine what he found so attractive about Valerie. Not the briefcase she carried with her like a second purse. Certainly not the way she popped antacid tablets, or the way she dressed in a sexless gray suit that disguised every feminine curve of her slender frame.

What appealed to him most was the contrast he sensed in her. Outwardly she appeared calm and collected, asking intelligent questions with the composure of someone inquiring about commonplace statistics instead of her father's chances of survival.

Colby hadn't been fooled. He noted how she gnawed on her lower lip even while her gaze steadily met his. Valerie had been badly shaken by her father's ordeal. There were depths of emotion in this woman, a real capacity for feeling that was—or so he guessed—usually kept hidden.

He also noticed the love in her eyes when he took her to see her father. He'd watched her struggle to keep her emotions at bay. Her fingers had trembled when they reached for her father's hand and her face had grown gentle. There was a strong bond between those two.

It hadn't been necessary to repeat David's comment about their marrying, and Colby wasn't sure why he had.

He suspected he'd been hoping to discover if she was involved with someone. Knowing that she was, or rather that she was about to be, should have reassured him. But it hadn't. If anything, he was more curious than ever.

Norah's arrival stirred Valerie into wakefulness early the following morning. She hadn't slept much, too exhausted and keyed up to let herself relax. Toward dawn she'd drifted into an uneasy slumber.

"How's Dad?" Norah asked, handing Valerie a white sack that contained breakfast.

"The same. I haven't been in to see him, but I've talked to the CCU staff several times." She'd paced the hospital corridor most of the night and as a result had received intermittent reports.

"He's been like this from the first, as though he's balancing on the edge of a cliff. He could fall either way."

"He'll live," Valerie said fervently, as if her determination would be enough to keep him alive.

"I hope you're right."

"I am," Valerie returned, forcing her voice to remain confident.

"Oh, before I forget," Norah said, sitting opposite Valerie, "there were two messages on the answering machine when I got home last night. The first was from Mr. Cassidy at CHIPS. He's your boss, isn't he?"

Valerie nodded, opening the bag her sister had brought. She removed a warm croissant and a cup of fresh coffee. The last time she could remember eating had been at O'Hare, and although her pizza had looked decent, she'd been too upset to feel very hungry.

"What'd Rowdy have to say?"

"Just that he'd heard about Dad's heart attack. He asked if there was anything he could do."

Valerie smiled to herself, pleased that Rowdy had taken a few minutes out of his busy schedule to call. It seemed to confirm her thoughts of the night before; she was increasingly convinced that his interest in her was more than business.

"Who else phoned?" she asked, purposely turning her mind from Rowdy. There'd be plenty of time later to mull over her recent revelation.

"Steff."

"How's she doing?" Valerie asked before biting into the flaky croissant.

"Not very well, I'm afraid." Norah's shoulders slumped forward slightly. "She sounded desperate."

"I take it she hasn't left Italy yet?"

"She can't. Apparently the whole country's at a standstill. Like I told you, she's trapped in this tiny village a hundred miles outside Rome. She'd gone there to spend a few days with a friend's family."

"Why doesn't she rent a car?"

"Seems everyone else thought of the same thing. There's not a car to be had."

"What about her friends?"

"From what I understand, the people she's with don't have a car. She and her friend got a ride there from someone else, and everyone she knows is away on spring break. She's very upset. I called her back, but she was out, so I left a message." Norah shook her head in frustration.

"What did you tell her?"

"That you'd arrived. That I'm on leave from my job as long as necessary. And…that Dad's condition is stable." It was a small lie, but necessary, Valerie agreed, for their sister's peace of mind.

"I'll try to give her a call later," Valerie said, sipping the rapidly cooling coffee. She glanced at her watch and calculated the time difference between Oregon and Texas. If she phoned now she might be able to catch Rowdy. If he was in the office, she'd ask him to locate the best heart surgeon in the state. No, on the West Coast.

She knew there were restrictions against using cell phones in hospitals, so she lined up at the pay phone, which didn't afford her much privacy. But that couldn't be helped. To her relief, she was immediately connected with her boss.

"Valerie," he said, his big voice booming over the wire. "Good to hear from you. How's your father?"

"We don't know yet. It could go either way."

"I'm sorry to hear that." Rowdy sounded genuinely concerned and again her heart warmed toward him. "If there's anything I can do, let me know."

"There is," Valerie said, lowering her voice in an effort not to be overheard. She looked around to make sure no staff members were within earshot. "I need the name and phone number of the best heart surgeon on the West Coast. Dad's too ill to be transferred to another hospital just yet, but the one here in Orchard Valley is small. I can't be sure he's getting the best possible care. I want to make other arrangements as soon as I can."

"Of course, I'll get right on it."

Not for the first time, Valerie felt a twinge of conscience. Colby Winston obviously cared about her father. If she hurt his professional pride by going behind his back, then she'd apologize. For now, though, her primary concern had to be her father, and if that meant offending a family friend, well, too bad. It couldn't be avoided.

"How can I reach you at the hospital?" Rowdy asked.

"It's easier if I call you back. In an hour or so?"

"Sure thing."

"I really appreciate this," Valerie told him.

A few minutes later, she strolled into the waiting room, where she'd left Norah. Colby had joined her and it struck Valerie a second time how perfect Norah would be for him.

Valerie should've been pleased by the idea. Excited, too. But she wasn't and she didn't know why.

Norah smiled at something Colby was saying, and Valerie realized with a small pang that her youngest sister was half in love with him already. If she could see it, then surely her father had, too. He was probably confusing the two of them in his mind, Valerie reasoned, which was certainly understandable under the circumstances.

"Dad's doing about the same," Norah said when she became aware that Valerie had entered the room. "Colby was just in to see him."

"Good morning," he greeted her, smiling briefly.

"Morning." Feeling guilty, she couldn't meet his eyes.

"You can take turns visiting your father if you'd like, but you can only stay five minutes, and I'd prefer that you waited an hour between visits."

"Fine," Valerie murmured. "Since I was with him last night, do you want to go first?" she asked Norah.

"All right."

Valerie assumed that Dr. Winston would go with her sister, but he stayed behind, pouring himself a cup of coffee from the freshly brewed pot. His back was to Valerie.

"Your father's going to require open-heart surgery,"

he said once he'd turned around to face her. "Right now his heart's too weak to withstand the additional stress, but we're fast approaching a crisis point, and you and your sisters need to prepare yourselves."

"Here?" Valerie challenged. "And who'd perform the surgery?"

"I will— I *am* a qualified cardiovascular surgeon. And Orchard Valley has one of the best heart units in the state," Colby said in a reassuring voice.

"I don't want *one* of the best, I want the *very* best! This is my *father* we're talking about." Valerie knew she sounded unreasonable, even rude, but her concern about David overrode all other considerations, including her embarrassment at misjudging Dr. Winston. Why had Norah never mentioned that the man was a heart surgeon? Still, it didn't matter; her father deserved the best-equipped facility and the best-trained specialist around. She spoke in a calmer voice. "If he needs surgery, then he'll have it, but not here. Not when there's a better hospital and more experienced…"

"Heart surgeons?" Colby finished for her.

She stiffened, wanting to avoid a confrontation and knowing it was impossible. "Exactly."

"You're welcome to a second opinion, Valerie. I'd be happy to review my credentials with you, as well."

Her arms cradled her middle. Her breakfast seemed to lie like a deadweight in her stomach.

Colby had begun to speak again. "Norah—"

"You already mentioned the possibility of open-heart surgery to Norah?" she flared, disliking the fact that he'd talked to her sister first.

He nodded. "Just now. While you were out."

That hurt her pride. She, after all, was the oldest, the decision maker, the strong one.

"If you'd like to talk to another specialist, I can recommend several."

"That won't be necessary," Valerie returned stiffly, feeling like a traitor. "I'm having a friend get me the names of the top heart surgeons on the West Coast."

A vacuum of silence followed her words.

"I understand."

She glanced toward him, surprised not to hear any resentment in his voice.

"It isn't that we don't appreciate everything you've done," she rushed to explain. "Norah's told me several times that if it weren't for you, we'd have lost Dad that first night. I'm grateful, more than you'll ever know, but I want to stack the odds in Dad's favor, and if that means bringing in another surgeon, I'll do it."

Her impassioned words were met with a cool but not unfriendly smile. "If David were my father I'd do the same. Don't worry, Valerie, you haven't offended me."

She was so relieved that she nearly sagged onto the sofa.

"Let me know who you want to call in and I'll be happy to confer with him."

"Thank you," she whispered. "Dad and Norah are right," she added, almost to herself.

"About what?" Colby asked on his way out the door.

She looked up, realizing he'd heard her. "You really are wonderful."

Their eyes met and in those few seconds an odd understanding passed between them. It wasn't a look lovers would exchange, she thought, but one close friends would.

Norah came back from the five-minute visit with their father, pale and clearly distressed. Slowly she lowered herself onto the sofa, her hands clasped tightly together.

"Dad's not doing well this morning?" Valerie ventured.

Norah nodded. "He's so weak…he's talking about dying and…" She paused, her light blue eyes glassy with tears.

"He isn't going to die," Valerie said vehemently, clenching her fists at her sides. She *refused* to let him die.

"He'd prefer if you and Steff and I were married, but that can't be helped now, he says. He told me he's sorry he won't be around to enjoy his grandchildren, but—"

"Norah," Valerie admonished briskly, "you didn't honestly listen to that garbage, did you? We can't allow him to talk like that."

"He seems to think you should marry Dr. Winston."

Valerie frowned. "So I heard. That just goes to show you how illogical he's become. If anyone should marry Colby Winston, it's you."

Norah lowered her eyes and an attractive shade of pink flowed into her cheeks. "Every female employee in the hospital's in love with Dr. Winston. Even the married women have a crush on him. He's so strong, yet he's gentle and caring. I—I don't know what I would've done the last couple of days without Colby."

"You really care about him, don't you?" Valerie asked, fighting down an unexpected sense of disappointment.

"I'm not in love with him—not exactly. I admire him the way everyone else does, and if he ever asked me out, I'd accept without thinking twice, but he hasn't."

Valerie was sure she would. She paced the small room, wondering what had prompted this sudden need for movement—her father's apparent death wish or Norah's feelings for Colby Winston.

"I've been busy this morning myself," she said, not looking at her sister. "I asked Rowdy Cassidy if he'd get us the name of the top heart surgeon on the West Coast. Dad has to have the finest medical—"

Norah's head shot up. "You *what?*"

"Listen, if you're concerned about offending Colby, I've already spoken to him and he agrees we should get a second opinion."

"But Colby teaches at Portland University. He's the best there is!"

"For Orchard Valley." Of that Valerie was confident, but there was a whole world Norah knew little or nothing about. Her sister's entire universe revolved around Orchard Valley and their five-hundred-acre apple orchard ten miles outside town.

"Colby's one of the best cardiovascular surgeons in the state." Norah didn't bother to disguise her irritation. "Do you know what you've done?" she demanded. "You've just insulted one of this country's most—"

"I didn't insult him," Valerie insisted, interrupting her sister's tirade. "I made sure of that. Furthermore, you never even let me know he was a heart surgeon— I thought he was just a G.P. And even if he's considered good here in Orchard Valley, Dad needs absolutely the best one available anywhere. Shouldn't you be concerning yourself with his problems and not worrying about offending your doctor boyfriend?"

Norah's eyes widened with shock and hurt. She stood and without a word walked out of the room, leaving Valerie swamped in remorse. She hadn't meant to snap at her sister, nor had she wanted to sound so overbearing. Referring to Colby as Norah's boyfriend had been childish and petty, which proved how badly her nerves were frayed.

An hour passed and Valerie hurried down to the lobby to call Rowdy on her cell phone.

"It's Valerie," she said breathlessly when he answered.

"Listen, you're in luck. There's an up-and-coming heart surgeon working out of Portland University. Apparently he's developed an innovative surgical technique. I've talked to three of the top heart specialists in the country and they all highly recommend him."

"Great." She groped through her purse until she found a pen and a notebook, which she positioned against the lobby wall. "Ready."

"His name is Dr. Colby Winston."

Valerie dropped her arm. "Dr. Colby Winston," she repeated.

"I've got his phone number here."

"Thanks, Rowdy," she said, pride and shame clogging her throat, "but I've already got it."

She hadn't been home for twenty-four hours and she'd already managed to alienate her sister, insult a family friend and at the same time disparage a highly regarded doctor.

"Just great, Valerie," she muttered to herself. "Can things get any worse?"

Three

"Steffie?" David Bloomfield's eyes fluttered open and he gazed up at Valerie.

"She'll be here as soon as she can," Valerie reassured him. It was now early evening, and during every previous visit that day, he'd been asleep, his heart's activity reported on the monitor.

How weak he sounded, she thought, as though death was only hours away. Her own heart clamored with dread and fear; she wanted to shout at him to fight, to hang on...

It wasn't that easy or straightforward—as Valerie knew. In the past two days she'd learned more about the functions of the heart than she'd ever imagined. In more ways than one... She'd learned that the symbolic heart, the center of human emotion, grew larger with the sorrows as well as the joys of love. And the physical heart was subject to its own stresses and risks.

Colby had strived to make the explanation as uncomplicated as possible. Simply put, her father was experiencing heart failure; his heart was pumping blood less efficiently than it should. The decreased strength of the muscles then resulted in distended blood vessels that leaked fluid into his lungs, which interfered with his breathing. Each hour he was growing weaker and closer to death.

"Can't…hold out much longer."

"Of course you can," Valerie insisted, railing against discouragement and defeat. "You're going to live long enough to be a problem to your children. Isn't that what you've always said? You've still got years and years. Good years, with a houseful of grandchildren."

Her father's smile was fleeting. "Go home, sweetheart," he whispered. "You haven't even been to the house yet."

"There's nothing there for me without you." She rubbed her thumb soothingly across the back of his hand, avoiding the IV needle. "Get well, Daddy, *please* get well. We all need you."

His eyes drifted shut, and the oppressive need to give in to the weakness of tears nearly overcame her. She blinked furiously in an effort not to cry, succeeding despite the enormous lump in her throat.

Valerie was grateful her features were outwardly composed when Colby entered the cubicle a few minutes later. He read over the clipboard that outlined her father's progress, then made a brief notation.

"He'll sleep now," he said, guiding her out of the room.

"What's happening?" she asked once they'd left the Coronary Care Unit. "Why is he so much weaker than before? It's like watching his life ebb away. Surely you can do something?" She heard the note of hysteria in her own voice and didn't care. Perhaps she was being selfish in wanting him to live when he so clearly wanted to be released from life. But she loved him so desperately. She *needed* him, and so did Steffie and Norah.

"We're doing everything we can," Colby assured her.

"I know—but it's not enough."

"Valerie, trust me, I love that crotchety old man myself. I don't want to lose him, either." He led the way to the elevator. "Come on, I'll buy you some dinner."

When she declined, he said, "Well, at least a cup of coffee."

She was on the verge of pointing out that there was coffee in the waiting room, then hesitated. He was right. She needed a break, even if it was only ten minutes in the hospital cafeteria.

They rode the elevator down to the basement and walked into the large, open room, which was mostly empty now. Colby reached for a serving tray and slid it along the counter, collecting a green dinner salad, a cellophane-wrapped turkey sandwich and coffee. Valerie surveyed the cottage cheese salad with the limp pineapple and instead grabbed a bottle of cranberry juice. She wasn't at all hungry, although she'd eaten very little in the past few days.

He withdrew his wallet and paid the cashier, then carried the tray to a table at the back of the room, near the window.

He chose one far removed from any of the occupied tables, and that started Valerie's heart pounding with a renewed sense of anxiety. Colby had brought her here to face the inevitable.

"I'm going to lose my father, aren't I?" she asked outright, determined to confront the truth head-on.

Colby looked up, his dark eyes filled with surprise. "Not if I can help it. What makes you ask?"

She slumped against the back of the chair, so relieved that it was all she could do not to weep openly. "I thought that was why you brought me here—what you intended to tell me." With trembling hands, she picked up the bottle of juice and removed the top.

"We aren't going to lose him." He spoke with such fierce conviction that she realized his will to keep her father alive was as strong as her own.

"How long have you known my dad?" she asked, leaning forward and resting her elbows on the table.

"A few years now."

Valerie vaguely recalled hearing Colby's name mentioned once or twice, but she couldn't remember when or for what reason. With her hectic work schedule she'd been home only intermittently. Her last visit had been nearly six months ago, although she phoned weekly.

"We met soon after your mother died," Colby explained. "Your father made a generous donation to the hospital in her name."

Valerie knew that David's contribution had been large enough for the hospital to begin construction of a new wing. The irony of the situation struck her for the first time, and she drew in a deep, painful breath. The new wing housed the Coronary Care Unit.

"By the way," she said, feeling obliged to apologize—or at least acknowledge his reputation. "I understand that I was, uh, mistaken earlier in what I assumed about your skills. I'm sorry about that."

"Don't worry." He shrugged. "It happens all the time. But back to your dad—he and I play chess once a week."

"You ever beat him?"

Colby grinned. "Occasionally, but not often."

Valerie was good at chess herself, which was hardly surprising since her father had taught her to play. One day, perhaps, when all of this was over, she'd challenge Colby to a game. Odd how easy it was to assume they'd continue to know each other....

"He's very proud of you," Colby said casually as he unwrapped his sandwich.

Valerie suppressed a sudden urge to giggle. "So... he mentioned me *before* his attack."

"At every opportunity." He frowned as he said it. He was, no doubt, thoroughly sick of the subject.

Valerie settled back and crossed her arms, enjoying herself. "In other words, Dad's preoccupation with matching the two of us up isn't something new."

Colby paused, averting his gaze. "Let's put it this way. He wasn't quite as blatant about it as he's been the past few days."

"You must've been curious about me."

"A little."

"And?" she said. "What do you think?"

Colby lifted his shoulders, as if to say she hadn't impressed him. Or was he saying she hadn't disappointed him?

"That doesn't tell me a thing," she complained.

"You're everything your father said and more," he muttered, obviously hoping to satisfy her and at the same time put an end to the conversation.

Valerie knew it was sheer vanity to be so pleased. Still, although he might have intended his remark as a compliment, she didn't read any admiration in his eyes. If Dr. Colby Winston was attracted to her, he concealed it well. She hated to admit how much that wounded her pride. The truth was, she wanted him to be fascinated with her. She wanted him to feel enthralled, enchanted, impressed—the way she was with him. Because, despite herself, and despite their awkward beginning, despite the prospect of a relationship with Rowdy Cassidy, she couldn't get Colby out of her mind.

In a strictly objective way, Valerie knew she was slim and attractive. No matter what her father said about her hair, it was styled in an exuberant tangle of russet curls that highlighted her cheekbones and unusual gray-green eyes.

Those eyes were her greatest asset in the looks department, although her mouth tended to be expressive. Being tall, almost five-eight, was a plus, too. Norah was barely five-three, and the entire world seemed to tower above her sister. When Valerie wore heels, there wasn't a man in her field she couldn't meet at eye level, which she considered a definite advantage.

"You don't like me, do you?" she asked bluntly.

Her question clearly took him aback, and he didn't immediately respond. "I don't dislike you," he finally said.

"I make you nervous?"

"Not exactly."

"Then what is it?" she prodded. "Don't worry. I'm not planning to fall in love with you. As I said before, there's someone else on the horizon. I'm just…curious."

"About what?"

"How you feel about me."

His mouth tightened, and Valerie could tell he wasn't accustomed to dealing with a woman as direct as she was. Most men weren't. Valerie didn't believe in suggestion or subtlety. The shortest distance between any two points was a straight line. She'd learned that in high-school geometry and it had worked equally well in life.

"I think you're very good at what you do."

He was sidestepping her question and doing a relatively competent job of it, but she wasn't fooled. "Which is?" she pressed.

"Functioning in a male-dominated field."

"Are you implying I've sacrificed my femininity?" She couldn't help sounding a bit sarcastic.

His lips tightened again. "You're good at putting words in someone's mouth, too, aren't you?"

"Sometimes," she agreed, "but only when it suits my purposes."

"No doubt."

"You're not sure how you feel about me, are you?"

"On the contrary, I knew the minute we met."

She cocked an eyebrow, waiting for him to finish. "Well?" she asked when he didn't supply the answer.

"You're bright and attractive."

"Thank you." It wasn't what she'd hoped to hear. He'd revealed no emotion toward her. She'd rarely met a man who was so…she searched for the right word. *Staid,* she decided. *Stoical.* He seemed to close himself up whenever he was around her, almost as though he felt he needed protection.

Valerie knew she could be overpowering and opinionated, but she wasn't cold or hard. Just straightforward. They were alike in that way, both sensible, seasoned professionals. It was common ground between them, yet Colby seemed determined to ignore their similarities.

He'd been kind to her, she reminded herself. But she sensed that he would have behaved in the same compassionate manner regardless of who she was. Valerie understood that, even applauded it.

So why was she looking for something that wasn't there?

She shook herself mentally. "All right, Dr. Winston," she began in a brisk voice. "Tell me about my father."

Norah was asleep on the sofa when Valerie returned from the cafeteria. She spread the blanket over her sister, wondering why Norah wasn't at home. Norah stirred, her eyes fluttering open.

"Hello, Sleeping Beauty," Valerie said, smiling tenderly.

"Where were you?" Norah asked, sitting up. She

swept tangled hair away from her face, and Valerie saw that her soft blue eyes were puffy, as though she'd recently been crying.

"Down in the cafeteria with Colby."

Norah blinked, looking mildly surprised.

"He hadn't had dinner yet and asked me along so we could talk."

"I feel bad about what happened this morning," Norah said. "I was upset about Dad and angry with you for going behind Colby's back. But then I realized I should have explained things better—you know, told you about his qualifications." She sighed. "I was angry that you hadn't talked to me first."

"If I had, I might have saved myself a lot of trouble," Valerie agreed. "Don't worry about it, sis—I would've been upset, too."

"If there was ever a time we need to stick together, it's now. We can't allow a quarrel to come between us."

Valerie nodded. Norah looked small and lost, and Valerie crossed the room to sit down beside her, placing a protective arm around her sister's shoulders.

"I wish Steffie was here," Norah murmured.

Valerie did, too, but in some ways perhaps it was best that their sister hadn't arrived yet. Her absence might well be the only thing keeping their father alive.

"What did you and Colby talk about?" Norah asked, pressing her head against Valerie's shoulder.

"Dad, and what's going to happen."

"Does Colby know?"

"No, but it looks like he may not have the option

of waiting until Dad's lungs clear before performing open-heart surgery."

"But his chances of survival would be practically nil if Colby went ahead with it now!"

Valerie had felt the same alarm when Colby described the procedure to her. He'd drawn a detailed diagram on a napkin and answered a multitude of questions. Although the surgery would be risky, it seemed to be the only alternative available to them. Valerie had understood and accepted Colby's reasoning, even though her father's chances were slim. She prayed the surgery could be delayed, but that was looking less promising every hour.

"The likelihood that he'll survive is a whole lot better with the operation than without," Valerie reminded her sister. "Still, he said he'd defer it as long as he could."

"Yes, but…oh, Val, it's so scary to think of what our lives would be like without Dad."

"I know." She stroked her sister's hair, offering what reassurance and comfort she could.

"Isn't Colby wonderful?" Norah asked after a while.

Valerie smiled to herself, then nodded. He'd made the surgery, with all its risks, seem the logical thing to do. For the first time since her arrival, she felt hopeful for her father's chances. She held on to that small surge of confidence with both hands. Colby had been patient, answering her questions, giving her reassurance and hope when she'd felt none.

"Now can you understand why everyone likes him so much?" Norah asked, her voice soft.

"Yes." She'd intentionally baited him, determined to find out how he really felt about *her*. She'd looked for some reaction, some sign, but he'd given her nothing.

The more reserved he was, the more challenged she felt. Valerie doubted he ever raised his voice or lost his cool, composed air. Even when she'd pressured him, he'd shown almost no emotion. Yet Valerie couldn't shake the conviction that he was a man of deep feeling—and strong passion.

Colby was smiling; he'd been smiling ever since he'd left the hospital. He wasn't sure what had prompted him to invite Valerie down to the cafeteria. But he suspected it was because...well, because he enjoyed being with her. He'd never known a woman who was so willing to speak her feelings. She was direct and honest and, damn it all, *interesting*. It wasn't that he found Sherry—or for that matter, Norah—boring. He enjoyed their company in an entirely different way.

But Valerie kept him on his toes. She didn't take anything at face value, but challenged and confronted until she was satisfied. He admired that. In fact, he admired *her*. But that wasn't the end of it. This was a woman he could grow to love.

He'd gone off the deep end, he told himself. Worked too many hours without a real break. He'd listened to David Bloomfield once too often. There could never be anything between him and Valerie. She wasn't what he needed in a woman; not only that, she'd never be content with life in Orchard Valley again.

He knew that as well as she did.

* * *

The next morning, with Norah at the hospital, Valerie felt comfortable about leaving for the first time since her arrival from New York. She desperately needed a change of clothes. She was still wearing the business suit she'd had on when she'd received Norah's message two—no, three—days earlier.

She drove to the family home, down the mile-long driveway that led to the colonial house. She took a moment to glance at the hundreds of neat rows of apple trees, all in fragrant blossom. Then she hauled her suitcase up to her old bedroom, showered and changed into a pair of jeans and a soft blue sweater.

When Valerie returned to the hospital she felt a thousand times better. Norah was still asleep, curled up on the sofa, her knees tucked under her chin. She was so blonde and delicate that Valerie had an almost overpowering recollection of their mother. She came to an abrupt stop. The words of greeting froze on her lips and she turned into the hallway.

Quietly she fought back the tears. She'd barely managed to compose herself before she saw Colby striding intently down the wide corridor, heading straight toward her, his face taut.

"Have you got a moment?" he asked stiffly.

"Sure," Valerie said, puzzled by his obvious tension. "Is something wrong? Is it Dad?"

"No, this is between you and me." Colby actually seemed angry. Furious, even, although he hadn't raised his voice. This was certainly the most emotion she'd seen in him.

He marched toward the elevator, with Valerie following, and then down the narrow passageway to the back entrance of the hospital and the employee parking lot. He was several yards ahead of her.

"Where are we going?" she demanded. His pace was too swift for her to keep stride with him.

"Outside."

"In case you hadn't noticed, we already are."

"I don't want anyone to hear this."

"Hear *what?*" she practically shrieked, losing her patience.

Colby whirled around to confront her. "I want to know *exactly* what you said to your father."

Valerie was confused. "About what?"

"Us." The simple little word resonated with anger, contempt, disgust.

Well, so much for her assumption that Colby Winston felt any attraction for her.

"Us?" she repeated. "Don't be ridiculous. There isn't any us."

"That's precisely my point," he snapped. "Perhaps you can tell me why your father suddenly announced that you were falling in love with me—and that he expected me to *do* something about it."

"He *what?*" she exploded.

"You heard me. What in the name of heaven did you say?"

"Nothing." Except for the time she'd seen him yesterday evening, her father had been asleep. At least, his eyes had been closed and his breathing was shallow but regular.

"He knew we'd talked in the cafeteria," Colby informed her coolly.

"He did?"

"He mentioned it himself."

"Maybe Norah—"

"Norah, nothing. It came straight from the horse's mouth. That and a whole lot more."

Valerie frowned, staring down at the ground in an effort to think.

"Valerie!"

"I…thought he was asleep."

"What did you say?" he demanded a second time.

She was flustered now, which happened so rarely that it unnerved her even more. "Uh…just that we'd spoken the other night and I…"

"Go on," he insisted, his jaw muscles tightening.

"I, uh, have this tendency to talk when I'm upset. I don't mind telling you Dad's condition has really scared me. So if he's asleep, like he's been most of today, I sit by his side and tell him the things I've been thinking about."

"Which included me?"

Reluctantly, she nodded. Rarely could she recall being more embarrassed. Color burned in her cheeks.

"Valerie, what did you say to him?" Colby asked for the third time. His voice was quiet but his face had sharpened with tension.

She closed her eyes. She didn't remember everything she'd mumbled, but what she did recall made her cringe. She'd rambled on during those five-minute stretches, saying whatever came into her mind, and most of her thoughts seemed to concern Colby. Not for a second had she believed her father was awake enough to understand a word of it.

"I told him how impressed I was with you," she began hesitantly. "Although I don't know you well, I sense a strength in you. I told him how grateful I was to you because I've felt so helpless the last couple of days."

She chanced a look in his direction but his expression was impassive. Not knowing what else to do, she continued. "In any family crisis there's always one person who has to be strong, and everyone else leans on that person for support. I'm the oldest and I feel responsible for the others. But when I saw my father that first time, I just…couldn't cope. It's even harder for Norah. I realized that the strong one in this situation is you. I told Dad that…and some other things."

"What other things?"

It wasn't getting any better. "That I…found myself attracted to you. Not physically," she rushed to explain, conscious that she was lying. "I'm attracted to the emotional stability I sense in you. Only I didn't say all that to Dad because I didn't think he could hear me anyway.

"Was that so terrible?" she asked, when Colby remained silent.

"No," he finally admitted in a hoarse voice.

"What did Dad say to you?" she asked curiously.

Colby's gaze touched hers, then withdrew. "That you'd fallen head over heels in love with me. And that's a quote."

"What?" Valerie said incredulously. "No wonder you were so upset!"

"Upset's not the word for it. I'm worried about how this is going to affect David's recovery, especially since he seems to have all kinds of expectations now—expectations that are going to be disappointed. Eventually he'll just have to realize you're not the kind of woman I intend to marry."

"Believe me, Dr. Winston, you have nothing to worry about," she murmured, annoyed now. "If I *was* going to fall in love, it would be with a man who was a little more sensitive to my pride."

"I apologize," he said, shrugging indifferently. "Your father unfortunately read too much into your... remarks. I'm afraid you'll have to say something to him."

"Me?"

"You're the one who started this."

"Why can't we just let the whole thing drop? By tomorrow he'll have forgotten I said anything."

"That's not likely," Colby said in a grim voice. "He asked me to bring a preacher so we could be married at his bedside."

Valerie couldn't help it, she burst out laughing. It was as though all the tension, all the waiting and frustration, had broken free inside her. She laughed until the tears streamed down her face and her sides ached, and even then she couldn't stop. Clutching her stomach, she wiped the moisture from her cheeks.

"Colby, darling," she said between giggles. "What shall I wear to the ceremony?"

Colby apparently didn't find her antics humorous.

"I'll want children, of course," she told him when she'd managed to stop giggling. "Nine or ten, and I'll name the little darlings after you. There'll be little cheeses running around our happy home—Cheddar and Parmesan and—"

"I have absolutely no intention of marrying you."

"Of course you don't right *now,* but that'll all change." She enjoyed teasing him, and the laughter was a welcome release after the tension of the past few days.

"You're not serious, are you?"

Valerie sighed deeply. "If you want me to say something to Dad, I will."

"I think that would be best."

"I'm really not so bad, you know," she felt obliged to tell him. She was disappointed in his reaction, although she'd never admit it. If she was going to make a fool of herself over a man, she didn't need to travel halfway across the country to do so!

"We don't have a thing in common and shouldn't pretend we do."

"Well, but—"

"Let's leave it at that, Valerie."

His attitude hurt. "Fine. I'm not interested in you, either," she muttered. Without another word, she turned around and marched back into the hospital.

The man had his nerve. He made a relationship with her sound about as attractive as one with a…a porcupine! Colby acted as though she'd purposely set a trap for him, and she resented that.

Norah was awake when she got back to the waiting room. Her younger sister looked up, smiling, as Valerie hurried in and began to pace.

"What's wrong?" Norah asked, pouring herself a cup of coffee. She gestured toward the pot, but Valerie shook her head.

"Have you ever noticed how opinionated and high-handed Colby Winston can be?" she asked, still pacing furiously.

"Dr. Winston?" Norah repeated. "Not in the least. I've never known him to be rude, not even when someone deserved it."

Valerie impatiently pushed the sleeves of her sweater past her elbows. "I don't think I've ever met a man who irritated me more."

"I thought you liked him."

"I thought I did, too," she answered darkly.

"Steffie phoned," Norah said, cutting off Valerie's irritation as effectively as if she'd flipped a light switch. "She got through to the nurses' station here when she couldn't reach either of us at the house or on our cells."

"Where is she?" Valerie asked. "Is the transportation strike over?"

"No," Norah replied. "She's still trapped in whatever that town is. If she was in one of the big cities she wouldn't be having nearly as much trouble. She asked about Dad, and I told her everything's about the same. She sounded like she was close to tears."

"Poor Steffie."

"She said she'd give everything she owns to find a

way home." Norah sighed. "If something doesn't break soon, I think Steff's going to hike over the Alps."

She'd do it, too; Valerie didn't doubt that for a moment.

"I was with Dad earlier," Norah said, changing the subject again. "He was more alert than before."

Valerie frowned, well aware of the reason. Her dear, manipulative father seemed to think he was about to get his wish. Little did he realize she had no intention of marrying Dr. Colby Winston. Or that Colby was no more interested in her than she was in him.

Four

David Bloomfield's condition didn't change throughout the day that followed. Valerie saw Colby intermittently. He was in surgery most of the afternoon and
came by, still wearing his surgical gown, to check on
her father early that evening. Valerie happened to be
there at the time, and she recognized the weariness in
Colby's face. Without saying anything to her father,
she trailed Colby out of the room.

"What about a cup of coffee?" she suggested, and
when he hesitated, she added lightly, "I thought you
might like to know how I warded off the preacher."

He grinned, then rubbed a hand across his eyes. "All
right," he said, glancing at his watch. "Give me fifteen
minutes and I'll meet you in the cafeteria."

Valerie headed downstairs with her briefcase and
her laptop. That afternoon she'd had her assistant email
the contents of several files to her. Even if she had to be
out of the office while her father was ill, there were still
matters that required her attention. She'd spent much

of the afternoon answering emails. Working out of the hospital waiting room wasn't ideal, but she'd managed.

She was at a table in the cafeteria, reading over some notes on her laptop, when Colby arrived. As he pulled out a chair, she straightened, shut down the computer and closed it.

After a somewhat perfunctory greeting, Colby reached for the sugar canister in the middle of the table and methodically poured out a teaspoon, briskly stirring it into his coffee. "I wanted to apologize," he began.

His words took her by surprise. "For what?"

"I was out of line, coming down on you the way I did about the marriage business. I should've realized your father was stretching whatever you said out of proportion. I took my irritation out on you."

She dismissed his apology with a shake of her head. "It was understandable. As far as I'm concerned, it's forgotten."

His eyes met hers as though he couldn't quite believe her. "You spoke to him?" he asked abruptly.

Valerie nodded, trying to conceal her amusement. "My poor father was distraught, or at least he tried to persuade me he was. But—" she sighed expressively "—he'll get over it just as I will." She fluttered her eyelashes melodramatically, teasing Colby just a little.

His eyes shot to hers, and a slow grin moved across his face, relaxing his features. "Disappointed, were you?"

"Oh, yes. I've always dreamed of a traditional white wedding gown—one that matches the sheets on my father's hospital bed." She smiled and relaxed, too, feeling at ease with him now. She'd been angry, but that was over, and she had to admit she actually liked this man. She certainly admired him.

Colby sipped his coffee, and once again she noted the lines of fatigue that marked his eyes and mouth.

"Rough day?"

He nodded. "I lost a patient. Joanne Murphy. She died this afternoon in surgery. We knew there was a risk, but…" He shrugged heavily. "No matter how often it happens, I never get used to it."

"I'm so sorry, Colby." Her hand slid over to his in a gesture of friendship and support.

His fingers gripped hers as if to absorb the comfort and consolation she offered. At the feel of his hand closing over hers, Valerie felt a thrill of happiness, and even more inexplicably, a sense of *rightness*. She didn't know how else to describe it. Yet almost immediately, the doubts and uncertainties flowed into her mind.

They were friends, nothing more, she reminded herself. And very recent friends at that. Neither of them was looking for anything else. Neither of them *wanted* anything else. But if that was really the case, why would she experience this deep ache of longing? For one impulsive moment she yearned to throw herself into his arms, rest her head against his shoulder and immerse herself in his strength. Lend him hers.

Valerie decided she had to ignore these uncharacteristic sensations. She withdrew her hand, hoping he wouldn't notice its trembling.

"I'd better get back before Norah wonders where I

am," she said firmly. Valerie knew she was a woman who needed to be in control, who looked at a problem from all angles and worked toward the most favorable solution. But Colby Winston wasn't a problem to be solved. He was a man who left her feeling vulnerable and confused.

She was already on her feet, briefcase in one hand, laptop in the other, when Colby spoke. "Don't leave… not yet." His voice was low, hesitant.

Valerie stared at him, unsure whether to stay or go.

"Oh, never mind." Colby shook his head, eyes suddenly guarded. "Actually, I should be leaving myself," he said quickly, bounding to his feet. He drank down several gulps of coffee, then strode out of the cafeteria, with Valerie close behind.

"Colby." She stopped him in front of the elevator. "What is it you don't like about me?" The question was out before she had time to analyze the wisdom of asking.

"I do like you," he answered, frowning.

"But you wouldn't want to marry someone like me?"

"No," he agreed calmly. "I wouldn't want to marry someone like you."

"Because?" Valerie wasn't sure why she continued to probe, why it was necessary for her to understand his reasons. She only knew that she felt a compelling urge to ask.

"You have a brilliant future ahead of you," he said, not meeting her eyes. "Your father's proud of your accomplishments, and rightly so. I admire your drive, your ambition, your ability."

"But." She said it before he could. There had to be a *but* in there somewhere.

"But," he said with the slightest hint of a smile. "I'm not interested in getting involved with an up-and-coming female executive. When I commit myself to a woman and a relationship, I want someone who's more…traditional. Someone who'll consider making our home and rearing our children her career."

"I see." He was wise to acknowledge that she wasn't the type who'd be content to sit quietly by the fireplace and spin her own yarn. No, Valerie would soon figure out how to have that yarn mass-produced, then see about franchising it into a profit-making enterprise. Business was in her blood, the same way medicine was in his.

"I don't mean to offend you," he said.

"You haven't," she assured him, and it was the truth.

The elevator arrived and they stepped inside together. Neither spoke as Colby pushed the appropriate button. The doors silently glided shut.

Valerie wished they weren't alone. It seemed so intimate, so private, just the two of them standing there.

"Valerie, listen…"

"It's okay," she said, smiling up at him. "Really, I asked, didn't I? That's how I am. You were honest with me, and I appreciate that. It's true I'm attracted to you, but that's probably fairly common in our circumstances, since you saved my father's life and all. Being attracted doesn't mean I'm in love with you."

"I know, it's just that—" He broke off hastily, his eyes probing hers. "Oh, what the hell," he murmured,

the words so low that Valerie had to strain to hear him.
Then his hands were taking hold of her shoulders and
drawing her toward him. His mouth unerringly found
hers and without conscious intent, she responded to
his kiss, feeling none of the awkwardness she experienced with other men. The kiss was much like the
man. Warm, deliberate, devastating.

She heard a soft moan from the back of her throat.

His head shifted restlessly before he released her. He
dropped his arms, looking completely shocked. Valerie
didn't know what had distressed him most—the fact
that he'd kissed her or that he'd enjoyed it.

"Valerie, I…" Her name was a whisper.

Just then the elevator doors opened, and Colby cast
an accusing glare at the nurse who entered. Grabbing
Valerie's hand, he jerked her onto the floor before the
elevator doors closed again.

"This isn't CCU," she protested, glancing around.
Good grief, they were on the maternity floor. Down
the hall, a row of newborns was on display behind a
glass partition.

But Colby didn't give her a chance to get a closer
look. Still holding her hand, he led her to the stairwell.
He held open the door, then released her and dashed
up the steps. He was halfway up the first flight before
he seemed to realize she was no longer beside him. He
turned back impatiently.

"Colby," she objected. "If you want to run up the
stairs, fine, but you're in better physical condition than
I am. I sit at a desk most of the day, remember?"

"I didn't mean for that to happen."

"What, racing up the stairs?"

"No, kissing you!"

"It was nice enough, as kisses go," she said, out of breath from the exertion, "but don't worry, you won't have to marry me because of a simple kiss." The only way she could deal with this experience was to deny how strongly it affected her, push aside these unfamiliar, unwelcome feelings. She suspected that was how Colby felt, too.

"Our kiss may have been a lot of things, but simple wasn't one of them," he muttered.

"You're worrying too much about something that really isn't important."

His eyes held such a quizzical expression that Valerie continued talking. "You're tired, and so am I," she said, making excuses for them both. "We're under a great deal of stress. You've had a long, discouraging day and your guard slipped a little," she went on. "My being so pushy didn't help, either. You kissed me, but it isn't the end of the world."

"It won't happen again." He spoke with absolute certainty.

Pride stiffened Valerie's shoulders. "That's probably for the best." Colby was right. Her personality was all wrong for someone like him. A doctor's work was emotionally demanding and physically draining; she couldn't blame him for seeking a wife who'd create a warm cocoon of domesticity for him. A home filled with comfort and love and peace. Valerie couldn't fault his preference. She wished him well and determined to put the kiss out of her mind.

* * *

The next afternoon, Valerie went downtown. The streets of Orchard Valley greeted her like a long-lost friend. She felt heartened by the sight of the flower-filled baskets that hung from every streetlight.

The clock outside the Wells Fargo Bank was still ten minutes slow, even after thirty years. When Valerie was thirteen, a watchmaker from somewhere out East had been hired to repair the grand old clock. He spent most of a day working on it, then declared the problem fixed. Two days after he'd left town, the clock was back to running ten minutes late and no one bothered to have it repaired again, although it came up on the town council agenda at least once a year.

The barbershop with its classic red-and-white-striped pole whirling round and round was as cheery as ever. Mr. Stein, the barber, sat in one of his leather chairs reading the *Orchard Valley Clarion,* waiting for his next customer. Valerie walked past, and when he glanced over the top of the paper, she smiled and waved. He grinned and returned the gesture.

The sense of homecoming was acute, lifting her spirits. She passed the newspaper office, two doors down from the barbershop; looking in the window, she noted the activity inside as the staff prepared the next edition of the *Orchard Valley Clarion*. She hadn't gone more than a few steps when she heard someone call her name.

She turned to find Charles Tomaselli, the paper's editor, directly behind her. "Valerie, hello. I wondered how long it'd take before I ran into you. How's your dad doing?"

"About the same," she answered.

"I'm sorry to hear that." He buried his hands in his pants pockets and matched his pace to hers. "I haven't seen Stephanie around."

"She's still in Italy."

Although he gave no outward indication of his feelings, Valerie sensed his irritation. "She didn't make the effort to come home even when her father's so ill? I'd have thought she'd want to be with him."

"She's trying as hard as she can," Valerie said, defending her sister. "But she's stuck in a small town a hundred miles outside of Rome—because of that transportation strike. But if there's a way out, Steffie'll find it."

Charles nodded, and Valerie had the odd impression that he regretted bringing up the subject of her sister. "If you get the chance, will you tell your father something for me?"

"Of course."

"Let him know Commissioner O'Dell called me after last week's article on the farm labor issue. That'll cheer him up."

"The farm labor issue?" Valerie repeated, wanting to be sure she understood him correctly.

Charles grinned almost boyishly, his dark eyes sparkling with pleasure. "That's right. I don't know if you're aware of this, but your father would make one heck of an investigative reporter. Tell him I said that, too. He'll know what I mean."

"Sure," Valerie agreed, wishing she knew more about the article and her father's role in it.

"Nice seeing you again," Charles said, turning to head back to the newspaper office. He hesitated. "When you see Stephanie, tell her hello from me," he said over his shoulder.

"Of course. I'll be happy to." Thoughtfully, Valerie watched him walk away. Charles not only edited the *Clarion,* he wrote a regular column and most of the major features, like the farm labor story he'd just mentioned. Considering his talent and energy, she was surprised he'd stayed on with a small-town paper; he could have gone to work for one of the big dailies long before now. But then, these days, with major newspapers folding, maybe he'd been smart not to leave.

She found it interesting that he'd asked about Steffie. Several years ago, Valerie had suspected there was something romantic developing between them. Steffie had been a college student at the time and Charles had just moved to Orchard Valley. She remembered Steffie poring over every article, every column, exclaiming over Charles's skill, his style, his wit. To Valerie, it had definitely sounded like romance in the making. His comments about Stephanie now suggested it hadn't been entirely one-sided, either.

But then, romance was hardly a subject she knew much about. So if there *was* something between Steffie and Charles, it was their business and she was staying out of it. She knew just enough about relationships to make a mess of them. A good example of that was how she'd bungled things with Colby.

She felt a twinge of regret. Since their kiss, he'd been avoiding her. Or at least she assumed he was. Until then, he'd made a point of coming by and chatting with her when he could. They'd always been brief visits, but their times together had broken up the monotony of the long hours she'd spent at the hospital. She hadn't realized how much those short interludes meant to her until they stopped.

Norah was the one who'd sent Valerie on the errand into town. Some flimsy excuse about picking up some photos from a roll of film their father had left for developing. He was admittedly old-fashioned when it came to cameras and photography; Valerie had wanted to buy him a digital camera last Christmas but he'd insisted that he preferred his forty-year-old Nikon, which had served him well all these years. Asking her to collect the pictures now was a blatant attempt to get her out of the hospital, not that Valerie minded. She was beginning to feel desperate for fresh air and sunshine.

Although most of the orchards were miles out of town, she could've sworn that when she inhaled deeply she caught a whiff of apple blossoms.

Spring was her favorite time of year. But although she'd been home intermittently over the past decade, she'd never spent more than a day or two and had never visited during April or May. She wondered if she'd been unconsciously avoiding Orchard Valley during those months, knowing that the charm and the appeal of her home would be at their strongest then. Perhaps she'd feared she might never want to leave if she came while the white and pink blossoms perfumed the air.

Not wanting to examine her thoughts too closely, Valerie continued down the street, past the feed store and the local café until she arrived at her destination. Al's Pharmacy.

Al's was a typical small-town drugstore, where you could buy anything from cards and gifts to aspirin and strawberry jam. At one end of the pharmacy Al operated a state-run liquor store and in the opposite corner was a small post office. The soda fountain, which specialized in chocolate malts, was situated at the front. It had been there since the fifties, the kind of thing rarely seen outside of small towns anymore. Valerie had lost count of the number of times she'd stopped in after school with her friends. She wondered if "going to Al's for a chocolate malt" remained as popular with local teenagers these days as it had been when she was growing up. She suspected it did.

"Valerie Bloomfield," the aging pharmacist called to her from behind the counter. "I thought that was you. How's your dad doing?"

"The same."

"Norah phoned and said you were on your way. I put those snapshots aside for you and just wrote it up on the bill. You tell your dad I'm counting on him to go fishing with me come July, and I won't take no for an answer."

"I'll tell him," Valerie promised.

She took the package and wandered outside. Curiosity got the better of her, though, and she paused on the sidewalk to open the envelope. Inside was an array of snapshots her father had taken that spring.

Valerie's heart constricted at the number of photos he had of her mother's grave site. In each, a profusion of flowers adorned the headstone. There were a couple of pictures of Norah, as well. The first showed her sitting in a chair by the fireplace, a plaid blanket around her knees and an open book on her lap. The second was taken outside, probably in late March. The wind had whipped Norah's blond hair about her face, and she was laughing into the sun. In both photographs her resemblance to their mother was uncanny.

Grief and pity tore at Valerie's heart as she imagined her father taking those pictures. He was so lost and lonely without his Grace, and the photographs told her that in an unmistakable and poignant way.

Her thoughts oppressive, Valerie walked aimlessly for a few minutes. When she saw that she was near the community park, she strolled in, past the swimming pool, now drained and empty, and followed the stone walkway that meandered through the manicured lawns. As she reached the children's playground, a breeze caught the swings, rocking them back and forth.

Memories of her childhood crowded her mind, and she sat in one of the old swings, almost wishing she could be a little girl again. It would've been easy to close her eyes, pretending she was eight years old. She allowed herself a minute to remember Sunday afternoons spent in this very park, with David pushing her and a tiny Stephanie on these swings, catching them at the bottom of the slide. But she was thirty-one now and her father, whom she adored, was in a hospital room, fighting for each breath he drew.

She refused to even consider the possibility of losing him. Was she being selfish? She didn't know. Her father had said he was ready to die, ready to relinquish his life.

She dragged the toe of her shoe along the ground, slowing the swing to a halt. When the time came to let go of her father, Valerie prayed she could do it with acceptance and strength. When death came to him, she wanted it to be as a friend, not an enemy with a score to settle. *But don't let him die yet. Please, not yet.*

As she drove back to the hospital, past the strip malls that marked the highway, she caught sight of a recent addition. A movie theater, a six-plex. It astonished her that little Orchard Valley could have six movies all playing at once, especially in the era of DVDs and movies you could download from the internet. She supposed that in a small town, going to the movies was still a major social event. The downtown theater she remembered so well from her teenage years still operated, but to a limited audience; according to Norah the features were second-run and often second-rate.

Orchard Valley had its share of national fast-food restaurants now, too, many of them situated along the highway. But as far as Valerie was concerned, hamburgers didn't get any better than those at The Burger Shack, a locally owned diner.

The summer she was sixteen, Valerie had worked there as a waitress, serving customers for minimum wage, thinking she was the luckiest girl in town to have landed such a wonderful job. How times had changed! How much *she'd* changed.

As she neared the hospital, Valerie felt a surge of reluctance. For nearly a week now, she'd practically lived on the CCU floor with only brief visits home to shower and change clothes. It had been a strange week, outside ordinary time somehow. Four years ago, when her mother was dying, she'd experienced something similar. But then her father and both her sisters had been there to share it. Now there were only two—Norah and her. And Colby…

She pulled into the parking lot and found a vacant spot, then walked toward the main entrance, sorry to leave the sunshine.

The minute she entered the lobby, Norah sprang up from the sofa she'd been sitting on. "I didn't think you'd ever get back," she said breathlessly. "What took you so long?"

"I stopped at the park. What's the matter?"

"Steffie called from Rome. She's flying home by way of Tokyo. I know it sounds crazy, but it was the most direct flight she could get. She's hoping to arrive sometime tomorrow night. She wasn't sure exactly when, but she said she'd let us know as soon as possible."

"How'd she make it to Rome?"

"I asked her that, but she didn't have time to explain. I told Dad she'd probably be here by tomorrow night."

Valerie felt herself relax. Until now, she hadn't realized just how tense she'd been over Steffie's situation.

"Colby wants to see you," Norah informed her next.

"Did he say why?"

Norah shook her head, frowning a little. "You two didn't have an argument, did you?"

"No. What makes you ask?"

Norah shrugged vaguely. "Just the way he looked when he asked for you."

"Looked?"

"Oh, I don't know." Norah was clearly regretting that she'd said anything. "It's like he was eager to see you, but then relieved when I told him you'd gone into town. That might seem absurd, but I can't think of any other way of describing it."

"I'll catch him later." For some reason, Valerie wasn't quite ready to see him yet.

"I'm sure he'll stop by this evening."

"How's Dad doing?" Valerie asked as they headed for the elevator.

"Not so good. His breathing is more labored and the swelling in his extremities isn't any better. That's not a good sign. Colby's doing everything he can to drain his lungs, but nothing seems to work. In the meantime, Dad's growing weaker by the hour."

"He misses Mom even more than we knew," Valerie whispered, thinking about the snapshots she'd picked up at Al's Pharmacy. She wondered how often he'd visited their mother's grave. How often he turned to speak to the woman he'd spent a lifetime with, remembering too late that she was gone.

"What will we do if anything happens to Dad?" Norah asked quietly.

A few days earlier, Valerie would've rejected that possibility, adamantly claiming their father wasn't going to die. She'd stubbornly refused to consider it. She wasn't as unyielding now.

"I don't know," she admitted, "but we'll manage. We'll have to."

They were seated in the waiting room when Colby arrived. Valerie glanced up from a business publication she was reading and knew instantly that something was wrong. Terribly wrong. His eyes, dark and troubled, met hers. Without being conscious of it, she stood, the magazine slipping unnoticed to the floor.

"Colby?" His name became an urgent plea. "What is it?"

He sat down on the sofa and reached for Valerie's hands, gripping them tightly with his own. His gaze slid from her to Norah. "Your father's suffered a second heart attack."

"No," Norah breathed.

"And?" Valerie's own heart felt as though it were in danger of failing just then. It pounded wildly, sending bursts of fear through her body.

"We can't delay the surgery any longer."

Norah was on her feet, tears streaking her face. "You can't do the surgery now! His chances of survival are practically nil. We both know that."

"He doesn't have *any* chance if we don't." Although he was speaking to Norah, it was Valerie's gaze he held, Valerie's eyes he looked into—as if to say he'd do anything to have spared her this.

Five

Colby had been with her father in the operating room for almost six hours, but to Valerie, it felt like six years.

While she waited, she recalled the happy times with her father and, especially as she entered adolescence, the not-so-happy ones. Her will had often clashed with his, and they'd engaged in one verbal battle after another. Valerie had found her father stubborn, high-handed and irrational.

Her mother had repeatedly told Valerie the reason she didn't get along with her father was that the two of them were so much alike. At the time Valerie had considered her mother's remark an insult. Furthermore, it made no sense. If they were alike, then they should be friends instead of adversaries.

It wasn't until her mother became ill that Valerie grew close to her father. In their love and concern for Grace, they'd set aside their differences; not a cross word had passed between them since.

Valerie couldn't say which of them had changed, but

she figured they'd both made progress. All she knew was that she loved her father with a fierceness that left her terrified whenever she thought about losing him.

The passage of time lost all meaning as she paced, back and forth, across the waiting room floor. It wasn't the waiting room she was so familiar with, since Surgery was on the hospital's ground level; a small brick patio, bordered with a waist-high hedge, opened off glass doors. Every now and then, Valerie or Norah would wander outside to breathe in the cool air, to savor the peace and tranquility of the night. There'd been no other patients in surgery that evening, no other families waiting for news.

Somehow word got out about her father's crisis. Pastor Wallen from the Community Church stopped by and prayed with Valerie and Norah. Charles Tomaselli was there for an hour, as well. Various friends, including Al Russell from the pharmacy, came, too.

At midnight, an exhausted Norah had curled up on the sofa and fallen into a troubled sleep. Valerie envied her sister's ability to rest, but found no such respite from her own fears.

Pacing and sucking on hard candy to relieve her nerves were the only methods she had of dealing with the terrible tension. She stared out the window at the bright moonlit night, then turned suddenly when she heard a soft footfall behind her. Colby stood there, still wearing his surgical greens.

Valerie's eyes flew to his, but she could read nothing.

"He made it."

She nearly slumped to the floor with relief. Tears welled up, but she blinked them back. "Thank God," she whispered, raising both hands to her mouth.

"I nearly lost him once," Colby said hoarsely, shaking his head. How exhausted he looked, Valerie noted. "I didn't think there was anything more we could do. It seemed like a miracle when his heart restarted. In some ways, it was. Only so much of what happens on the operating table is in my hands."

"I'm sure it *was* a miracle," Valerie whispered, hardly able to speak. She walked to the sofa on unsteady legs and bent to wake Norah. Her sister woke instantly—her training as a nurse, no doubt—and Valerie told her, "Dad made it through the operation."

"The danger's not over yet," Colby cautioned. "Not by a long shot. I wish I could tell you otherwise, but I can't. If he survives the night—"

"But he survived the surgery," Norah said, her voice rose with hope. "I didn't think that was possible. Surely that was his biggest hurdle?"

"Yes," Colby agreed, "but his condition is critical."

"I know," Norah answered, but a faint light began to glow in her eyes. From the little Norah had said, Valerie realized her sister hadn't expected their father to live through the ordeal. Now that he had, she was given the first glimmer of promise.

"I'll be back in a few minutes," Colby said, rubbing his eyes in an oddly vulnerable gesture. He must be running on pure adrenaline, Valerie thought. He'd been in surgery earlier in the day and he'd lost a patient; he'd feared he was about to lose another one. He still could. He didn't need to say it aloud for Valerie to know.

Colby didn't think her father would live until morning.

"I wish Steffie was here," Norah said after Colby had left.

Valerie nodded. "I do, too."

Colby had been gone a few minutes when a male nurse appeared. He knew Norah and greeted her warmly, then told them they could each see their father, but for only a moment.

Valerie went first. She'd assumed she was emotionally prepared, but the sight of her father destroyed any self-control she might have attained. Seeing him lying there so close to death affected her far more acutely than she'd expected.

Hurriedly she turned and left, feeling as though she could barely breathe. She walked past Norah without a word. She stumbled onto the patio, hugging her middle with both arms, dragging in one deep breath after another in a futile effort to compose herself.

The tears, which she'd managed to resist all evening, broke through in a flood of fear and anger. It was *unfair*. It was so unfair. How could she lose her father so soon after her mother?

She didn't often give in to tears, but now they came as a release. Huge sobs shook her body. Slowly, she lowered herself onto a concrete bench, then rocked back and forth as the hot, unstoppable tears continued to fall.

A hand at her back felt warm and comforting. "Go ahead and let it out," Colby whispered.

He sat beside her, his arm around her shoulders, and gradually drew her to him. She had no strength or will to refuse. Nestling her face against his jacket, Valerie sobbed loudly, openly. Colby rubbed his cheek along her hair and whispered indistinguishable, soothing words. His arms were strong and safe, and she desperately needed him and he was there.

When there were no more tears left to shed, a deep shudder racked her body. She straightened and used her sleeve to wipe her damp face.

"Feel better?" Colby asked, his hand on her hair.

Valerie nodded, embarrassed now that he'd found her like this. "Norah?"

"She's talking to Mark Collins. One of the nurses who assisted me in surgery."

"I...thought I was prepared...didn't know I'd fall apart like this."

"You've been under a lot of stress."

"We all have." She edged away from him, and taking the cue, he dropped his arm. She offered him a trembling smile, her gaze avoiding his.

"I wish I could guarantee that your father's going to make it through this," he said, his voice heavy. "But I can't do that, Valerie."

"I know." Spontaneously, as though he'd silently willed it, she raised her eyes to his. His hands grasped her shoulders, tightening as he urged her closer. His eyes seemed to darken as his mouth made a slow descent toward hers, stopping a mere fraction from her lips.

Valerie closed her eyes, and his warm breath caressed her face. She inhaled the pungent scent of surgical soap and something else, something that was ineffably him.

"We shouldn't be doing this," he whispered.

It certainly wasn't what she'd expected him to say. "I...know," she said, but she was beyond listening to common sense. She needed Colby. His warmth, his comfort, his touch. And she wouldn't be denied.

"Please," she whispered.

The driving force of his kiss parted her lips, and Valerie was instantly caught in a whirlwind of sensation. Her hands reached for him, sliding up his solid chest, her fingers locking at the base of his neck.

He moaned, and she did, too. There was no resistance in Valerie, none. She surrendered herself to his kiss, to his need and her own.

With what seemed like reluctance, he broke away and slipped his mouth from hers.

She felt cold when he lifted his face. Opening her eyes, she glanced toward the waiting room, grateful to see that it was empty. They were alone in the shadows of the hedge, but a few seconds earlier it wouldn't have mattered if they'd been standing in the middle of the bustling emergency room.

"I shouldn't have let that happen. We both—"

Valerie placed her finger over his lips, silencing him. "Don't say it. Please." Her hands cupped his face and she gazed into his eyes, dark now with desire. "I need you. Right or wrong, I need you. Just hold me."

A faint quiver went through her as he brought her back into his arms. Closing her eyes again, Valerie surrendered to the strength and safety she felt in his embrace.

He kissed her forehead lightly. His breath was uneven, and she found pleasure in knowing that he was no less affected by their encounter than she was.

As she'd already told him, Valerie didn't want to question the right or wrong of it now. Neither of them was in any real danger of falling in love. Colby had explained the reasons a relationship between them was unfeasible. And she agreed with him. But their calm, rational words didn't take into account what she was experiencing. This excitement, this weightless sense of release and longing. She didn't want it to end. Apparently Colby didn't, either, because he made no move to let her go.

"You shouldn't feel so good in my arms," he told her.

"I'm sorry." But she wasn't, not really. Soon they'd both regret this, but she'd save all the remorse for another day.

While she was in Colby's embrace, she didn't have to think about the future. She didn't have to worry about facing the world without anyone to guide and support her. For the first time since she'd come home to Orchard Valley, Valerie didn't feel inadequate or alone.

True, Norah was with her and Steffie was due to arrive soon. The three of them had each other, yet Valerie couldn't quite escape the old roles; she was the one they'd always depended on for encouragement, guidance, a sense of strength. Only Valerie didn't feel strong. She felt shaken, knocked off balance. She felt completely helpless....

"Norah's looking for you," Colby said.

Valerie sighed and grudgingly broke away from him. She peered into the waiting room and noticed her younger sister. Norah's eyes found her at the same time. She didn't do a good job of concealing her shock.

Valerie stood and turned to Colby. "Thank you."

He remained sitting on the concrete bench and sent her a smile full of private meaning.

Norah met her at the door, eyes shifting from Valerie to Colby. "Is everything all right?"

Valerie nodded. "Dad's holding his own at the moment."

"I didn't mean Dad. I meant with you."

"Of course," Valerie answered, forcing a casual tone. "I...just needed a good cry, and Colby lent me his shoulder."

Norah slipped her arm around Valerie's waist. "His shoulder, you say?" she asked, with more than a hint of a smile. "It looked like more than that to me."

It was the following night, and once again Valerie and Norah had taken up residence in the waiting room. Several small groups of people were scattered about the area, either silent or speaking quietly.

"Dad's been asleep for nearly twenty hours." Valerie voiced her concern to Norah, who was far more knowledgeable about what was and wasn't usual after this kind of surgery. "Isn't that too long? I realize the anesthesia has a lot to do with it, but I can't help worrying."

"He's been awake for brief periods off and on today," Norah said. "He's doing very well, all things considered."

Her father wasn't Valerie's only concern. It was now after nine in the evening, and she'd been waiting since morning for some word from Steffie, who was supposed to be arriving sometime that day. But no one had heard from her, and Valerie felt anxious.

"Dad tried to talk the last time I was with him," Norah told her.

"What did he say?"

She shrugged. "It didn't make any sense. He looked up at me and grinned as if he'd heard the funniest joke in years and said 'six kids.'"

"Six kids?"

"I don't get it, either," Norah murmured. "I'm going to ask Colby about it when I see him, but we keep missing each other."

Valerie sat down and thumbed through the frayed pages of a two-year-old women's magazine. It was a summer issue dedicated to homes and gardens, which only went to prove how desperate she was for reading material that would take her mind off her fears.

She glanced at photographs of bright glossy kitchens and "country" bedrooms, wicker-furnished porches and "minimal" living rooms—all of them attractive, none of them quite real. None of them *home*.

And she knew with sudden certainty that home was *here*. Here in Orchard Valley at the family house. In the upstairs bedroom at the end of the hallway. Home was curling up with a good book by the fireplace in her father's den, and it was eating meals around the big oak table in the dining room her mother had loved.

That was home. She *lived* in her Houston condo in an exclusive neighborhood. She'd had a decorator choose the color scheme and select the furniture, since she didn't have the time for either task. A housekeeper came in twice a week to clean. The condo was a place to sleep. An address where she could pick up her mail. But it wasn't a place of memories and it wasn't home.

She read an article in the same magazine about herb gardens. Gardening had always been her mother's hobby, but every now and then Valerie had helped her weed. The times they'd spent working in the garden were among the fondest memories she had of her mother.

Perhaps in an attempt to recapture some of that simple happiness, Valerie had bought several large plants for her condo. But the housekeeper was the one who watered and fertilized them, since Valerie traveled so much.

Neither a home, at least not like the one she'd been raised in, nor a garden seemed to be in her future. Colby had recognized that from the beginning. Just as well, although it hadn't warded off the magnetic attraction between them.

Valerie's mind wandered to their exchange the night before. Their kissing was undoubtedly a mistake, but it was understandable and certainly forgivable. Both were emotionally drained, their resistance to each other almost nonexistent. Yet Valerie couldn't bring herself to regret the time she'd spent in Colby's arms.

It hurt a bit that he was avoiding her, because it told her he didn't share her feelings. In those moments with Colby, Valerie had experienced something extraordinary. She'd always considered romantic love a highly overrated commodity. Dr. Colby Winston was the first man who'd given her reason to reevaluate that opinion—despite the fact that a relationship between them had no possible future.

Just when she was beginning to think he planned never to seek her out again, Colby surprised her. Norah had gone to talk with the nurse who'd been assigned to care for their father, and Valerie sat alone in the SICU waiting room, shuffling through her thoughts. Colby was on her mind just then—not that he was ever far from it.

She happened to glance up as he walked in. He was wearing a dark gray suit; she didn't think she'd ever seen a handsomer man. Not even Rowdy Cassidy...

Their eyes met and held. "Hello," she said, with a breathless quality to her voice. Over the course of her career, Valerie had made presentations before large audiences. Her voice carried well, yet with Colby she felt like a first-grader asked to stand before the class and confess a wrong.

"Valerie." He paused and cleared his throat, then began again, sounding stilted and formal. "I've tied up everything here and I'm addressing a seminar this evening at the university. However, I have time for a bite to eat before I leave. Would you join me?"

"I'd be happy to," she answered.

"I thought we should eat someplace other than the cafeteria." His voice was more relaxed now. "There's an Italian restaurant near here that serves excellent food."

"Great." Valerie brightened until she realized he hadn't chosen the restaurant because he had a craving for spaghetti. He wanted to talk to her somewhere away from the hospital. Somewhere he could be assured none of his peers would be listening.

After leaving a message for Norah, they left the hospital in his car, a late-model maroon sedan. Sitting beside him, watching his strong, well-shaped hands on the steering wheel, gave Valerie a sense of intimacy, a feeling of familiarity.

The restaurant, a fairly new place she'd never visited before, was elegantly decorated in black and silver. The lighting, low and discreet, created a welcoming ambience.

"You didn't need to pay for my dinner to apologize, you know," Valerie said, reading over her menu. She quickly decided on a bowl of minestrone soup and fettuccine with fresh asparagus. No wine, because it would send her to sleep.

"Apologize?" Colby repeated.

Valerie lowered her menu and, crossing her arms, leaned toward him. "Not apologize exactly. You brought me here to tell me you're sorry about what happened last night, didn't you? I mean, it's fairly obvious, since you've been avoiding me all day. But don't worry about it," she said offhandedly, "I understand."

He scowled and set aside his menu. "Sometimes I forget how direct you can be."

"I'd rather have everything out in the open. There's no need to concern yourself with...what happened. I—needed you, and you were there for me."

His scowl intensified. "In other words, any man would have suited your purposes?"

"No," she said. "Only you. What we shared was very...sweet. I'll always be grateful to you for letting me cry."

"It's not the crying that concerns me."

"The kissing was very special, too," she said softly.

"Yes, I suppose it was. But it might be best to forget that, uh, particular part of last night."

The waitress approached with pad and pen in hand. They placed their orders, then Valerie resumed the conversation. "Maybe you can forget the kissing," she said in a mild tone, "but I don't think it'll be possible for me."

Colby's gaze left hers. "Personally, I don't think I'll be able to forget it, either," he said.

They both fell silent but a faint smile curved her lips as she savored his words. He'd tried to dismiss the attraction between them and couldn't. Neither could she.

"It doesn't change anything," he told her, his voice calm and resolute.

He'd meant everything he'd said earlier; that much Valerie understood. She couldn't change who she was. Easy as it would be to fall in love with him, Valerie knew she'd never be truly happy as a homemaker. She had too much ambition, too many dreams. A business career was what she wanted, where her skills lay, and she couldn't relinquish that any more than Colby could give up his medical practice.

"Your father's doing remarkably well," Colby told her in an obvious attempt to change the subject.

Valerie was delighted. Norah had told her repeatedly what excellent progress their father was making, and it was thrilling to have it confirmed.

"I've got him listed as critical at the moment," Colby went on, "but I have a feeling he's going to surprise us all and live to be a hundred."

Valerie beamed Colby a happy smile, hardly able to speak for the emotion clogging her throat. "We owe you so much, Colby."

He shrugged off her thanks and seemed grateful that the waitress appeared just then to deliver the first course of their meal.

The soup was delicious, but after a few spoonfuls Valerie was finished, her appetite gone. She managed only a taste of her fettucine. Colby glanced over, frowning, when she pushed the plate aside.

"Is something wrong?"

She shook her head. "No."

"You hardly touched your meal."

"I know."

"What's wrong?" he pressed.

Valerie lowered her eyes. "I was just trying to decide how I was going to leave you, Colby, and not cry." She hadn't meant to sound quite so serious; she'd meant to sound wryly amused.

Her words silenced him. His eyes met hers, and

when he spoke, his voice revealed his sincerity. "You'd be very easy to love."

"But." She said the dreaded word for him.

"But we both know it wouldn't work."

"You're right," she said convincingly. Why wouldn't her heart listen?

"Valerie." Her father smiled weakly as she entered the cubicle in SICU. His hand reached for hers, brought it to his lips. "I wondered when I'd see you."

"I…went out for dinner."

"All by yourself?"

"No." But she didn't want to tell him she'd been with Colby.

Besides, there were other things to discuss. Norah had told Valerie the most unbelievable story. Apparently while Valerie was out for dinner, their father had told Norah about a vision he'd had. A vision? Valerie didn't know what to make of that, any more than Norah did.

"What's all this Norah was telling me?" she asked.

Once again her father smiled, only this time it was brighter and there was a sparkle in his tired eyes. "I died, you know. Ask Colby if you don't believe me."

Vaguely Valerie remembered Colby saying something about her father's heart stopping and restarting, and considering it a miracle. "I know we're very fortunate to have you with us."

"More fortunate than you realize. Now, I don't want you getting all excited the way your sister did, but I don't expect you will. I had what those television reporters call a near-death experience."

"The long dark tunnel with the light at the end?" Valerie had certainly heard about the phenomenon.

"Nope," he said, shaking his head. "I was in a garden."

"The Garden of Eden?" she asked lightly.

"Might've been. I couldn't say."

He hadn't been aware that she was joking. "I didn't notice the trees so much, but there might've been an apple. What I did notice was the pretty woman tending the roses."

"Mom?" Valerie breathed the question, hardly knowing where it came from.

David smiled and shut his eyes. "We had a good, long talk, your mother and I. She convinced me it wasn't my time to die, that there's still plenty for me to do on this earth. I wasn't pleased to hear it because I've been thinking for some time now that I'd rather be with her."

"Daddy, I don't—"

"Shush now, because I have a lot to tell you and I'm getting weaker."

"All right."

"Your mother loves you and is very proud of everything you've accomplished, but she said you should take time to enjoy life before it passes you by."

That sounded like something her mother would say.

"She also told me I was an old fool to try and match you up with Colby."

"But—" She snapped her mouth closed, unwilling to say more.

"Grace feels my pushing the two of you to marry was ridiculous. Said I should apologize for that."

Valerie remained silent.

"There's more," David continued, "lots more. Grace wanted to be sure she gave me plenty of reasons to come back to this world."

"I'm very glad she convinced you."

Her father's eyes drifted shut, but he opened them again with apparent effort. "She talked to me about Stephanie and Norah, too."

"Good, Daddy," she said softly, patting his hand. "You can tell me all about it next time."

"Want to explain now..."

"Shh, sleep."

"You're all going to get married. Your mother assured me all three of you would."

"Of course we will. Eventually."

"Soon. Very...soon."

"I'm glad," she whispered, although she wasn't sure he heard her.

So her father had gone through a near-death experience. Valerie didn't know how much credence to put in what he was saying. Marriage was the farthest thing from her mind at the moment. Obviously, marrying Colby was out of the question. And—without even noticing—she'd lost interest in the idea of a relationship with Rowdy Cassidy.

"She gave me twelve reasons to live," her father announced sleepily. "Twelve very good reasons."

Valerie recalled that Norah had said something about the number six. She couldn't imagine why her father was speaking in figures all of a sudden.

"Twelve reasons," Valerie echoed, then leaned forward to kiss his cheek.

Her father's eyes fluttered open and he grinned boyishly. "Yup, my grandchildren. You, my darling Valerie, are going to give me three. All within the next few years."

Six

"When's the last time you spoke to your father?" Colby asked Valerie when she arrived at the hospital the next morning, carrying an armful of apple blossoms for the nurses' station. He seemed to be waiting for her, and none too patiently.

She sighed, realizing what must have happened. "I take it Dad told you about his experience in the Garden of Eden?"

"It was the Garden of Eden?"

"Figuratively, I suppose."

"So you know, then," Colby muttered. A hint of a frown flickered across his expression.

"Look at it this way—at least Dad's given up his matchmaking efforts." Valerie had assumed Colby would be happy about that, so his reaction puzzled her.

His scowl deepened. "He apologized for even making the suggestion."

"See, what'd I tell you?" Valerie said, her mouth quirking with a smile. "We're both in the clear."

Apparently, this wasn't what Colby wanted to hear, either. "He also claimed you'd be married before the end of the summer—and that you'd present him with three grandchildren."

"In the next few years. It looks like I'm going to be busy, doesn't it?" Valerie hadn't taken her father's announcement too seriously; he'd had some kind of pleasant hallucination, and if it made him feel better, if it gave him a reason for living, then that was fine. She'd go along with it, although she wouldn't actively encourage him.

Besides, it was highly unlikely she'd marry anytime soon, and even if she did, she had no intention of leaping into this motherhood business. Marriage would be enough of an adjustment. She enjoyed children, and naturally assumed she'd eventually want a family, but definitely not in the first year or two following her marriage.

"Did he say *who* you're supposed to marry?"

"No. He wouldn't tell Norah, either, although he seemed to enjoy letting her know she's going to have six kids. Three boys and three girls, if you can believe it. You don't really buy any of this, do you?"

His mouth twisted into a wry grin. "That would be ridiculous, only... Never mind," he finished abruptly.

"No, tell me."

He shrugged, clearly regretting that he'd said anything. "Another patient of mine, an older woman, had a near-death experience. It was all rather...strange."

"She came back thinking she knew who her children would marry and how many grandchildren she was going to have?" Valerie asked sarcastically.

"No." Colby threw her an annoyed glance.

"What happened then?" She was curious now, unable to disguise her interest.

"She seemed to know certain things about the future. She—predicted, I guess is the word—certain political events. She wasn't entirely sure how she knew, she just did."

"So what was that all about?"

Colby obviously wasn't comfortable outlining the details of his patient's experience. "She didn't have any more than an eighth-grade education, and she'd never taken much interest in history or politics. But after that near-death phenomenon, she was suddenly able to discuss complicated world problems with genuine insight and skill. She didn't understand it herself, and I didn't have any medical explanation to offer her. The whole thing was as much a mystery to me as it was to her."

Until then, Valerie had to admit, she'd found her father's experience somewhat…entertaining. She'd been willing to tolerate it, since whatever had happened had been very real to David. This "dreamtime" with her mother had given his life a new purpose, and she was grateful for that, if nothing else.

"What are you saying?" she asked Colby.

"I don't actually know."

Suddenly none of this seemed quite as amusing. "Dad insists I'll be married before the end of the summer."

"He told me the same thing," Colby said. "About

you, I mean." He paused. "Is it likely? I mean, is there someone back in Texas you've been seeing on a regular basis?" He clasped his hands behind his back and strolled slowly down the corridor. "Someone other than this person you were hoping to start dating soon?"

She puffed out her cheeks, debating how much to tell him about Rowdy Cassidy. "Not really, but…"

"Go on," he urged.

"My boss, Rowdy Cassidy." She shifted the spray of apple blossoms, conscious of their heady aroma in the antiseptic-smelling hospital corridor.

"The owner of CHIPS?"

Valerie nodded. "I've never gone out on a formal date with him, although until recently we saw each other nearly every day. We've often traveled together, and attend business dinners together. It wasn't until I got here and Dad started talking about you and me marrying that—well, Rowdy seems the natural choice for me. He's as dedicated to his career as I am and… we get along well."

"He's a wealthy man. Prominent in his field."

"Yes."

Colby clenched his jaw as though he disapproved.

"Do you know something about Rowdy that I don't?"

"I've never met the man. Everything I know about him I've read online or in the papers. But from all outward appearances, the two of you should be an ideal couple." His words were indifferent. Then without saying anything else, he turned and walked away from her.

"Colby," Valerie called, once she'd recovered from

her initial surprise. She hurried after him. "What's wrong? You're acting like I've done something to offend you."

"I'm not angry," he said, his voice low. His gaze held hers with a disturbing intensity. "I remember what you said yesterday about wondering how we were going to say goodbye. I was just thinking the same thing. I don't know how I'm going to be able to stand by and watch you marry another man."

To her the solution was simple. He could marry her himself. But...they'd both already decided that wouldn't work.

"What about you?" she asked, needing to know. "Is there someone special you've been seeing?"

"Yes."

Her heart felt as if it had done a nosedive, colliding with her stomach. Her face must have revealed her shock because he elaborated.

"Sherry Waterman. I thought Norah might have mentioned her."

"A nurse?" she guessed.

Colby nodded. "Sherry has her nursing degree and she's also trained as a midwife. That's what she's been doing for the past five years. She's good with children and she enjoys weaving and gardening." His voice was brisk and matter-of-fact as he listed Sherry's qualifications.

"She...sounds exactly right for you." The aching admission was torn from her throat. Although it was painful to think of Colby with another woman, Valerie knew he'd chosen well in Sherry Waterman. Domestic, talented, perfect in all the ways Valerie wasn't.

"We've been dating for the last year."

"A year," Valerie repeated slowly, surprised he hadn't proposed to Sherry long before now. "You shouldn't keep her waiting then."

"I keep telling myself the same thing."

His words hurt, although Valerie pretended otherwise. "I'm delighted for you, Colby."

"Rowdy Cassidy will make you a good husband." His eyes probed hers.

Valerie smiled and nodded, then they both turned and walked in opposite directions. And although she was tempted, she didn't look back.

Valerie's cell phone vibrated, and she took the call in the hospital lobby.

"Valerie, it's Rowdy. Thought I'd check and see how everything's going with your father. No one's heard from you in a while."

When had she last reported into CHIPS headquarters? Two days before, she calculated. Two whole days! Valerie found that hard to believe. Until recently, her job had been all-consuming, but it wasn't that way now. She'd completely overlooked her work responsibilities, forgotten everything that had once been so important. It seemed impossible that she could have allowed so much time to slip past.

"My father had open-heart surgery."

"How's he doing now?"

"Fabulously well. His recovery in the last twenty-four hours has been remarkable." She didn't tell him that much of the improvement was a result of a change in attitude. Since his "conversation in the garden" with Grace, David Bloomfield's will to live was stronger than ever. If there was anything to worry about now, it was the fact that Steffie hadn't arrived yet and no one had heard from her. Valerie had spent part of the morning calling the airlines to find out which flight she was on, to no avail.

"We miss you around here," Rowdy said in that casual way of his. Valerie could picture him sitting in his office, leaning back in his plush leather chair, cowboy boots propped on the mahogany desk. She couldn't remember ever seeing Rowdy without his boots and hat. She always thought of him as the Texan of frontier legend, the man who tackled life with robust energy, who considered no problem insurmountable. He worked hard, played hard and lived hard.

"I miss CHIPS, too."

"Any idea when you'll be back?"

"I'm sorry, no, but if you need me because of the Old West Bank deal—"

"No, no," Rowdy said, breaking in. "We're handling that from our end, so don't you worry about a thing. I just wanted you to know I miss you."

The personal pronoun didn't escape Valerie's notice. Rowdy *was* attracted to her. "My father wanted me to thank you for the flowers," she said. "Th-they got here yesterday morning." She'd hardly been aware of it at the time, although the nurses had all exclaimed over the lavish bouquets. Now, she felt flustered and nervous with him, something that had never happened before. Their relationship was moving into new territory, and Valerie found the ground unstable and a bit frightening.

"Actually the flowers were for you. I thought you needed something to brighten up your day."

"It was very thoughtful of you."

"It's the least I could do for my favorite executive. You hurry back, you hear?"

"I will. And, Rowdy, thanks for calling." She closed her cell phone and let her breath rush out in a deep sigh.

Norah was already in the waiting room when Valerie returned there. "That was Rowdy Cassidy," she explained unnecessarily.

"Are you in love with him?" Norah asked without preamble. "I thought you and Dr. Winston might be hitting it off, but..."

"Colby's involved with Sherry Waterman." Valerie kept her voice steady, making a strenuous effort to feign disinterest.

One glance at Norah told her she hadn't succeeded. "You'll recall that I never bothered to mention Sherry. There's a reason."

"Oh?" Valerie shrugged. "I wondered... I mean, even Colby seemed to think you had, or rather that you should have." She'd wanted to ask her sister, but had hesitated, almost preferring not to know.

"Those two have been dating for a year. If Colby was serious about Sherry he would've asked her to marry him before now. Even Sherry's given up on them, although Colby doesn't seem to have figured that out yet. The last I heard, she was seeing someone else. Not that I blame her," Norah was quick to add. "It must be the most frustrating thing in the world to be crazy about a guy and have him lukewarm toward you."

"I'm sure it must be."

"You still haven't answered me," Norah pressed. "What about Rowdy? Are you in love with him?"

Valerie shrugged again, uncomfortable with the subject of her boss, unsure of her own feelings toward him. "Yes and no."

"You're beginning to sound like Colby. I think he loves everything Sherry represents. She's a nurturing, kindhearted woman. She fits the image of what Colby wants in a wife."

"Then what's stopping him?"

Norah gnawed on her lower lip for a moment. "My guess is that she bores him. Don't get me wrong, Sherry's not a boring person. Actually when I think about it, Sherry and I are a lot alike. She's a homebody like me, and little things mean a lot to her. She doesn't need an active social life or fancy clothes. Given the choice between a stay-at-home date with a rented movie or dining in a world-class restaurant, she'd opt for the movie."

"I see."

"You're much better suited to Colby."

"Me?" Valerie asked, her voice rising in astonishment. Hadn't Norah just finished describing the kind of woman Colby wanted—a woman completely unlike Valerie?

"I've seen the looks the two of you exchange," Norah continued thoughtfully. "I'm not blind, you know. I can feel the attraction between you. It's mutual—and it's hot."

"Really," Valerie said, becoming preoccupied with the crease in her wool trousers.

"Yes, really!"

"Yes, well, I'll admit we're attracted to each other, but nothing's going to come of it." She glanced at her watch, wanting an excuse to leave. "I'm going to stop in and see Dad."

Norah's smile seemed all-knowing. "Okay."

David Bloomfield's color was better, and he grinned happily when he saw his eldest daughter.

"Hello, Dad," she said in a cheerful voice as she leaned over to kiss his cheek.

"Valerie," he whispered, holding out his hand to her. "Listen, sweetheart, you're spending too much time at the hospital. Take the day and get out in the sunshine. You're beginning to look pale."

"But..."

"It'll do you good. No more sleeping on some dilapidated couch in the waiting room, either."

She'd slept in her own bed in her own room for the first time the night before. In the morning, she'd been astonished at how well rested she felt. And she'd indulged in a long, hot shower, followed by a good breakfast—cooked by Norah.

The crews were just beginning to spray the apple trees under the direction of Dale Howard, the orchard manager. She'd heard the familiar sounds of men working in the orchards. It brought back memories of years past, of racing down the long, even rows, and climbing onto the low limbs of the trees, sitting there like a princess surveying her magical kingdom. Orchard Valley *was* magical, a town set apart.

For Valerie, coming home was like escaping to the past. The people were friendly, the neighbors neighborly, and problems were shared. It was a little piece of heaven.

"I wasn't at the hospital last night," she told him, pulling herself out of her musings. She loved Orchard Valley more than any place on earth, but she'd never be satisfied living here. There wasn't enough challenge, not enough to tax her mind. No, Houston was her future and she accepted that with only one regret. Colby.

"So I heard," her father answered. "I saw Colby earlier."

Valerie watched his expression, hoping for—what?—some sign, some indication of her father's thoughts. And of Colby's...

There was none.

"Well? What did the good doctor have to say?"

"Nothing much."

"Did he mention me?" she couldn't prevent herself from asking.

"Nope, can't say he did. Does that disappoint you?"

"Of course not."

"Is there any reason he *should* mention you?"

Valerie was sorry she'd brought up the subject. "Not that I know of."

Her answers seemed to make him smile. "So you like my doctor?"

"He's been wonderful to you," Valerie said.

"I wasn't talking about me," David told her gruffly. "I'm referring to *you*. You're attracted to him, aren't you, Valerie? You were never very good at hiding your feelings."

"I've never met a man who appeals to me more," Valerie said truthfully. There was no point in trying to deceive her father. He knew her all too well, and he understood her better than anyone, sometimes better than she understood herself.

"He feels the same way?" The question was calm, as though he were speaking to a child.

Valerie lowered her eyes before shaking her head. "It'd never work, and we both know it."

She expected an argument from her father, was even looking for one. She wanted him to tell her she was wrong, that love *could* work when two people were committed to each other. That it wouldn't matter how dissimilar they were, how differently they viewed life. That nothing mattered but the love they shared…

Her father, however, didn't respond.

Discouraged, Valerie said goodbye and returned to the waiting room. On her way, she saw that Norah sat talking to another doctor at the end of the hallway. She was grateful her sister had left, because she needed time alone to think.

If she wanted evidence that people with very different personalities could fall in love and make the relationship work, she need look no further than her own parents. The story of how they'd met and fallen in love was like a fairy tale, one that, as a child, she'd never tired of hearing.

Her father had gone to university and obtained his degree in business administration. Armed with his dreams, he'd built a financial empire and became a millionaire within a few years. Then he'd collapsed with rheumatic fever, nearly losing his life. While he was in the hospital recuperating, he'd met a young nurse. David knew the moment he met Grace Johnson that he was going to love her. It never occurred to him that she'd refuse his marriage proposal.

Several months of relentless pursuit later, he'd convinced Grace to marry him. Despite the fact that she was deeply in love with David, Grace had been afraid. She was a preacher's daughter who'd lived a simple life. David was a business tycoon who'd taken automation technology to new industry heights. Grace's fears about a marriage to David Bloomfield were warranted. But over the years, love had proven even the most hardened skeptics wrong, and the two had lived and loved together until her mother's death a few years before.

Her own romance wasn't going to have a fairy-tale ending, the way her parents' had. Her father knew it, too, otherwise he would've been the first to encourage her.

Her father, however, had said nothing.

Valerie was working in the den on her laptop, putting files in order, when she saw the red car hurtle down the driveway. She thought, for one hopeful moment, that it might be Colby, but then remembered he drove a maroon Buick. Still, she hastened to answer the door.

It was Charles Tomaselli, looking tired and frustrated.

"Have you heard from Stephanie?" he demanded without so much as a greeting.

Her sister's absence had been weighing on Valerie's mind, too. She'd done everything she could think of; she'd even placed a call to the American Embassy in Rome, with no results.

"I haven't heard a word. I don't know what could've happened to her."

"How late *is* she?"

Valerie had to think for a moment. In the past week, she'd lost all track of time. "Norah was the last person to speak to Steffie," she explained. "Let me see—that was just before Dad's surgery. Steffie thought she'd be home within twenty-four hours."

"That was forty-eight hours ago."

He didn't need to remind her, Valerie thought irritably. "She's coming by way of Tokyo."

"Tokyo? She's flying to Oregon via *Japan?*" Charles snapped.

"I gather she didn't have much choice."

"Don't you think you should be making some inquiries?" he asked gruffly.

"I already have. Tell me who else I should call and I'll be happy to do so."

Charles settled down on the top porch step, resting both elbows on his knees. "I have to tell you, Valerie, I'm worried. She should've been here before now."

"I know."

"I have some friends, some connections," Charles

said absently, "and I've checked with them. But they can't find any trace of her on the flights scheduled out of Rome. If she isn't here by tomorrow afternoon, I don't think you have any alternative but to contact the authorities."

Valerie swallowed tightly, then nodded. She could slap Steff silly for putting them through all this worry.

"She's okay, Charles," Valerie said after a moment.

"What makes you so sure?" He turned to look up at her.

"I...don't know, I just am."

Charles stood agilely, his gaze leveled on the long narrow driveway that led in from the road. "I hope you're right, Valerie. I hope you're right."

Valerie hoped so, too. And she wondered if his concern for Stephanie meant as much as she thought it did.

Norah came back from the hospital a half hour later, talkative and lively. "I can't get over how much Dad's improved in such a short time."

Valerie took the shrimp salad she'd prepared for their dinner from the refrigerator. Salads were her specialty. That, and folding napkins. She could do both without a hitch.

For the first time since her arrival, Valerie had spent most of the day away from the hospital. When her father had suggested she leave, she'd initially felt a bit annoyed. But as she revisited the life that had once been hers in this quiet community, she accepted the wisdom of his advice. She *had* needed to get out, to breathe in the serenity she found in Orchard Valley and exhale the fear that had choked her from the moment she'd received Norah's frantic message. Then, after her walk, she'd come back to the house, and because she'd never been idle in her life, she'd set up a communications center in her father's den.

"I'm going back to work, starting tomorrow," Norah announced between bites of lettuce, shrimp and slices of hard-boiled egg. "The hospital's understaffed, but then when isn't it? I'll still be able to see Dad, maybe even more often than before. You don't mind, do you?"

"Of course I don't mind. You do whatever you think best."

"You're not going to leave, are you?" Norah asked, rushing the words. "I wouldn't do this if the hospital didn't need me so badly."

"I realize that."

Norah took another forkful of salad. "You're quiet tonight. Is anything wrong?"

"Not really." She didn't want to worry Norah about Steffie's disappearance.

"Colby asked about you."

She felt her stomach churn with contradictory emotions. Part of her was thrilled that he'd even mentioned her, yet she experienced a growing sense of apprehension.

"He wanted to know where you were."

"Did you tell him?"

"Of course," Norah answered blithely. "He said he thought it was a good idea for you to get out of the hospital more. You've practically been living there ever since you arrived." She slowly chewed another bite of her salad. "He asked me what I knew about Rowdy Cassidy," she said.

Valerie put down her fork, her appetite having fled. "What did you tell him?"

"The truth. That I've never met the man, but Dad seems to think he's wonderful. You probably weren't aware of this, but Dad's been following CHIPS ever since you started working there. He thinks Rowdy's a genius. Funny, though—I got the impression that wasn't what Colby wanted to hear."

"The shrimp was on sale at Vern's Market," Valerie said, changing the subject abruptly, not wanting to talk about Colby. Not now when she felt so vulnerable, so conscious of the attraction between them. "Vern said he cooked it himself this morning."

"You don't want to talk about Colby?"

Valerie grinned. Her sister hadn't graduated magna cum laude for nothing.

"You're not going anyplace tonight, are you?" Norah asked next.

"I thought I'd drive in to the hospital and visit Dad, but other than that, no. Do you need me to do something?"

Norah shrugged. "I may be wrong, but I think Colby wanted to talk to you. I have a feeling he might call."

Norah was right.

When Valerie returned from her trip to the hospital, her sister had left a note taped to her bedroom door.

COLBY PHONED. SAID HE'D TALK TO YOU IN THE MORNING.

Valerie read the message with mixed feelings.

Thrill and dread went at it for round two, again evenly matched. She determined to forget everything—love, Colby, the future—for tonight. The morning would be soon enough to resume her worries. She craved the forgetfulness of sleep, the escape from thought and feeling.

Valerie had assumed she'd fall asleep with the same ease she had the previous night. For a solid hour she beat her pillow, tossed and turned in an effort to find a comfortable position. Finally giving up, she reached for the light on the bedside table and read until her eyes closed and the business journal slipped from her fingers.

But Valerie's exhausted sleep wasn't the restful oblivion she'd longed for. Colby wandered into her dreams like an uninvited guest.

He looked handsome, dressed in the suit he'd worn the night he'd taken her to the Italian restaurant.

"You're not going to be able to forget me, are you?"

In her dream, Valerie said nothing, but only because she had no argument. She merely stared at him, adoring every feature, every movement.

A noise disturbed her, distracting her from Colby. Irritated, she looked over her shoulder to see what it was and when she looked back, he was gone. She cried out in frustration, the sound of her own voice jerking her awake. She was sitting upright in the bed, heart pounding furiously.

It took her another moment to realize there was some sort of commotion going on downstairs. She climbed out of bed and grabbed her robe.

From the top of the stairs, she saw Norah, laughing and crying at once. A battered suitcase stood on the floor, along with a leather coat and an umbrella.

"Steffie!" Valerie cried excitedly, racing down the stairs.

Her sister was home.

Seven

Colby picked up the clipboard at the foot of David Bloomfield's bed, scanning the notations the nursing staff had written through the night. Although his eyes were lowered, he couldn't help being aware of David Bloomfield's cocky grin.

"You must be feeling more like your old self this morning," he observed genially.

David's smile widened. "I'm feeling more chipper each and every day. How much longer do you intend to keep me prisoner here? I'm itching to get home."

"Another week," Colby answered, replacing the clipboard. "Perhaps less, depending on how well you do."

"A week!" David protested. "Are you sure you aren't holding me up just so you'll have an excuse to visit with Valerie?"

Colby's hackles rose, and he was about to defend his medical judgment when he realized the old man was baiting him—and enjoying it.

"I'm going to have you transferred out of the Surgical Intensive Care Unit this morning," Colby continued, "but first I want you up and walking."

"I've been up."

Colby glanced back at the chart, surprised to see no indication of the activity.

"I just didn't let anyone know. I felt a bit dizzy, so I only walked around the bed. Not much of a trip, but it tired me out plenty."

"You're not to get out of this bed again unless there's someone with you, understand?" He used his sternest voice.

"All right, all right," David agreed. Stroking his chin, he studied Colby. "She's pretty as a picture, that oldest daughter of mine. Isn't she, Doc?"

Colby ignored both the comment and the question. "I'll have one of the physio staff come down in a few minutes and we'll see how well you do with your exercises. I imagine that by this afternoon you'll have conquered the hallway."

"From what I hear, that Rowdy Cassidy's been calling her two, three times a day."

Colby stiffened at the mention of the other man's name. He'd tried to tell himself that Valerie would be happier married to Cassidy. They shared the same attitudes, beliefs and ambitions; together they'd take the business world by storm. Rowdy was exactly the type of dynamic personality who'd help Valerie fulfill her goals and dreams. She'd never be content as a physician's wife, he told himself again. Nevertheless, he was having trouble accepting the obvious.

He'd never thought of himself as romantic. His career had consumed his life from the time he was a high-school sophomore. His much-loved grandfather had died of heart disease, and it was then that Colby had decided to become a doctor. Everything else had been subordinated to that goal. Only in the past year or so had he felt the desire to marry and start a family.

He'd acted upon that desire with methodical thoroughness, mentally tabulating a list of his wants and needs. He'd looked around at the single women in Orchard Valley and decided to date Sherry Waterman. If things didn't work out with Sherry, Norah Bloomfield was next on his list, although he was concerned about their age difference.

Things *had* worked out with Sherry, at least in the beginning. He'd found her refreshing and genuine and fun. Problems crept up later, when he discovered that she was entirely predictable. Involved with a woman who embodied every trait he wanted in his life's partner, he'd been…bored. He wasn't sure anymore that he needed someone quite so even-tempered and domestic.

According to the schedule he'd set for himself, he should have been married by now.

He wasn't.

To irritate him further, the only woman he'd been strongly attracted to in the past year was Valerie Bloomfield, and anyone with a lick of sense could see they weren't the least bit compatible.

For months, long before his heart attack, David Bloomfield had found excuses to drag his oldest daughter's name into their conversations. By the time he met Valerie, Colby was thoroughly sick of hearing about her. He hadn't even expected to *like* her. Instead, his heart and his head had been spinning out of control from that first moment.

It was time to put an end to such nonsense, before either of them took this attraction business too seriously.

"Cassidy would be a good match for a woman like Valerie," he said as offhandedly as he could. The last thing he wanted was for Valerie's father to know how attracted he was to her, although he suspected David already knew. The old man seemed to have a sixth sense about things like this.

"Rowdy will, at that," David returned matter-of-factly. "I should know, too." The cocky grin was back in place.

Colby's chest tightened, his anger simmering just beneath the surface. David hadn't referred to his dream lately, the one he'd termed his near-death experience. But from bits and pieces of conversation, Colby had learned that David was still predicting Valerie's wedding. It made sense that the man he expected her to marry was Rowdy Cassidy.

All the better. He—

"Stephanie's home," David said conversationally, cutting into Colby's thoughts. "I saw her briefly this morning. What a lovely sight she was to these tired old eyes."

Colby nodded, finding it difficult to dispel the image of Valerie married to her employer. Well, he'd better get used to the idea, because it was likely to happen soon. And because he refused to deliberately ruin his life by marrying the wrong woman.

He'd call Sherry this afternoon, Colby decided with renewed determination, and ask her out to dinner. One thing was certain; he intended to steer clear of Valerie Bloomfield, regardless of how hard that was.

So much for the best-laid plans, Colby mused as he left the Surgical Intensive Care Unit. Valerie was standing in the corridor waiting for him. As always, when he saw her, his heart was gladdened. An old-fashioned expression, perhaps, but he didn't know how else to describe what he felt when he was with Valerie.

He remembered the time he'd sought her out after losing Joanne Murphy. Just being with her had taken the sharp edge off the pain of that unexpected death, had helped him deal with the frustration, the sense of powerlessness. When she'd suggested coffee, his first inclination had been to refuse, but he'd found he couldn't. Sharing his concerns with her had, in some indefinable way, comforted him.

It seemed to him that their conversation had helped her, too, in coming to terms with her father's illness.

They'd helped each other. In thinking about those moments together, Colby understood why he couldn't simply dismiss his fascination with her as sexual attraction. That was part of it, all right. But more than any woman he'd ever known, Valerie Bloomfield was his equal. In intelligence, in emotional strength, in commitment to those she loved.

Every time Colby had been with her since, he experienced an elation, a small joy that left him feeling bewildered. Left him wanting to be with her even more.

Yet he knew he couldn't afford to pursue a relationship that had no chance of lasting.

"You wanted to see me?" Valerie asked, her eyes meeting his expectantly.

He frowned and shook his head. "No."

"Norah left a note for me last night, saying you'd phoned."

"Oh, that. It was nothing." He wanted to kick himself for that phone call now. He'd been looking for a reason to talk to her. His day had been long and tiring, and his defenses down, so he'd made up an excuse to hear the sound of her voice.

"I just wanted to tell you I'm transferring your father from SICU this morning," he went on quickly. "His progress has been nothing short of remarkable. If it continues like this, he'll be out of the hospital inside a week."

Valerie's eyes sparkled with relief. "That's wonderful news! It seems everything's happening at once. I don't know if you heard, but Steffie got home last night."

"So I understand." Colby watched her closely. Although she said nothing else, he realized that something was troubling Valerie. Her brow had furrowed, ever so briefly, when she mentioned her sister's name. Colby suspected she wasn't aware of the tiny, telltale action.

"Something going on with your sister?"

Her eyes widened in surprise. "Yes, just now. She was sitting in the waiting room reading a copy of the *Clarion* when she jumped to her feet, demanding to know if I'd read it. Before I could say anything, she dashed out, taking the paper with her. I can't remember ever seeing Steffie so angry. I'm not sure what got into her, but I'm guessing it has to do with Charles Tomaselli."

"I'm sure she'll tell you eventually."

"I'm sure she will, too, although I have a feeling this is connected to an article he wrote with Dad's help. I just don't understand what she found so offensive. I read it and I didn't see any problem. Those two can't seem to get along. They never could. It's always surprised me, because she seemed to be so keen on him and I was beginning to think he felt the same way."

The temptation to linger, even to suggest they have coffee together, was overwhelming, but Colby resisted. He was doing a lot of that where Valerie was concerned. Resisting. He only hoped his willpower held firm until she went back to Texas—and to Cassidy—where she belonged.

"Valerie," Steffie said, standing in the doorway outside Valerie's bedroom. "Have you got a moment?"

"Sure." Valerie was sitting up in bed reading, but her mind wasn't on the latest computer technology she'd had every intention of studying. With infuriating frequency, her thoughts drifted away from high resolution monitors and narrowed in on Colby. She welcomed her sister's visit, not least as a distraction.

Steffie crossed the room and sat on the edge of Valerie's bed. "I made a complete fool of myself this morning," she said, her eyes downcast.

Valerie waited for her to explain, but further details didn't seem to be forthcoming. Her curiosity was aroused, but she didn't want to pry.

"With Charles," Steffie finally said, drawing her knees up and circling them with her arms. "It isn't the first time, either. He's the one person in the world I swore I'd never speak to again and then, the first few hours I'm home, I make an idiot of myself over him."

Valerie set aside her business journal and drew up her own knees. "He's been worried about you."

"You've talked to him? When? What did he say?" Steffie's head came up. Her long dark hair fell to the middle of her back, and her eyes probed Valerie's. Although Steff was almost twenty-seven, she looked closer to eighteen. Especially now, when she felt so embarrassed.

"Charles asked about you shortly after I got home, and later he was concerned because you didn't arrive when we expected you. Apparently he made some inquiries, trying to track you down. Both Norah and I were so caught up in what was happening with Dad that we weren't as worried about your late appearance as we should've been. Charles, however, seemed terribly anxious."

"He was just hoping I'd get home in time to make an idiot of myself, which I did."

Valerie thought that was unfair of Steffie. "Charles has been wonderful," she protested, still wondering exactly what Stephanie had done.

"To you and Norah. I'm the one he can't get along with." Steffie's shoulders rose as she gave a deep, heartfelt sigh. "How do you know when you're in love, really in love?" she asked plaintively.

Their mother should be the one answering that question. Not Valerie. She hadn't figured out her relationships with Colby *or* Rowdy. Bemused, she shook her head. She could outsmart the competition, put together some of the biggest deals in the industry, but she didn't know how to tell if she was in love.

"I wish I could answer that," Valerie said quietly. "I know next to nothing about love. I was sort of hoping *you'd* be able to enlighten *me*."

Steffie frowned. "Don't tell me we're going to have to talk to Norah about this."

"We can't," Valerie said, then started to laugh.

"What's so funny? Listen, Val, this isn't a time for humor, or even pride. If Norah knows more than we do, which she probably does, then we should forget she's the youngest and come right out and ask her."

"We can't ask Norah about love, because she isn't here," Valerie said. "She's on a date."

Steffie started to laugh, too, not because it was particularly funny, but because it was a rare moment of shared closeness.

"Reading between the lines of your letters, I assumed you'd fallen in love with your boss," she said next. "You never said as much, but the two of you seemed to be spending a lot of time together."

"I think I might've been half in love with him until I met Colby."

"Dad's heart doctor?"

Valerie nodded. "When I first got home, Dad was

fully expecting to die. He actually seemed to be looking forward to it, which annoyed everyone. Although not being able to get home must have been a nightmare for you, it might be the one thing that kept him hanging on as long as he did."

"You're sidestepping the issue. Tell me about Colby."

"It started with Dad's matchmaking efforts, which I found rather amusing and Colby found utterly frustrating, but then as we got to know each other we realized there was a spark." More of a blowtorch than a spark, really, but she wasn't going to say that.

"If you're in love with Colby, then why do you look like you're going to cry?"

"Because we both know it wouldn't work. He's a small-town doctor, who also lectures at Portland University. Although he could practice anywhere, he wants to stay right here in Orchard Valley."

"And you don't?"

"I don't think I could be happy here," Valerie said miserably. "Not anymore. And there are other problems, too...."

"But if you truly loved each other, you'd be able to find a solution to your differences."

"That's just it. I don't know if this *is* love, and I don't think Colby does, either. Everything would be much easier if we did."

"Yes, but if he's the right person..."

"I don't know. I'm attracted to him. I think about him constantly, but is that enough for me to forsake all my ambitions? Give up my career? I don't know," she said again, "and it's got me tied up in knots. How do I decide? And if I *did* quit CHIPS and found some other job around here, how do I know I wouldn't resent him five years down the road? How do I know he wouldn't end up resenting *me* for not being a more traditional kind of woman—which is what he wants? Besides, even if I do love Colby, how can I be sure he feels the same way about me?"

"I wish Mom was here."

"So do I," Valerie said fervently. "Oh, Steffie, so do I."

Valerie didn't see Colby for several days. Four, to be exact. As her father's health improved, she spent less and less time at the hospital, therefore decreasing her chances of casually running into him. She was working out of the house, and that helped. Being in a familiar place, doing familiar tasks, allayed her fears and tempered her frustrations.

She knew she should think about returning to Texas. The crisis had passed, and by remaining in Orchard Valley she was creating one of a different sort. CHIPS, Inc., needed her. Rowdy Cassidy needed her. She'd already missed one important business trip, and although Rowdy had encouraged her to stay in Orchard Valley as long as necessary, he'd also let her know he was looking forward to her return.

Valerie had almost run out of excuses for staying in Oregon. Her father was going to be discharged in record time and Valerie, with her two sisters, planned a celebration dinner that included Colby.

She was surprised he'd accepted the invitation. Surprised and pleased. She was hungry for the sight of him. He was in her thoughts constantly, and she wondered if it was the same for him.

All afternoon, she'd been feeling like a schoolgirl. Excited and nearly giddy at the prospect of her father's homecoming—especially since Colby would be driving him back.

Norah had been in the kitchen most of the afternoon, with Stephanie as her assistant. Since Valerie's culinary skills were limited to salad preparation and napkin folding, she'd been assigned both jobs, along with setting the table.

"What time is it?" Steffie called from the kitchen.

Valerie, who was carefully arranging their best china on the dining-room table, shot a glance at the grandfather clock. "Five."

"They're due in less than thirty minutes."

"Do I detect a note of panic?" Valerie teased.

"Dinner isn't even close to being done," Steffie told her.

They'd chosen a menu that included none of their father's favorites. David Bloomfield was a meat-and-potatoes man, but that was all about to change. Colby had been very definite about that. From now on, David would be a low-cholesterol-and-high-fiber man.

"The table's set," Valerie informed the others. As far as she knew, it was the first time they'd brought out the good china since their mother's death. But their father's welcome-home dinner warranted using the very best.

Fifteen minutes later, Valerie glanced out the living-room window to see Colby's maroon car coming down the long driveway. "They're here!" she shouted, hurrying to the front porch, barely able to contain her excitement.

This moment seemed like a miracle to her. She'd come to accept that she was going to lose her father, and now he'd been given a second chance at life. This was so much more than she'd dared hope.

Steffie and Norah joined her on the porch. Colby climbed out of the car first and came around to assist David. It was all Valerie could do not to rush down the steps and help him herself. Although her father had made phenomenal progress in the eight days since his surgery, he remained terribly pale and thinner than she'd ever seen him. But his eyes glowed with obvious pride and satisfaction as he looked at his three daughters.

He turned to Colby and said something Valerie couldn't hear. Whatever it was made Colby's eyes dart toward Valerie. She met his gaze, all too briefly, then they looked hurriedly away from each other, as though embarrassed to be caught staring.

"I'm afraid dinner's not quite ready," Norah said as Colby eased David into his recliner by the fireplace.

"I've been waiting two weeks for a decent meal," David grumbled. "Hospital food doesn't sit well with me. I hope you've outdone yourself."

"I have," Norah promised, smiling at Valerie. Their father wasn't expecting poached salmon and dill sauce with salad and rice, but he'd adjust to healthier eating habits soon enough.

"Can I get you anything, Dad?" Valerie asked, assuming he'd request the paper or a cup of coffee.

"Walk down and see if the Howard boy is still in the orchard, would you, Val?"

"Of course, but I don't think you should worry about the orchard now."

"I'm not worried. I just want to know what's been going on while I was laid up. I promise I'm not going to overdo it. Colby wouldn't let me. I tried to die three times, but he was right there making sure I didn't. You don't think I'd want to ruin all that work, do you?"

Valerie grinned. "All right, I'll check and see if the foreman's still around."

"Colby," David said, raising his index finger imperiously, "you go with her. I don't want her walking in the orchard alone."

The request was a shamefully blatant excuse to throw them together, but neither complained.

Colby followed her out the front door and down the porch steps. "You don't need to come," she said, looking up at him. "I've been walking through these orchards since I was a toddler. I won't get lost."

"I know that."

"Dad was just inventing a way for us to be alone."

"I know that, too. He told me while we were driving here that he intended to do this."

"But why?"

"Isn't it obvious?"

"Yes, but…" Her father had hinted more than once that he anticipated a prompt wedding between her and Rowdy Cassidy. He'd apparently dropped the idea of her marrying Colby—so did he want her to clarify that in person? He seemed downright delighted at the prospect of Rowdy as a son-in-law, talking about her marriage as if it were a foregone conclusion.

"How have you been?" Colby asked. They strolled in the late-afternoon sunshine toward the west side of the orchard, where the equipment was kept. There was a small office in the storage building, as well, and if Dale Howard was still in the orchard that was the most likely place to find him.

"I've been fine. And you?" Valerie could tell him the truth about her feelings or she could tell him a half-truth. She chose the truth. "I've missed you."

Colby clasped his hands behind his back, as she'd seen him do before. It might have been wishful thinking on her part, but Valerie thought he did so in an effort to keep from touching her.

"I understand your boss is calling you every day," he said stiffly.

"I understand you took Sherry Waterman out to dinner this week," she retorted.

"It didn't help," he muttered. "The whole time we were together I kept thinking I'd rather be with you. Is that what you were hoping to hear?"

Valerie dropped her gaze to the dirt beneath her feet. "No, but I'll admit I'm glad."

"This isn't going to work."

How rigid his words sounded, as though he was holding himself in check, but finding it more and more difficult. "What isn't?"

"You…being here."

"Here? You didn't have to come with me! I've already explained that I'm perfectly capable of finding my way—"

"CHIPS stock went up two dollars a share last week."

Colby was leaping from one subject to the next. "That's great," she said cautiously. "I'm sure Rowdy's thrilled."

"You should be, too."

"As a stockholder myself I am, but what's that got to do with anything?"

"Houston is where you belong, with Rowdy Cassidy and all his millions."

Rowdy had been telling her the same thing. Not in quite the same words, but he wanted her in Texas. With him. Not a day passed that he didn't let her know how much he missed her. Rowdy wasn't romantic; fancy words weren't his forte. He was as straightforward as Valerie herself. He missed her, he said, missed the time they spent together and the discussions they'd shared. He hadn't realized how much until she'd left.

"When are you going back?" Colby demanded.

Valerie understood that this was the whole purpose of their being alone together. This was the reason he'd fallen in with her father's schemes and had walked in the orchard with her. He wanted her out of Orchard Valley and out of his life.

"Soon," she promised, and her voice cracked with pain. The intensity of it took her by surprise; embarrassed, she increased her pace to a half trot, wanting to escape.

"Valerie." His voice came from behind her.

"No, please… You're right. I'll—" She wasn't allowed to finish her thought. Colby caught her by the upper arm and turned her to face him, bringing her into his warm embrace.

He took her wrists and placed them around his neck as though she were a rag doll, then circled her waist with his arms and brought her tight against him. Before she had a chance to catch her breath, his mouth was on hers.

Valerie felt as though she'd drown in the sheer ecstasy of being in his arms again. It wasn't supposed to be like this. It wasn't supposed to feel so right, so good. His mouth was eager and she opened to him as naturally as a flower to the sun.

She clung to him, and then he suddenly jerked his head away. Valerie pressed her face into his shoulder and shuddered. She might've been able to forget him, forget these feelings, if he hadn't kissed her again, if he hadn't taken her into his arms.

"Valerie, can't you see what's happening?"

She nodded. "I'm falling in love with you."

"We can't let this continue."

"But—"

"Are you willing to risk everything we've both worked all our lives to achieve? Are you going to change, or do you expect me to? The fact is, you know that *neither* of us wants to give anything up. So we've got to put an end to this. Because, Valerie, we have nothing in common."

Offhand, Valerie could think of several things they had in common, but she didn't mention them. There was no point. She understood what Colby was saying. If they went on as they were, it would lead to the inevitable, and they'd be so deeply in love that they'd forget what was keeping them apart. They'd choose to forget that Valerie had a brilliant career waiting for her back in Houston. They'd choose to forget that Colby wanted a woman who'd be a dedicated homemaker. They'd overlook even the most obvious differences. For a while, their love would be enough, but that wouldn't last, not for long.

"It's time to go back," Colby said, releasing her.

"Dad won't be worried."

"I'm not talking about your father. I'm talking about you, Valerie. Go back to Texas," he said, his dark eyes holding hers, "before it's too late." He turned and walked away. It was the second time he'd pleaded with her to leave, and this time hurt even more than the first.

Eight

"Colby's taken Sherry Waterman out three nights in a row," Norah said casually over a cup of coffee Saturday morning. "They've gone out every night since Dad's been home." She nibbled her toast, but her gaze managed to avoid Valerie's, as though she felt guilty about relaying the information.

"I assume there's a reason you want me to know this."

"Yes," Norah murmured. "Sherry was at the hospital, and we had a chance to talk. She says she can't understand why Colby keeps asking her out. The spark just isn't there. They enjoy each other's company, but they're never going to be more than friends. It almost seems as if Colby wants to make it something it's not."

"Perhaps Sherry's reading more into the situation than is there." Valerie didn't actually believe that, but she felt compelled to suggest it. She knew exactly what Colby was doing—escaping her, fighting everything he felt for her.

"Sherry realizes Colby's in love with someone else, and she also knows he's fighting it." Norah's words were an eerie echo of her own thoughts. "It's you, isn't it, Val? Colby's in love with you."

"I can't speak for him," Valerie insisted, munching furiously on her toast.

"Do you love him?"

She gave a careless shrug and answered the question with one of her own, always a good business move. "What do I know about love?"

"You know enough," Norah argued. "Please, do everyone a favor and put the poor guy out of his misery."

"How would you suggest I do that?" Valerie asked, genuinely curious. She was miserable, too, but no one seemed to take *that* into consideration. In other circumstances, she would've talked to Steffie, but her middle sister was obviously having relationship problems of her own—not that she was forthcoming with the details.

"For the love of heaven," Norah cried, "just marry him. He's crazy about you. Any fool can see that, and you're in love with him, too."

"Sometimes love isn't enough."

"Yes, it is," Norah insisted.

Perhaps to Norah, who was young and idealistic. But there were too many complications Valerie couldn't afford to ignore in her relationship with Colby. Besides, he'd been pretty explicit about wanting her to leave.

"I think you should quit your job, move back home and marry Dr. Winston," Norah said decisively.

"And do what?" Valerie asked. "Take up politics?

Learn to knit? If I was *really* lucky, I might find some job in town that's about a tenth as interesting as the job I have now. Listen, I've been an active business-woman for the past eight years. Do you honestly think I'd be happy sitting at home knitting sweaters for the rest of my life?"

"You would eventually. It'll take a little adjusting, that's all."

"Oh, Norah." Valerie sighed and gave her starry-eyed sister a pitying smile. "You make everything sound so simple. It just isn't. Colby isn't exactly pin-ing away for me, not if he's spending all that time with Sherry. If he wants me to stay, he'll ask."

"What if he doesn't? Are you willing to throw away a chance at happiness because you've got too much pride? You should tell him you're willing to stay," Norah said heatedly. "Why does everything have to come from Colby?"

"It doesn't, believe me. But it's too late."

"What's too late?" their father asked from the kitchen doorway. He was dressed in his plaid house-coat, the belt cinched tightly at the waist. He ran a hand through his disheveled hair, looking as though he'd only just awakened.

Norah automatically stood and guided him to a chair.

"What are you two arguing about?" he asked. "I could hear you all the way in the back bedroom."

Their father was sleeping downstairs because Colby didn't want him climbing stairs yet. Although he hadn't complained, Valerie knew her father was anxious to return to his own room.

"We weren't arguing, Dad," Valerie said, paying no attention to Norah's angry look.

"I heard you," David countered, smiling up at Norah as she brought him a cup of coffee. "Seems to me I heard Norah suggest you should marry Colby. That's what I've been saying for weeks. So has everyone else who's got a nickel's worth of sense."

Valerie's throat seemed to close up on her. "He has to ask me first. And…and you acted as if you felt Rowdy and I—"

"Phooey. Rowdy Cassidy's a good man, but he's not for you. If it sounded like I thought you should marry Rowdy, that was just to get you—and that stubborn doctor—thinking. As for Colby not asking you, ask him yourself."

"Dad…" The list of objections was too long to enumerate. The best thing to do was ignore the suggestion.

"You've never been shy about going after what you want. I've always admired that about you. You love him, don't you? So ask him to marry you—or at least to give a relationship with you a chance. You might be pleasantly surprised by what he says," Norah told her.

"It wouldn't work," Valerie said sadly. "Colby's as traditional as they come. When he's found the woman he wants to marry, he'll propose himself."

Neither Norah nor her father offered a rebuttal, which suited Valerie. A few minutes later she left the kitchen and went up to her room to dress, but she didn't get far. Sitting on the end of her bed, she closed her eyes and tried to think. Was she being unnecessarily stubborn? Was Norah right? Was she allowing pride to impede happiness? Questions came at her from all directions, and she felt at a loss to answer them.

There seemed to be only one way of learning what she needed to know and that was to confront Colby. For years she'd been finding solutions in all kinds of unlikely situations. It was her greatest strength in business; however, when it came to her own life, she drew a blank. There had to be an answer that suited them both, but she couldn't figure out what it was.

She was obviously the last person Colby expected to see when he answered his door. Valerie saw the astonishment in his eyes and felt encouraged. She'd hoped to catch him off guard and had succeeded.

"Hello, Colby," she said.

"Valerie…hello."

She'd dressed carefully, taking time to select the perfect outfit for her purposes. Something that would remind him that she was a woman—but not a pushover. She'd chosen a lovely pale pink sweater dress Steffie had brought with her from Italy.

"Would it be all right if I came in for a few minutes?" she asked when he didn't immediately invite her inside.

"Of course. I didn't mean to be rude. I was writing."

"Writing?" She followed him into his living room and when he gestured toward the sofa, she sat there, hoping she appeared cool and serene. As though her visit was nothing more than a social call, when in fact the direction of her whole life depended on it. She had too much experience in negotiating to permit her feelings to show, but she was more nervous about this meeting than any business deal she'd ever accomplished.

"I've been working on an article for the *American Journal of Medicine,*" he elaborated. "The editor asked me six months ago if I'd be willing to contribute a piece and I'm only getting around to it now."

Valerie felt a surge of pride. Colby had an impressive future ahead of him. The world would be a better place because of his dedication and caring. Their eyes met, and Valerie wanted to tell him how much she respected him, how proud she was of him, but she couldn't. She didn't want anything she said now to sway his decision later.

"I have something to ask you," she said, standing abruptly. She glanced around, then sat down again.

"Yes?" His gaze fell to her hands and she realized she was rubbing her palms together. She stopped, embarrassed by this display of nervousness.

"The last time I saw you," she began in a voice that was more hesitant than she'd intended, "you asked me to leave Orchard Valley."

"Yes," he said harshly.

"Why?"

"You know the answer to that as well as I do. Your father's recovery has been a lot faster than we could've hoped. Eventually you're going back, so I can't see any reason to prolong this…interlude. Texas is where you belong."

"In other words, if a man's going to hold me and kiss me, it should be Rowdy Cassidy."

A brief flash of anger showed in his eyes, but was almost immediately quelled. "That's exactly what I mean," he returned smoothly.

"I can't help asking myself something," she said, her voice growing smaller despite her efforts. "Is my leaving what you *really* want?"

"What do you mean?"

"I could stay in Orchard Valley." Her gaze clung to his, hopefully, eagerly. "This is my home. It's where I was born and raised, where I attended school. Some of my friends still live here and I know just about everyone in town." The words were rushed, practically tumbling over one another.

Colby breathed in deeply and seemed to hold his breath. His hands tightened into fists. "Why would you do that?"

Valerie had wondered how he'd respond. She knew what she wanted him to say—that he needed her in his life. Instead, he'd responded with a cruelly flippant question.

"Why would I stay?" she repeated slowly, her eyes never wavering from his. "Because you're here."

Her words were met with a brief, tension-wrought silence as though her frankness had shocked him. He looked away.

"Are you saying you love me?" he demanded in a tone that suggested this wasn't what he wanted to hear.

"Yes." Her own voice was husky with something close to regret. "All morning I've been wishing I'd dated more in high school and college, because then I'd know what to say. I've always been too…direct. I can't help it. It's just part of my nature."

Colby didn't respond, which made her hurry to fill the silence.

"This is when you're supposed to admit you love me, too," she prompted anxiously. "That is, if you do… I may not have been a Homecoming Queen, but I'm woman enough to know you care for me, Colby. The least you can do is admit it and let me salvage what little pride I have left."

"Loving you has never been the problem."

"Thank you for that," she whispered.

"But love isn't enough."

"How do we know that?" she asked, although she'd said the same thing herself less than two hours earlier. "We haven't even tried. It seems to me no one would've gotten anywhere in this world if they'd decided to quit before even trying."

"You make it so tempting."

"I do? I really do?" His words thrilled her. They gave her the first sign of encouragement since her arrival. "I was thinking…there are companies in the Pacific Northwest I could work for…companies that would be glad to have me."

Colby stood and moved across the room. Not knowing what else to do, Valerie followed him.

"I think you should kiss me," she said hoarsely.

"Valerie." He turned as he said her name. He wasn't expecting her to be so close behind him, because he nearly collided with her. His hands reached for her shoulders to steady her.

It was exactly what Valerie had hoped would happen. She moved automatically into his embrace, wrapping her arms around his waist, hugging him close. She raised her mouth expectantly to his and wasn't disappointed.

With a groan, Colby claimed her lips. His hands were in her hair as he tilted her head back and kissed her with a hunger that left her breathless and weak.

"Valerie...no." Reluctantly he stepped away from her, bracing his hands against her shoulders.

"But why?" she pleaded.

Deftly Colby stepped farther back, putting as much distance as possible between them. "What's wrong with you?" he asked angrily.

"Wrong?" she repeated, still trapped in the excitement his kiss had aroused.

"Did you think coming here and seducing me would mean an offer of marriage? It's not very original, Valerie. I would have thought better of you."

"Seduce you?" Hot color sprang instantly to her cheeks. "I wasn't... I had no intention—"

"Well, that's the way it looked to me."

If he was trying to upset her, he was certainly doing an effective job. She forced herself to take several deep breaths. "I didn't come here to seduce you, Colby, nor am I going to let you annoy me into starting an argument. I came because I had to know. I had to find out for myself if there was a chance for us. If not, tell me so right now and I'll leave. I'll walk out that door and we'll both forget I was ever here." She paused. "Is that what you want?"

He frowned, his expression fierce, but he didn't answer.

"Say it," she demanded. "Tell me you don't want me. Tell me to get out of your life and I'll go, Colby. I won't even look back."

She remained on the far side of the room, frozen in misery.

Still Colby said nothing. Nothing.

"You don't need to worry about any unpleasant scenes. I'll pack up my belongings, drive myself to the airport, and you'll never hear from me again." Her voice remained steady despite the hoarseness of pain.

Silence.

"Just say it," she cried. "Tell me to go…if that's what you want. But if you had an ounce of sense, you'd ask me to stay right here and marry you. You don't have any sense, though. I know—because you're going to do what you think is the noble thing and send me away. Well, I won't make it easy for you, Colby. If you want me out of your life, you're going to have to say it."

"I might if I could get a word in edgewise."

Valerie choked on a sob and swallowed the laughter. "I love you! Doesn't that mean anything to you?"

His hands clenched into fists again, and his eyes, his beautiful eyes, didn't stray from her.

"Say it!" she shouted. "Tell me you don't want me. Better yet, tell me you're crazy in love with me and that you're willing to find a way to make everything right for us. Tell me that instead."

He closed his eyes.

"This is it, Colby. If I walk out that door, whatever was between us is over. I'll go about my business and you'll go about yours. I refuse to waste the rest of my life waiting for you." She dashed the tears from her cheeks with the back of one hand.

"You'll always be someone very special in my life." The words were so soft she barely heard them.

"That's not good enough," she sobbed. "Tell me to get out of your life. Make it really clear so I'll know you mean it, so I won't question it later. So *you* won't question it later."

"You don't belong here."

"That's better." She gulped. "But still not good enough. Haven't you ever heard of being cruel to be kind? Just make sure you mean what you say, because this is the only chance you'll have." Her voice broke. "You don't even have to promise to marry me. Just ask me to stay."

"No!" It was shouted at her, as though something had snapped inside him. "You want me to be cruel, is that what it takes? Does it have to come to this? You're an intelligent woman, or so I assumed, but this…this performance is ridiculous. I owe you nothing. You want me to tell you to go? Then go. You don't need my permission." He stormed to the other side of the room and held open the door for her. "Go back to Texas, Valerie. Marry your cowboy."

Stunned, she was afraid to move, afraid her legs would no longer support her. She nodded. She moved shakily past him.

"Goodbye," she whispered and then, unable to resist, brushed her fingertips down the side of his face. When she looked back at this moment, there would be no regrets. She'd offered him everything she had to give, and he was turning her away. There was nothing more she could do.

Colby glanced at his hands, the very hands he used to save lives, and saw they were trembling with the force of an emotion so strong it was all he could do not to smash them into a concrete wall.

When Valerie left, he'd been furious. He would have preferred it if she'd packed her bags and quietly disappeared. That was what he'd envisioned. Not this dreadful scene. Not dragging out their emotions, prolonging the pain.

It shouldn't have been so difficult for him. This wasn't a new decision, but one he'd made long before he'd ever kissed her, long before he'd held her in his arms and comforted her.

The phone rang and he seized it, grateful for the reprieve from his thoughts. "Hello," he snapped, not meaning to sound so impatient.

"Colby, is this a bad time?"

"Sherry…of course not. I was just thinking…" He let the rest fade.

"I'm sorry, but I won't be able to make our dinner tonight, after all."

How sweet she sounded, Colby mused. Why couldn't he feel for her the things he felt for Valerie Bloomfield? Heaven knew he'd tried in the past few days. He'd done whatever he could think of to spark their interest in each other, but to no avail.

"My aunt Janice arrived and my parents asked me to take her over to my brother's place," Sherry explained. "I hope this isn't inconvenient for you."

"No problem." He heard something else in her voice, a hesitancy, a disappointment, but he chose not to question it.

"Colby."

"Yes?" The irritation was back, but it wasn't Sherry who'd angered him. It was his own lack of feeling for her. This past week, he'd spent four evenings with her. He'd held her and kissed her, and each time her kisses had left him cold and untouched.

"I don't mean to be tactless, but I don't think we should see each other anymore."

Her words shocked him. "Why not?" he asked, although he knew the reasons and didn't blame her.

"It's not me you're interested in, it's Norah's sister. I like you, Colby, don't get me wrong, but this just isn't working. We've been seeing each other for over a year now, and if we were going to fall in love it would've happened before now."

"We haven't given it a real chance." Colby didn't understand why he was arguing with her when he was in full agreement. Sherry would make some man a wonderful wife. Some *other* man.

"You're using me, Colby."

He had nothing to say in his own defense. He hadn't realized until she'd said it, but Sherry was right. He *had* been using her. Not to make Valerie jealous, or in any devious, underhanded way, but in an effort to prove to himself that he could happily live without Valerie.

The experiment had backfired. And now he was alone, wondering how he could have let the only woman he'd ever loved walk out of his life.

"What's this I hear about you going to Texas?" David Bloomfield asked when Valerie joined him on the front porch following the evening meal. She sat on the top step, her back pressed against the white column while her father rocked in his old chair. She looked at the blooming apple orchard, breathed in the scent of pink and white blossoms perfuming the air. The setting sun cast a golden glow across the sky.

Valerie hadn't said anything at dinner about returning to Texas, and was surprised that her father was aware of her intentions. She'd sat quietly in her place at the table, pushing the food around her plate and hoping no one would notice she wasn't eating.

"It's time for me to go back, Daddy."

"It hurts, doesn't it?" he asked, his voice tender.

"A little." *A lot,* her heart cried, but it was a cry she'd been ignoring from the moment she left Colby's home. "Your health's improved so much," she said with forced cheerfulness. "You don't need me around here anymore."

"Ah, but I do," her father countered smoothly, continuing to rock. "Colby needs you, too."

His name went through her like the blade of a sharp sword, and her breath caught at the unexpected pain.

Her father was the reason she'd come home, but Colby was the reason she was leaving.

"Love is funny, isn't it?" she mused, wrapping her arms around her knees the way she had as a young girl.

"You and I are so much alike," her father said. "Your mother saw it before I did, which I suppose is only natural. I'm proud of you, Valerie, proud of what you've managed to accomplish in so short a time, proud of your professionalism. Cassidy's lucky to have you on his team, and he knows it—otherwise he wouldn't have promoted you."

"I've got a terrific future with CHIPS." She said it to remind herself that her life did have purpose. There was somewhere to focus all her energy. Something that would help her forget, give her a reason to go on.

"Your mother's and my romance wasn't so easy, either, you know," her father said, rocking slowly. "She was this pretty young nurse, and I was head over heels in love with her. To my mind, she was lucky to have me. Problem was, she didn't seem to think so. I was a business success, a millionaire. But none of that impressed your mother." His smile was wryly nostalgic, his eyes gazing into a long-ago world. "Convincing Grace to marry me was by far the most difficult task I'd faced in years."

"She didn't love you?" That was impossible for Valerie to comprehend.

"She loved me, all right, she just didn't think she'd make me the right kind of wife. I was wealthy, socially prominent and, as you know, your mother was a preacher's daughter from Oregon. Before I contracted rheumatic fever I was one of the most sought-after bachelors in California, if I do say so myself. But I hadn't met the woman I wanted to marry until your mother became my nurse."

How achingly familiar this sounded to Valerie. She'd been content with her own life until she met Colby. Falling in love was the last thing she'd expected when she returned home.

"There were other problems, too," David went on. "Your mother seemed to think my work habits would kill me, and she wasn't willing to marry me only to watch me work myself to death."

"But you solved everything."

"Eventually." A wistful look stole over him. "I loved your mother from the first moment I opened my eyes and saw her standing beside my hospital bed. I remember thinking she was an angel, and in some ways she was." His face shone with the radiance of unending love. "I knew if she'd ever agree to marry me, I was going to have to give up everything I'd worked so hard to achieve. That meant selling my business and finding something new to occupy my time."

"You did it, though."

"Not without a lot of deliberation. I'd already made more money than I knew how to spend, but I realized I wasn't going to be happy retiring before the age of forty. I had to have something to do. It took a couple of years—and Grace's help—to figure out what that should be."

Valerie nodded. "I feel the same way. I'd never be happy just sitting at home— I'm too much like you."

The extent of his sacrifice shook her. "How could you have given up everything you'd worked all those years to build?"

"Without your mother my life would've been empty. My work didn't matter anymore. Grace was important, and the life we were going to build together was important. I gave up one life but gained another, one I found far more fulfilling."

"But didn't you ever get bored or restless?"

"Some, but not nearly as much as I expected. When we'd been married a year or two, your mother saw I had too much time on my hands and we looked around for something to occupy me, some new interest. That was when we bought the orchard and moved here." He grinned. "My own Garden of Eden."

"I don't think I ever understood how much you'd changed your life to marry Mom."

"It was a sacrifice, and at the time it seemed like a huge one, but as the years passed, I realized she'd been right. I would've killed myself if I'd continued in business. Your mother brought balance into my life, the same way Colby will bring balance into yours."

She allowed a moment to pass before she spoke. "I'm not marrying Colby, Dad. I wish I could tell you I was, and that we were going to seek the same happiness you found with Mom, but it isn't going to happen."

It was as if she hadn't said a word. "You'll be so good for him, Valerie. He loves you now, and you love him, but what you feel for each other doesn't even begin to approach the love you'll experience over the years, especially after the children arrive."

"Dad, you're not listening to me." He seemed to be in a dream world that shut out reality. She had to make him stop, had to pull him out of the fantasy.

"He needs you, too, you know, even more than you need him. Colby's lived alone too many years. Only recently has he recognized how much he wants a woman in his life."

"He doesn't want *me*."

Her father closed his eyes and smiled. "You don't truly believe that, do you? He wants you so much it's eating him alive."

She lacked the strength to argue with her father, not after her confrontation with Colby earlier in the day. Nor did she have the energy to explain what had passed between them. In her mind, it was over. She'd told him she wouldn't look back and she meant it. She'd swallowed her pride and gone to him and he'd cast her out of his life.

She didn't hate him for being cruel; she'd asked for that. Nor had she made it easy for him to reject her. But he'd done it.

David sipped his coffee, and his smile grew even more serene. "You have such happiness awaiting you, Valerie. This problem with my heart is a perfect example of good coming out of bad. My attack was what brought you racing home. Heaven only knows how long it would've been before you met Colby if it weren't for this bum heart of mine."

Valerie reached for her own mug of coffee and took a sip. "You want anything else before I go inside?"

"So soon? It's not even dark."

"I have a lot to do."

"Are you going to think about what I said?"

She hated to disappoint him, hated to disillusion a romantic old man whose judgment was clouded by thirty years of loving one woman.

"I'll think about it," Valerie promised, but it was a lie. She intended to push every thought, every memory of Colby completely from her mind. That was the only way she'd be able to function. She got slowly to her feet.

"Good." He nodded, still smiling. "Stay with me, then. There's no need for you to hurry inside."

Valerie hesitated. This conversation was becoming decidedly uncomfortable. Despite her father's illusions, she had to face what had happened between her and Colby, accept it as truth and get on with her life. Pining away for him would solve nothing. And listening to her father only added to the pain.

"I need to do a few things before I leave." The excuse was weak, but it was all she could think of.

"There's plenty of time. Sit with me a spell. Relax."

"Dad…please."

"I want to tell you something important."

"What is it, Dad?" she asked with a sigh.

"I know for a fact that you're going to marry Colby," he said, smiling up at her, his eyes bright and clear. "Your mother promised me."

Nine

"Dad," Valerie said, suppressing the urge to argue with him. "If it's about your dream, I don't think—"

"It was more than a dream! I was dead. I told you— ask Colby if you don't believe me. I crossed over into the valley of shadows. Your mother was waiting for me there and she wasn't pleased. No, sir. She was downright irritated with me. Said it wasn't my time yet, and I was coming home much too early."

"I'm sure this seemed very real to you—"

"It *was* real." His voice had grown louder. "Now you sit down and listen, because what I'm about to tell you happened as surely as I live and breathe."

Trapped, Valerie did as her father asked, lowering herself to the top porch step. "All right, Dad, I'll listen."

"Good." He smiled down at her, apparently appeased. "I've missed your mother, and I didn't want to continue living in this world without her. She told me my thinking was all wrong. She promised me the years

I have left will be full and happy ones, with nothing like the loneliness I've endured since she's been gone."

"Of course they will." Valerie didn't put much stock in this near-death experience of her father's, but he believed it and that was the important thing.

"Problem was, I didn't much care about my life back here," he went on, almost as if he hadn't heard Valerie. "I was with Grace, and that was where I wanted to be. As far as I was concerned, I wasn't going back."

Valerie was familiar with her father's stubbornness; she'd inherited a streak of it herself.

"Your mother told me there was a reason for me to return. To tell you the truth, I'd already decided I wasn't going to let her talk me into it. She was darn good at that, you know. She'd drag me into the most outlandish things and make me think it was my idea."

Her father was grinning as he spoke, his eyes twinkling with a rare joy.

"That was when she told me about you girls. Your mother and I were standing by a small lake." He frowned, evidently trying to remember each detail of his experience. "She asked me to look into the water. I thought it was an unusual request, considering the discussion we were having."

"What did you see?" Valerie was picturing trout and maybe some bass, knowing how much her father enjoyed lazing away a summer afternoon fishing.

"I saw the future."

"The *future?*" This sounded like something out of a science fiction novel.

"You heard me," he said irritably. "The water was

like a window and I could look into the years ahead. I saw you and your sisters, and you know what? It was the most beautiful scene I could ever have imagined. So much joy, so much laughter and love. I couldn't stop looking, couldn't stop smiling. There were my precious daughters, all so happy, all so blessed with love, the same way your mother and I had been."

"It sounds lovely, Dad." Her father had undergone traumatic surgery and just barely survived. If he believed in this dream, if he maintained he'd actually spoken to her mother, then Valerie couldn't bring herself to disillusion him. Nor did she want to argue. Especially not now, when her own emotions had taken such a beating.

"I remember every single moment of that meeting with your mother. I didn't see a single angel, though. I don't mind telling you, that was a bit of a disappointment. Nor did I hear anyone playing the harp."

Valerie hid a smile.

"You understand what I'm saying, don't you?"

"About angels?"

"No," he returned impatiently. "About you and Colby. He's the one I saw you with, Val. You had three beautiful children."

"Dad, why now?" At his quizzical gaze, she elaborated. "Why are you trying so hard to convince me to marry Colby? After the surgery, you seemed to have given up the idea. What happened to change your mind?"

"You did."

"Me?"

"You're both so darned stubborn. I hadn't counted on that."

"But you apologized for the matchmaking, remember?"

"Of course I remember. I gave it up on Grace's advice, but only because I felt you two wouldn't need any help from me. But I quickly found out you need my help more than ever. That's why I talked about Cassidy so much. To get you thinking about what you really wanted. And to make Colby a little jealous. Face it, Val. Eventually you're going to marry him."

"Dad, please, I know you want to believe this, but it just isn't going to happen." Without realizing what he was doing, her own father was making everything so much more painful.

"Don't you understand, child? Colby loves you, and you love him, and you're going to have a wonderful life together. Naturally there'll be ups and downs, but there are in any marriage."

"I'm not marrying Colby," she said from between gritted teeth. "For heaven's sake, I only met him a few weeks ago!"

"You think I'm an old man whose elevator doesn't go all the way to the top, but you're wrong." He gave her a lazy smile. "I know what I saw. All I'm asking is that you be patient with Colby and patient with yourself. Just don't do anything foolish."

"Like what?"

"Going back to Texas. You belong here in Orchard Valley now. It's where you're going to raise your children and where Colby's going to continue his practice."

"It's too late."

"For what?"

Valerie stood, her chest aching with the effort to breathe normally. She felt so empty, so alone. More than anything, she wanted to believe her father's dream, but she couldn't. She just couldn't.

"I've already booked my flight. My plane leaves in the afternoon." She didn't wait for her father to disagree with her, to tell her what a terrible mistake she was making. Instead she hurried into the house and up the stairs, not stopping until she was inside her room, with the door firmly closed.

She hauled her suitcase from the closet. There wasn't much to pack, and the entire process took her all of five minutes. She didn't weep. Her tears had already been spent.

When she returned to Texas, she'd be more mindful of love. It had touched her life once; perhaps it would again. In time. When her heart had healed. When she was ready.

With that thought in mind, she reached for the phone on the nightstand and held it in her lap, staring sightlessly at the keys. After an endless moment, she tapped out the long-distance number.

"Hello." The deep male voice sounded hurried and impatient.

"Hello, Rowdy," she said quietly.

"Valerie." He seemed delighted to be hearing from her. "I'm glad you phoned. I tried to reach you earlier in the day, but your sister told me you were out. Did she mention my call?"

"No. Was it something important?" Norah must have been the one who answered, since Steffie was out most of the day. Romantic Norah, who so badly wanted Valerie to marry Colby and live happily ever after.

"It wasn't urgent. I just wanted to see how soon CHIPS could have you back. There's been a big hole here since you left."

"I realize my being gone has been an inconvenience—"

"Don't be silly. I wasn't referring to the workload, I was talking about *you*. Like I told you before, I got used to having you around," he said gruffly, as though he was uncomfortable saying such things. "Doesn't seem right with you not here. You're an important part of my team. That's how come I'm giving you a ten percent raise—just so you'll know how much you're appreciated."

Valerie gasped. "That isn't necessary."

"Sure it is. Now, when are you flying home?"

Home. Home wasn't in Texas, it never really had been, but Rowdy wouldn't understand that.

"Valerie?"

"Oh, sorry. That was actually the reason for my call. I've booked my flight for tomorrow. I'll arrive early in the evening and be at the office Monday morning." She forced some enthusiasm into her words.

"That's great news! It's just what I was hoping to hear. We'll celebrate. How about if I pick you up at the airport and take you to dinner?"

The invitation surprised her, although she supposed it shouldn't have. "Ah…" She didn't know what to say.

She'd already promised herself she wasn't going to spend the rest of her life pining away for Colby Winston. Yet when the opportunity arose to put the past firmly behind her and begin a new life, she hesitated.

"I don't think so," she told him regretfully. "Not just yet. I'm going to need some time to readjust after being away for so long." It had been less than three weeks, but it felt like a whole lifetime.

"You've been gone *too* long," Rowdy said, his voice low and resonant. "I've missed you, Valerie. I haven't made a secret of it, either. When you get back, I'd like the two of us to sit down and talk."

Sudden dread attacked her stomach, her nerves. This wasn't what she wanted to hear. "I—I don't know if that'd be a good idea, Rowdy. I don't mean to be—"

"I know what you're thinking," Rowdy cut in. "And I have to admit, I share your concern. An office romance can lead to problems. That's why I want us to talk. Clear the air before we get involved."

It obviously hadn't occurred to Rowdy that she might not be interested. But only a little while ago, the prospect of a relationship with him would have filled her with excitement.

Colby had hardly ever spent a more uncomfortable night. He hadn't been able to sleep and, finally giving up, had gone downstairs to read. Another hour ticked slowly by, and still his mind refused to relax. Feeling even more disgruntled, he set the novel aside.

It would have helped if Sherry had kept her dinner date, but she'd cancelled. Not only that, she'd let him know she didn't want to see him again. She was right to have done it, too—a fact that didn't improve his disposition.

When it came to his relationships with women, Colby just wasn't getting anywhere. Okay, so he was behind schedule. He'd underestimated the difficulty of finding the type of wife he wanted.

His requirements were very specific, which was why he'd intended to conduct his search in a methodical, orderly manner. It wasn't as though he'd discovered any shortage of "old-fashioned" girls, either. Unfortunately, most of them didn't appeal to him.

This only served to confuse him further. Obviously there was a flaw in his plan. Of one thing he was certain—Sherry was out of the picture. For that matter, so was Valerie.

Valerie.

Her name seemed to be engraved on his mind, but by sheer force of will, he turned his thoughts in another direction. He got up and moved into his den to print out the article he'd been working on earlier that day. Although he'd shrugged off its importance when he spoke to Valerie, he was well aware that the invitation to submit it was a real honor. He'd done exhaustive research, and every word he'd written had been carefully considered.

But right then and there, Colby realized it meant nothing. Nothing. With an angry burst of energy, he crumpled the sheets and tossed them in his wastebasket.

Colby rarely acted in anger. Rarely did he allow

himself to display any emotion. He'd schooled himself well; he'd needed to. He dealt with death so often, with fear, with grief. It became crucial, a matter of emotional survival, to keep his own feelings strictly private. Over the years, that had become second nature. For the first time in recent memory, he deplored his inexperience at expressing emotion.

He had no trouble recognizing that his inability to sleep, his lack of interest in a good novel, his discontent with the article he was writing, were all caused by what had happened between him and Valerie that morning.

He'd done what he had to do. It hadn't been easy— for either of them—but it was necessary. She'd made him angry with her demand that he be cruel. She wouldn't accept anything less. By the time she left, he'd been furious. She'd prodded and pushed and shoved until, backed into a corner, he'd had no choice.

Every harsh word he'd spoken had boomeranged back to hit him. She'd insisted repeatedly that he tell her to get out of his life. And he'd done it....

It was over, which was exactly what he wanted. Valerie would go back to Texas and he'd continue living here in Orchard Valley.

Her sad gray eyes would haunt him. And it had taken all afternoon to forget the feel of her fingertips as they grazed his face.

His intention had been to send her away, hurt her if he had to, so the break would be final. He hadn't grasped how much that would cost him.

Twenty hours later, he was still angry. Still in pain. Walking back into his living room at 2:00 a.m.,

Colby sank into the recliner and reached for the television remote control. Surely there'd be some movie playing that would hold his attention for an hour or two.

He was wrong. All he could find—other than infomercials and vapid talk shows—was a 1950s love story, filmed in nostalgic black-and-white. The last thing Colby was in the mood to watch was a sentimental romance with a happy ending. He turned off the television and stood up.

He hadn't been out to the Bloomfields' in three days. Although David was home and they'd scheduled an appointment at the office early in the week, it wouldn't be a bad idea to stop by and see how the older man was recovering. They were friends, and it was the least Colby could do—for the sake of a long-standing friendship.

That decision made, he found himself yawning loudly. Fatigue greeted him like an old comrade, and in that moment Colby knew he'd be able to sleep.

Valerie was dressed, her suitcase packed. She'd lingered in her room far longer than necessary. Her flight wasn't until 1:00 p.m.—not for another four hours—so she had plenty of time, yet she felt an intense need to be on her way. But there was another feeling that ran even deeper, even stronger: she dreaded leaving.

"Valerie?"

She turned to see Steffie standing in her bedroom doorway, frowning as she glanced at the suitcase. "Are you sure you're doing the right thing?"

Valerie gave her a wide and completely artificial smile. "I'm positive."

"How can you smile?"

"It's such a beautiful morning, how could I possibly *not* smile? Dad's home and thriving, you're here, and Norah's in seventh heaven because she's got someone to cook for."

Steffie grinned. "Yeah, I know. But I can't help feeling you shouldn't go."

"My life's in Texas now."

Steffie wandered into the room and sat on the edge of the bed. "If you're running away, it's a mistake. I made the same one myself three years ago. I embarrassed myself in front of Charles Tomaselli, and then because I was so mortified and because I couldn't bear to face him, I decided to study in Europe."

"You had a wonderful opportunity to travel. Do you honestly regret it?"

"Yes. Oh, not the travel and the experience. But leaving was wrong. I didn't realize it then, but I do now. I went into hiding. I know that sounds melodramatic, but it's the truth. At the time it seemed like the only thing to do, but I understand now that I should have swallowed my pride instead of walking away from everything I loved."

"Sometimes we don't have any choice."

"And sometimes we do," Steffie said. "Don't make the same mistake I did. Don't run away, because at some point down the road, you're going to regret it, just like I did."

Her sister's eyes were intent, silently pleading with Valerie to reconsider. If she hadn't gone to Colby the day before, Valerie might have hesitated, but there was no reason now for her to stay. There was no reason to hope Colby would change his mind.

"Someone's coming," Steffie said, walking over to look out Valerie's bedroom window.

Valerie moved aside the white curtains and peered outside. Steffie was right. A maroon car was making its way down the long driveway.

Colby.

A surge of excitement shot through her. He'd come to tell her he'd changed his mind, to ask her not to leave. Only seconds before, she'd been so sure there was no hope and now it flowed through her like current into an electrical wire. Try as she might, she couldn't squelch it.

"It—it's Colby," Valerie said, when she found her voice.

Steffie gave a cry of sheer joy. "I knew it! I knew he wouldn't be able to let you go. Everyone knows how he feels about you, how you feel about him. He'd be a fool if he let you go back to Texas."

"He didn't know I was leaving today," Valerie said calmly, although he must have figured it out for himself. He must've recognized that she wouldn't stay in Orchard Valley any longer than necessary.

"I'll find out what he wants," Steffie said, her voice high and excited. "Let's play this cool, okay? You stay up here and when he asks for you, I'll casually come and get you."

"Steffie…"

"Valerie, for heaven's sake, be romantic for *once* in your life."

"There could be plenty of other reasons Colby's here."

"Are you going to make him suffer, or are you going to forgive him right away? Personally, I think he should suffer…but only a little."

The doorbell chimed and Steffie hurried downstairs without another word.

Valerie couldn't keep her heart from racing, but she refused to play this silly game of wait-and-see. She reached for her suitcase and started resolutely down the stairs, the way she'd originally intended.

She was on the top step when she heard Colby ask to see her father. *Her father—not her.* If it hadn't hurt so much, Valerie would have laughed at Steffie, who looked completely stunned. Her sister stared at Colby, her mouth open, hand frozen on the door, blocking his entrance.

"My father," Steffie repeated after a shocked moment. "You're here to see Dad?"

"He is my patient."

"I know, but…"

Some slight sound must have alerted Colby that Valerie was standing at the top of the stairs. His gaze rose and linked with hers before slowly lowering to the suitcase in her hand. Valerie detected a frown, as though he'd been caught by surprise.

"Valerie's leaving for the airport this morning," Steffie announced in a loud, urgent voice, implying that Colby had better do something fast.

What Steffie hadn't grasped was that Colby didn't

want to do anything—other than bid her a relieved farewell.

"You should tell Dad that Dr. Winston's here," Valerie said mildly. "He's probably in the kitchen."

Steffie left, and Valerie gradually descended the stairs.

"Looks like you're packed up and ready to go," he said in a conversational tone.

She nodded. "My flight leaves at one."

"So soon?"

"Not soon enough, though, is it, Colby?"

He ignored the question, and Valerie regretted the pettiness that had prompted her to ask. He stood before her, his expression unreadable. She was grateful when her father appeared. Grateful because she wasn't nearly as expert at hiding her feelings as Colby. She was afraid he could read much more of her emotional turmoil than she wanted him to.

"Colby, my boy, good to see you. You've been making yourself scarce the last few days." David steered Colby into the kitchen, then glanced back at Valerie, scowling at the suitcase in her hand. "You've got plenty of time, Val. Come and have a cup of coffee before you leave."

For her father's sake, she resisted the temptation to argue. Shrugging, she set her luggage aside and dutifully followed Colby and David into the large family kitchen.

The two men sat at the table while Norah served them coffee. Valerie didn't sit with the others, but pulled out a stool in front of the counter and perched on that.

"I thought I'd check in and see how you were feeling," Colby was saying.

"Never felt better," her father said in response.

Valerie noticed how Colby avoided looking in her direction. He was uncomfortable with her; his back was stiff, his shoulders rigid with tension. Perhaps he'd expected her to have left by now.

Valerie sipped her coffee and briefly closed her eyes, wanting to savor these last few moments with her family. Norah, an apron tied around her waist, was busy pulling hot cinnamon rolls out of the oven. Homemade ones, from the recipe their mother had used through the years. The scent of yeast and spice filled the kitchen, and it was like stepping back in time. Their kitchen had always been where everyone gathered, a place of warmth and laughter and confidences shared.

Steffie couldn't seem to stand still. She paced to one side of the room, then crossed to the other, as though debating her next course of action.

Valerie found it endearing that her sister cared so much about what happened between her and Colby, especially when Steffie's own romance was so problematic. Valerie sensed that things weren't going well between her sister and Charles Tomaselli, but she wasn't in any position to be offering advice.

Steffie paused, her eyes pleading with Valerie. She seemed to be begging her to stay in Orchard Valley. To listen to her heart...

After a moment Valerie couldn't meet her sister's gaze and purposely looked away.

Conversation floated past her, but she wasn't aware of what was being said or who was saying it. The sudden need to leave was too powerful to ignore. If she didn't do it soon, she might never be able to. Slipping down from the stool, she deposited her mug, still half full of coffee, in the sink.

"The rolls will be ready to eat any minute," Norah said, looking at her anxiously. She, too, seemed to want Valerie to stay.

"Don't worry, I'll pick up something at the airport later."

"Are you going?" her father asked, as if this was news to him. "You've still got lots of time."

Valerie gave the first excuse that came to mind. "I've got to get the rental car back to the agency."

"You're *sure* you want to go?" Steffie asked forlornly, moving toward her sister.

"I'm sure," Valerie answered in a soft voice, throwing her arms around Steffie in an affectionate hug. "It isn't like I'll never be back, you know?"

"Don't let it take you three years, the way it did me," Steffie whispered into Valerie's ear. "I just can't help thinking you're making a mistake."

"What I'm doing is for the best," Valerie said.

Norah stood behind Steffie, waiting her turn to be hugged, her pretty blue eyes as sad as Steffie's. "I can't believe you're really going. I loved having you home."

"It's been good, hasn't it, Dad?" Valerie said, trying to lighten the atmosphere. "I'd like to suggest another family reunion, only next time let's plan things a bit differently. If I'm going to take three weeks away from CHIPS, I'd prefer to see more than a hospital waiting room."

David Bloomfield stood, his gaze holding Valerie's. He seemed to be asking her to remain a little longer, but she firmly shook her head. Every minute was torture.

She dared not look in Colby's direction. That made it easier to pretend he wasn't there.

"I have a great idea for a family reunion," Steffie said eagerly. "Why don't we all take a trip to Egypt? I've always wanted to ride a camel and see the pyramids."

"Egypt?" Norah echoed. "What's wrong with a camping trip? We used to do that years ago, and it was fun. I remember us sitting around the campfire singing and toasting marshmallows."

"Camping!" Steffie cried. "You can't be serious. I remember mosquitoes the size of Alabama."

"But we had fun," Norah reminded them.

"Maybe you did, but count me out," Valerie said, laughing quickly. "My idea of roughing it is going without room service." She glanced from one sister to the other, loving them both so much she thought she'd start to cry. Blinking rapidly, she stepped forward and flung her arms around her father's neck.

"Take care of yourself," she whispered.

"The dream," he returned, his eyes bright and intense. "I was so sure...."

Valerie didn't need to be reminded of her father's dream. "Maybe someday it'll happen." But she didn't believe it, any more than she believed the dead could come back to life.

"You're going to say goodbye to Colby, aren't you?" her father urged.

She'd been hoping to avoid it. But she realized it would be impossible to leave without saying something to Colby, who was her father's doctor, her father's guest. David released her and she saw that Colby was on his feet and moving toward her. Her pride would've been salvaged, at least a little, if he'd revealed even a hint of sadness. But from all outward appearances she was nothing more to him than a passing acquaintance. It was as if he'd never held her in his arms, never kissed her.

"Goodbye, Colby," she said as cheerfully as she could. "Thank you for everything you did for Dad—for all of us. You were...wonderful." She extended her hand, which he took in his own. His fingers tightened on hers, his grip almost painful.

"Goodbye, Valerie," he said after a moment. As before, it was impossible to read his expression. "Have a safe trip."

She nodded and turned away, afraid that if she didn't leave soon, she'd do something utterly stupid, like burst into tears.

Everyone followed her to the front porch. Eager to get away now, Valerie hurried down the steps. Not bothering to open the trunk, she set her suitcase on the backseat.

"Phone once in a while, would you?" Steffie called.

Valerie nodded. "Take care of Dad, you two."

"Bye, Val." Norah pressed her fingers to her lips and blew her a kiss.

Rather than endure another round of farewells, Valerie slid into the driver's seat and closed the door. She didn't look at the porch for fear her eyes would meet Colby's.

Escaping was what mattered. Fleeing before she made a fool of herself a second time over a man who didn't want her.

She started the car, raised her hand in a brisk wave and pulled away. The tightness in her chest was so painful it was almost unbearable. For a moment she didn't know if she'd be able to continue. The thought that she needed a doctor was what dispersed the horrible pain. It broke free on a bubble of hysterical laughter.

She needed a doctor, all right, *a heart doctor.* With the sound of her amusement still echoing in her ears, Valerie looked back one last time, her gaze seeking Colby's.

Hard as it was, she managed a slow smile, a smile of gratitude for what they'd shared.

She drove away then and didn't glance back.

Not even once.

Ten

For long minutes, no one said a word. Colby stood frozen on the Bloomfield porch, his eyes following Valerie's rental car as it sped down the driveway. His hands knotted into tight fists at his sides, and his chest throbbed with suppressed emotion.

The timing of this visit couldn't have been worse. He'd had no idea Valerie was leaving that morning, and like a fool he'd stumbled upon the scene. He cursed himself for not calling first.

He wasn't sure what he'd been thinking when he'd decided to come here. No, that wasn't true. Visiting David had been an excuse. He'd come to see Valerie. He'd hoped, perhaps, to find a private moment to talk to her. But for the life of him, he didn't know what he'd intended to say. He certainly hadn't changed his mind, hadn't planned to sweep everything under the proverbial rug and pretend that love would conquer all. He'd leave that kind of idealism to the world's romantics. He wasn't one of them; he was a physician and he dealt with reality. He had no intention of deluding himself into believing he and Valerie had a chance together, even if she did entertain thoughts like that herself.

"I can't believe this," Stephanie cried, glaring at Colby. Tears swam in her eyes. He'd always considered weeping females cause for alarm; he never knew what to say to them.

But there'd been that time with Valerie, the night of David's surgery, Colby reminded himself. She'd been sobbing out her grief and fear. With anyone else he would've sought another family member to offer the needed consolation. But he hadn't looked for Norah that night. Instead he'd gone to Valerie himself. He'd felt his own terrible loss. He couldn't hold out hope for her father's recovery, not when everything indicated that David probably wouldn't survive the night. And so he'd sat on the concrete bench beside her and placed his arm around her shoulders.

Valerie had turned to him, and buried her face against him. The surge of love he'd experienced in that moment was unlike anything he'd ever felt. Stroking her hair, he'd savored the feel of her in his arms.

"She'll be back," David said, interrupting Colby's memories.

"No," Stephanie argued in a trembling voice. "She won't. Not for a long time."

"Valerie's not like that," Norah said. "She'll visit again. Soon."

"Why should she, when everything she equates with home means pain? It's too easy to stay away, too easy to make excuses and be satisfied with a phone call now and then." Suspecting that David's second daughter was speaking from experience, Colby studied her.

She must have felt his scrutiny because she turned suddenly, undisguised anger blazing from her eyes.

"You might be a wonderful surgeon," she said, her gaze as hard as flint, "but you're one of the biggest idiots I've ever met."

Colby blinked in surprise, but before he could respond, Stephanie ran back inside the house. Shocked by the verbal attack, he looked at Norah. They'd worked together for a number of months and he'd always been fond of her.

"I couldn't agree with my sister more," Norah said with an uncharacteristic display of temper. "You are an idiot." Having said that, she stormed into the house as well.

David chuckled, and Colby relaxed. At least one member of this family could appreciate the wisdom of his sacrifice. Stephanie and Norah acted as if he should be arrested. Both seemed to think it'd been easy for him to let Valerie drive away, although nothing was further from the truth. Even now he needed to grab hold of the railing to keep from racing after her.

If only she hadn't turned at the last moment and looked straight at him. And smiled. The sweetest, most beautiful smile he'd ever seen. A smile that would haunt him to his grave.

"I love her," Colby whispered, his eyes never leaving the driveway, although Valerie's car was long out of sight. By now she was probably two miles down the road.

"I know," David assured him.

Something in the older man's tone made Colby glance at him. The inflection seemed to suggest that however much Colby might love Valerie, he didn't love her enough. But he did! He loved her so much that he'd sent her out of his life. It seemed that no one, not even David Bloomfield, could appreciate the depth of his sacrifice.

"Rowdy Cassidy will be a much better husband for her than I ever would," Colby said, steeling himself against the pain his own words produced.

"Maybe, but I doubt it," David responded, walking over to his wicker rocking chair and lowering himself into it. "I don't suppose you've noticed, but Valerie and I are a lot alike."

Colby grinned. The similarity hadn't exactly escaped him. Here were two people who each possessed a streak of stubbornness that was wider than the Mississippi. Both were intelligent, intuitive and ambitious. Hardworking. Single-minded.

"She'd never be happy living here in Orchard Valley," Colby said, his gaze returning to the driveway. He couldn't seem to make himself look away. It was as if that road was his only remaining connection to Valerie.

"You're right, of course. Valerie would never be content in a small town again. Not after living in Houston."

The reassurance should have eased the ache in his heart, but it didn't. He told himself there was no reason to linger. Carrying on a polite conversation was beyond him, yet he didn't seem to have the energy to leave.

"Did I ever tell you how I met Grace?"

"I believe you did." Valerie must be three or four miles down the road by now, Colby estimated.

"Our courtship was a bit unusual. It isn't every day a man woos a woman from a hospital bed."

Colby nodded. Before long, Valerie would be close to the interstate, and then it would be impossible to catch her. *Not* that he was going to chase after her.

"Grace wasn't keen on marrying me, for a number of reasons. All good ones, I might add. She loved me, that much I knew, but to her mind love wasn't enough."

David's words diverted Colby's attention from the road. He swiveled his gaze to the older man, who was rocking contentedly as though they were discussing something as mundane as the best bait for local trout.

"Grace was right. Sometimes love isn't enough," David added.

"In your case she was wrong," Colby mumbled, displeased. For the first time he understood where this discussion was leading. Valerie's father was going to force him to admit that he was as big an idiot as Stephanie and Norah had claimed. Though he might be a little more subtle about it.

"Not really. I knew I'd need to make some real changes before Grace would agree to marry me, but I was willing to make them because I knew something she didn't."

"What was that?"

A wistful look came over David, and his eyes grew hazy. "Deep in my soul, I knew I'd never love another woman the way I loved Grace. Deep in my soul, I recognized that she was the one chance I had in this life for real happiness. I could've done the noble thing and let her marry some nice young man. There were plenty who would've thanked me for the opportunity."

"I see."

"I have to tell you, though, it was the most difficult decision of my life. Marrying Grace was the biggest risk I ever took, but I never regretted it. Not once."

Colby nodded. David was telling him exactly what he wanted to hear. He, too, had made his decision; he'd set Valerie free to find what happiness she could. Rowdy Cassidy was waiting in the wings, eager to step into his place. Eager to help her forget.

Colby's mind flashed to Sherry Waterman. He liked her and enjoyed her company. He felt the same about Norah. But it was Valerie who set his heart on fire. Valerie who challenged him. Valerie whom he needed. Not anyone else, only Valerie.

"Don't you worry about her," David continued. "She'll be fine. In a while, she'll regroup and be a better person for having experienced love, even for such a short time. As for marrying Rowdy Cassidy, I don't think you need to concern yourself with that, either."

"Why not?"

"Because I know my daughter. I know exactly what I would've done had Grace decided against marrying me. I'd have gone back to my world, worked hard and made a decent life for myself. But I would never have fallen in love again. I wouldn't have allowed it to happen."

Colby didn't say anything. By now, Valerie was on the interstate. It was too late. Even if he did go after her, they wouldn't be able to stop. Not on the freeway with cars screaming past. It would be reckless and dangerous and beyond all stupidity to chase her now. Besides, what could he possibly have to say that hadn't already been said?

David stood. "You want another cup of coffee?"

"No, thanks. I should be on my way."

"I'll be in your office bright and early Tuesday morning, then."

Colby nodded. It was time to get back to his life, the life he'd had before he met Valerie Bloomfield.

Valerie refused to cry. She'd never been prone to tears and, except for a few occasions, had usually managed to fend them off. Even as a child, she'd hated crying, hated the way the salty tears had felt on her face.

What astonished her was how much it hurt to hold everything inside. It felt as though someone had crammed a fist down her throat and expected her to breathe normally.

In an effort to push aside the pain of leaving Colby, she focused her thoughts on all the good he'd brought into her life. Without him, she would have lost her father. Norah had told her as much that first evening. Colby was the one who'd convinced her father to go to the hospital. Colby was the one who'd performed the life-saving surgery.

If for nothing else, she owed him more for that than anyone could possibly repay.

But that wasn't all he'd given her. Dr. Colby Winston had taught her about herself, about love, about sacrifice.

She would always love him for that. Now she had to teach herself to release him, to let him go. Finding love and then freely relinquishing it might well prove to be a tricky business. She'd never given her heart to a man before. Loving Colby was the easy part. It felt as though she'd always known and loved him, as if he'd always been part of her life. It seemed impossible that they'd met only a few weeks ago.

Leaving him was the hardest thing she'd ever done.

The self-doubts, the what-ifs and might-have-beens rolled in like giant waves, swamping her with grief and dread.

Dragging in a deep breath, she fought the urge to turn the car around and head back. Back to Orchard Valley. Back home.

Back to Colby.

Instead, she exhaled, tried to relax, tried to tell herself that everything would feel much better once she got to Texas. She'd be able to submerge the pain in her job. When she resumed her position with CHIPS, she could begin to forget Colby and at the same time treasure her memories of him.

Valerie didn't realize there were tears in her eyes until she noticed how blurry the road in front of her had become. Hoping to distract herself, she turned on the radio and started humming along with a country-western singer lamenting her lost love.

"Stop it," Valerie muttered to herself, weeping harder than ever. Irritably, she snapped off the radio, then swiped at the tears with the back of one hand, reminding herself she was too strong, too independent, for such weak emotional behavior.

Not until she was changing lanes on the freeway did she see the Buick behind her. A maroon sedan, traveling at high speed, passing cars, going well over the limit.

Colby? It couldn't be.

More than likely it was just a car that looked like his. It couldn't be him. He'd never come after her. That wasn't his style. No, if he ever had a change of heart, something she didn't count on, it wouldn't be for weeks, months. Colby wasn't impulsive.

The Buick slowed down and moved directly behind Valerie's car and followed her for a moment before putting on the turn signal. If it hadn't been for the tears in her eyes she would've been able to make out the driver's features.

The car honked. It *had* to be Colby. He didn't expect her to stop on the freeway, did he? It wouldn't be safe. There was an exit ramp only a few miles down the road and she drove toward that, turned off when she could and parked. Luckily traffic was light, and the shoulders on both sides of the road were wide enough for her to park safely. When she did, Colby pulled in behind her.

She'd barely had time to unfasten her seat belt before he jerked open her door.

"What are you doing here?" she demanded.

"What does it look like? I'm chasing after you."

Legs trembling, she climbed out of her car and stood

leaning against it, hands on her hips. "This better be good, Winston. I've got a plane to catch."

"You've been crying."

"There's something in my eye."

"Both eyes apparently."

"All right, both eyes." She didn't know what silly game he thought he was playing, but she didn't have the patience for it. "Why are you here? Surely there's a reason you came racing after me."

"There's a reason."

"Good." She crossed her arms and shifted her position. Whatever Colby wanted to say was obviously causing him trouble, because he started pacing in front of her, hands clenched.

"This is even harder than I expected," he finally admitted.

Not daring to hope, Valerie said nothing.

"I can't believe what a mess I've made of this. Listen." He turned to face her, his expression as closed as always. "I want you to come back to Orchard Valley."

"Why?"

"Because I love you and because I'd like us to talk this through. You love me, too, Valerie. I don't think I realized how much until just now. It must've been so hard to come to me, to lay your heart out like that and then have me send you away. I—"

"You don't need to apologize," she broke in.

"I do."

Valerie had no idea, not the slightest, where all this was leading. She took a shaky breath. "All right, you've apologized."

"Will you come back?"

"If you want to talk, we can do it at the airport." That seemed like a fair suggestion.

"I want to do more than talk," he said. "I want you to show me how we're going to make this marriage work, because darned if I know. We haven't got one thing working in our favor. Not one."

"Then why even try?"

"Because if you leave now I'm going to regret it for the rest of my life. Sure as anything, I'm going to think back to this moment for the next fifty years and wish I'd never let you go. The problem is, I'm not sure what to do now—you've got me so tied up in knots I can't think straight."

"No wonder you don't look happy."

"You're right, I'm not happy. I'm furious."

Valerie grinned. "Love *is* rather frightening, isn't it?"

Colby grinned, too, for the first time. "But you know something? It's living without you, without your love, that frightens me."

"Oh, Colby…"

"Let's say we did get married," he said, the gravel under his feet crunching as he paced.

"All right, let's say we did."

"Are you going to want a job outside the home?"

"Yes, Colby, I will."

"What about children?"

"Oh, yes, at least two." She found it odd to be discussing something so personal while standing at the side of a road.

"How do you propose to be both a mother and an executive?"

"How do you intend to be both a father and a surgeon? Not to mention a husband? You have a career, too, Colby."

"You can't have it all, Valerie."

"Neither can you! Besides, it doesn't have to be either or. Half the women in America maintain a career *and* a family, but there have to be compromises. You're right, I won't be able to do everything. I couldn't even begin to try."

"I don't like the idea of farming our children out to strangers."

"Frankly, I don't, either, but there are ways of working around that. Ways of making the situation acceptable to both of us. For one thing, I could set up an office at home. It's pretty common these days with email and teleconferencing and everything. Rowdy might be willing to start a branch of the company on the West Coast, and I think he might be persuaded to pick Oregon—especially if a hardworking executive chose to live there."

Colby nodded and thrust his hands into his pockets.

"I know I'm not what you want in a wife, Colby. You'd rather I was the kind of woman who'd be content to stay home and do needlepoint and put up preserves. But that isn't who I am, and I can't change. I'd give anything to be the woman you want, but if I'm not true to myself, the marriage would be doomed before we even said our vows."

"I don't think we should be concerning ourselves

with some unrealistic image I've invented. What about the man *you* want?"

She smiled and looked away. "You're the only man I've ever wanted."

He reached for her then, wrapping his arms tightly around her, dropping a gentle kiss on the side of her neck. A deep shudder went through him as he exhaled.

"I'm never going to be able to stop loving you."

"Is that so terrible?" she asked in a whisper, her throat raw.

"No, it's the most wonderful blessing of my life." His eyes were warm and loving as he brought up his hands to clasp her shoulders. "I've been arrogant. Selfish. I nearly destroyed both our lives because I refused to accept the gift you offered me."

"Oh, Colby."

"There won't be any guarantees."

"If I wanted guarantees, I'd buy myself a new car. Everything in life is a risk, but I've never been more willing to take one than with you." She smiled. "I'm very sure of what I feel for you, even though it all developed so quickly."

"Like it sprang to life fully formed," he added.

"The most exciting thing is that we have a lifetime to get to know everything about each other."

"I'd say we're in for an adventure."

"Yes, but it'll be the grandest adventure of all." Valerie's arms went around his neck as he lowered his mouth to hers. One kiss wiped out the pain and the torment of these past few days. Colby must have felt it, too, because he kissed her again and again, their need insatiable, their joy boundless.

A car driving past honked noisily, disturbing them.

Valerie reluctantly broke off their kiss. "You might have chosen someplace a bit more private, Dr. Winston."

"Shall we try this again later, with champagne and a diamond ring?"

Valerie nodded because speaking when her heart was so full would have been impossible.

Her father was sitting on the porch when Valerie and Colby pulled up in front of the house late that afternoon.

"Did you tell Dad you were coming after me?"

"I didn't know it myself until I left here. Before I realized what I was doing, I was on the freeway, racing after you like a bat out of hell. I didn't have a clue what I was going to say when I found you."

Valerie tucked her hand in his and pressed her cheek to his shoulder. "You looked like you wanted to bite my head off."

"I looked like a man who was calling himself every kind of fool in existence."

"For coming after me?"

"No," he said quietly. "For letting you go."

Valerie rewarded him with an appreciative kiss on the corner of his mouth.

Colby groaned softly. "I'm not going to want a long engagement. The sooner we can arrange this wedding, the better."

"I couldn't agree more."

Colby kissed her lightly on the lips. "I have the sneaking suspicion your father hasn't moved since you took off for the airport."

They'd been gone for hours, returning the rental car to Portland, and then stopping for an elegant lunch in an equally elegant restaurant. Before leaving the city, they'd visited a well-known jewelry store where Valerie chose a beautiful solitaire diamond engagement ring. That very ring was on her finger now. It felt as if it had always been there.

"About time you two got back," her father said as Colby helped her out of his car. "I was beginning to worry."

"How'd you know we were coming?" Colby asked.

"I knew before you left here that you'd be back with Valerie before the end of the day."

"Dad, you couldn't possibly have known." She waited for a protest, but none came. Her father sat back in his rocker and grinned happily.

"Oh, I know more than that about what's going to happen to you two."

"He's going to talk about that dream again," Valerie murmured, slipping her arm around Colby's waist and smiling up at him. He brought her close to his side.

"Love's shocked you both," David said, wagging a finger at them. "But there are a few more shocks in store for you. Just wait and see what happens when my twin grandsons are born."

"Twins?" Colby echoed incredulously.

"You're going to name them after their two grandfathers. The blond one will be David, and he'll be the spitting image of me."

"Twins," Colby said again.

"I don't know," Valerie said with a laugh. "I could get used to a few surprises now and then, especially if it means I can be with you."

Colby gazed down at her and Valerie realized her father was right. Love had caught them unawares, but it was the best surprise of their lives.

* * * * *

STEPHANIE

For Heidi Pollard
A woman of letters

One

Home.

Stephanie Bloomfield lugged her heavy suitcase up the porch steps of the large white-pillared house. She moved quietly, careful not to wake her two sisters, although it occurred to her that they might be at the hospital.

She herself had spent the best part—no, the *worst* part—of the past two days either on a plane or standing at the counter in a foreign airport. Or was that three days? She couldn't tell anymore.

Norah, her younger sister, had managed to call her in Italy nearly a week ago about their father's heart attack. The connection had been bad and she'd had difficulty hearing, but Norah's sense of urgency had come clearly over the wire. Their father was gravely ill, and Steffie needed to hurry home—something that turned out to be much easier said than done.

Steffie had been living just outside Rome, attending classes at the university. She'd been participating in a special program, learning Italian and studying Renaissance history, culture and art. For three years she'd traveled effortlessly from one end of the country to the other. Now, when she desperately needed to fly home, the airports were closed by a transportation strike that paralyzed Italy. It didn't help that she'd been staying in a small, relatively isolated village hundreds of miles from Rome. She'd gone on a brief holiday, visiting a friend's family.

It had taken her several days and what felt like three lifetimes to arrange passage home. *Days,* when it should've been a matter of hours. This past week had been the most stressful of her life. She'd been in touch with her sisters as often as possible, and at last report Norah had said that their father was resting comfortably. Still, she'd heard the dread in Norah's voice. Her youngest sister had never been much good at hiding the truth. Although she'd tried to sound reassuring, Steffie was well aware that her father's condition had worsened. That was when she'd undertaken the most daring move of her life. She'd made contact with some men of questionable scruples, sold every possession of value and, at a hugely inflated price, obtained a means out of the country, by way of Japan, with layovers in places she'd never expected to visit. It was decidedly an indirect route to Oregon, but she was home now. Heaven only knew how much longer it would have taken if she hadn't resorted to such drastic measures.

After a whole day of waiting at the Tokyo airport, fighting for space aboard any available flight to the States, and then the long flight itself, Steffie was frantic for news of her father. Frantic and fearful. In some ways, not knowing was almost better than knowing....

She opened the front door and stepped silently inside the sleeping house. She'd adjusted her watch to Pacific time, but her mind was caught somewhere between Italy and Tokyo. She was too exhausted to be tired. Too worried to be hungry, although she couldn't remember the last meal she'd eaten.

Setting down her impossibly heavy suitcase, she stood in the foyer and breathed in the scent of polished wood and welcome.

She was home.

Her father's den was to her right, and she immediately felt drawn there. Pausing in the doorway, she flipped on the light switch and stood gazing at the room that was so much her father's. A massive stone fireplace commanded one entire wall, while two other walls were lined with floor-to-ceiling bookcases.

She looked at his wingback chair, the soft leather creased from years of use. Closing her eyes, Steffie breathed in deeply, savoring the scent of old leather and books and the sweet pungency of pipe tobacco. This was her father's room, and she'd never missed him more than she did at that moment.

His presence seemed to fill the den. His robust laugh echoed silently against the walls. Steffie could visualize him sitting behind the cherrywood desk, the accounting ledgers spread open and his pipe propped in the ugly ceramic ashtray   the one she'd made for him the summer she turned eleven.

The photograph of her mother caught her eye.

David Bloomfield could leave his daughters no finer legacy than the love he'd shared with their mother. He'd changed after Grace's death. Steffie had noticed it even before she left Orchard Valley. She'd guessed it from his letters in the years since. And she'd been especially aware of the changes when he came to visit her in Italy last spring. The spark was gone. The relentless passion for life that had always been so much a part of him was missing now. Each month his letters were more painful to read, more lifeless and subdued. Without his wife at his side, David Bloomfield was as empty as...as that chair there, his old reading chair, standing in front of the fireplace.

Steffie's gaze slipped to the newspaper spread across the ottoman. It felt as though, any minute, her father would walk through the door, settle back into his chair and resume reading.

Only he wouldn't.

He might never sit in this room again, Steffie realized, her heart constricting with pain. He might never reach for one of his favorite books and lovingly leaf through its pages until he found the passage he wanted. He might never sit by the fireplace, pipe in hand. He might never look up when she entered the room and smile when he saw it was Steffie—his "princess."

The pain in her chest grew more intense and the need to release her emotions burned inside her, but Steffie ignored it, as she had a thousand times before. She wasn't a weeper. She'd guarded her emotions vigilantly for three long years. Ever since that night with Charles Tomaselli when he'd—

She brushed the memory aside with the efficiency of long practice. Charles was a painful figure from her past. One best forgotten, or at least ignored. She hadn't thought of him in months and refused to do so now. Sooner or later she'd be forced to exchange pleasantries with him, but when she did, she'd pretend she had trouble remembering who he was, as though he were merely a casual acquaintance and not the man who'd broken her heart. That seemed the best way to handle the situation—to pretend she'd completely forgotten their last humiliating encounter.

If he did insist on renewing their acquaintance, which was unlikely, she'd show him how mature she was, how sophisticated and cosmopolitan she'd become. Then he'd regret the careless, cruel way he'd treated her.

There was a sound in the hallway, and Steffie moved out of the den just as Norah reached the bottom of the stairs.

"Steffie? My goodness, you're home!" Norah exclaimed, rushing to embrace her.

And then, with a small cry of welcome, Valerie, the oldest of the three, bounded down the stairs, her long cotton gown dancing about her feet.

"Steff, I'm so glad you're home," Valerie cried, wrapping her arms around both sisters. "When did you get in? Why didn't you let us know so we could meet you at the airport?"

"I flew standby most of the way, so I wasn't sure when I'd land. I caught the Air Porter and then a cab." She took a deep breath. "I'm just glad I'm here."

"I am, too," Valerie said with an uncharacteristic display of emotion, wiping the tears from her cheeks. Normally Valerie was a model of restraint. Seeing her this shaken revealed, more plainly than anything she could've said, how desperately ill their father was.

By tacit agreement, they moved into the kitchen. Valerie set about preparing a pot of tea. According to the digital clock on the microwave, it was a little past three. Steffie hadn't realized it was quite that late. She could hardly recall the last time she'd slept in a bed. Four days ago, perhaps.

"How's Dad?" It was the question she'd been yearning to ask from the moment she'd walked in the door. The question she was afraid to ask.

"He's doing just great," Norah said, her soft voice rising with delight. "We came really close to losing him, Steffie. Valerie and I were in a panic because things looked bad and Dr. Winston couldn't delay the surgery. And Dad pulled through! But…"

"But he…" Valerie began when Norah hesitated.

"He what?" Steffie prompted. Although she was thrilled with the news that her father had survived the crisis, she couldn't help wondering why both her sisters seemed reluctant to continue. "Tell me," she insisted. She didn't want to be protected from the truth.

"Apparently Dad had a near-death experience," Norah finally said.

"Isn't that fairly common? Especially during that kind of surgery? I've been reading for years about people who believe they traveled through a dark tunnel into the light."

"I wouldn't know how common it is to talk to someone in the spirit world, would you?" Valerie snapped.

"Dad claims he talked to Mom." Once again it was Norah who supplied the information.

"To Mom?" Steffie felt numb, unsure of how to react.

"Which we all know is impossible." Valerie hurried barefoot across the kitchen floor to pour boiling water into the teapot. She placed three mugs, three spoons and the sugar bowl on a tray; when the tea had steeped, she filled the cups, obviously preoccupied with her task. Carrying the tray to the table, she served her sisters, then leaped up to get a plate of Norah's home-baked cookies. "I think Dad needs to talk to a counselor," she said abruptly.

"Valerie." Norah sighed as though this was a well-worn argument. "You're overreacting."

"You would, too, if Dad was saying to you the things he says to me." Valerie stirred her tea without looking up.

Norah sighed again. "Dad honestly believes he spoke to Mom and if it makes him feel better, then I don't think we should try to discount his experience."

"What was Mom supposed to have said to him?" Steffie asked, intrigued by the interplay between her two sisters. She helped herself to a couple of oatmeal cookies as she spoke.

"That's what worries me the most." Valerie raised her voice, clearly unsettled. "He's got some ridiculous notion that we're all going to marry."

"Now, that's profound." Steffie couldn't hide her

amusement. The three of them were of marriageable age; it made sense that they'd eventually find husbands.

"But he claims to know *who* we're going to marry," Norah said, grinning sheepishly, as though she found the whole thing amusing.

"He's been wearing this silly smile for two days." Valerie groaned, dropping her forehead onto her arms. "He's been talking about a housefull of grandchildren, too. The ones *we're* supposed to present him with— and all in the next few years. If it wasn't so ludicrous, I'd cry."

"Has he said who I'm supposed to marry?" Steffie asked, curiosity getting the better of her.

Valerie lifted her head to glare at Stephanie, and Norah chuckled. "That's something else that irritates Valerie," she explained. "Dad hasn't told any of us, at least not directly. Not yet."

"He's acting like he knows this wonderful secret and he's keeping it all to himself, dropping hints every now and then. I swear it's driving me crazy."

"I don't mind it," Norah said. To someone else, she might have sounded self-righteous, but Steffie recognized her younger sister's compassion and knew that it edged out any hint of righteousness. "Dad's smiling again. He's excited about the future and even if he's becoming a bit…presumptuous about the three of us, I honestly can't say I mind. I'm just so glad to have him alive."

Valerie nodded, her argument apparently gone. "I guess I can put up with a few remarks, too."

"This is the first time one of us hasn't stayed all night at the hospital," Norah said, her mouth curving into a gentle smile. "Dr. Winston insisted there wasn't any need. Not anymore."

"Don't be fooled by that guy," Valerie muttered under her breath. "He may look like your average, laid-back country doctor, but he's got a backbone of steel."

He must have, if Valerie was reacting like this, Stephanie thought with sudden interest. It seemed that her sister had finally encountered a will as strong as her own. So, either Valerie had changed her ways or she had—could it be?—a soft spot for this Dr. Winston.

"In other words," Steffie said quickly, "I missed the worst of it. Dad's out of danger now and will eventually recover?"

"Yes," Norah said cheerfully. "Everything'll be back to normal."

"Not exactly." Valerie shook her head. "In a few weeks Dad will be the picture of health, but the three of us will be pulling out our hair after listening to all his talk about marriage, husbands and grandchildren!"

Bright sunlight poured through the open window of Steffie's bedroom when she woke. The house was quiet, but the sounds of the day drifted in from outside. Birds chirped merrily in the distance and a spring breeze set the chimes on the back porch tinkling and rustled the curtains lightly. She could hear work crews in the orchard—spraying the apple trees, Steffie guessed.

After those long days of struggling to get home, she exulted in the sensation of familiarity, wrapping the feel of it around her like a warm quilt. The crisis had passed. Her father would survive, and all the world seemed brighter, sweeter, happier.

Reluctantly she slid out of bed and dressed, pulling a pair of slacks and a light sweater from her suitcase.

She found a note on the kitchen table explaining that both Valerie and Norah were at the hospital. They were going to leave her arrival a surprise, so she could come anytime she was ready. No need to rush. Not anymore.

Selecting a banana from the fruit bowl on the kitchen counter, she ate that while reheating a cup of coffee in the microwave. As the timer was counting down the seconds, she walked into her father's den and reached for the newspaper, intending to take it with her to the hospital.

She would read it, Steffie decided, to catch up on the local news. But even as she formed this thought, she knew she was lying to herself.

There was only one reason she was taking the local newspaper with her. Only one reason she'd even picked it up. *Charles Tomaselli.* She turned to the front page. The *Orchard Valley Clarion.* She allowed her eyes to skim the headlines for a moment.

Emotion came at her in waves. First apprehension. She'd give anything to avoid seeing Charles again. Then anger. He'd humiliated her. Laughed at her. She'd never forgive him for that. Never. The agony of his humiliation smoldered even now, years later. Yet, much as she wanted to hate Charles, she couldn't. She didn't love him anymore. That was over, finished. He'd cured her of love in the most effective way possible. No, she reassured herself, she didn't love him—but she couldn't make herself hate him, either.

She could handle this. She had to. Besides, he was probably as eager to avoid any encounters between them as she was.

She gulped down half the steaming coffee. Then she tucked the paper under her arm and grabbed the car keys Norah had thoughtfully left on the kitchen table and headed out the door.

When she got to Orchard Valley General, Steffie paused, taken aback by a sudden rush of grief. The last time she'd gone through those doors had been the day her mother died. Steffie's heart stilled at the nearly overwhelming sadness she felt. She hadn't expected that. It took her a couple of minutes to compose herself. Then she continued toward the elevator.

When she arrived at the waiting room, she found Norah speaking to one of the nurses, while Valerie sat reading. It was so unusual to see her older sister doing anything sedentary that Stephanie nearly did a double take.

"Steffie!" Norah said, her face lighting when she saw her sister. "Did you get enough sleep?"

"I'm fine." That was true, although it would take more than one night's rest to recuperate from the past week.

"Did you fix yourself some breakfast?"

"Yes, little mother, I did. Can I see Dad now or is

there anything else you'd like to ask me?" She slipped an arm around her sister's trim waist, feeling elated. It was wonderful to be home, wonderful to be with her family.

"You're here," Valerie said, joining them. "Dad asked me earlier when we'd last heard from you. I told him this morning."

"He's going to be moved out of the Surgical Intensive Care Unit tomorrow," Norah said happily. "Then we'll all be able to see him at once. As it is now, only one of us can visit at a time."

"Norah, would you like me to take your sister in to see your father?" Another nurse had bustled up to them.

"Please," Steffie answered eagerly before Norah could speak. The nurse led her through a hallway with glass-walled cubicles. Every imaginable sort of medical equipment seemed to be in use here, but Steffie barely noticed. She was far too excited about seeing her father. The nurse stopped at one of the cubicles and gestured Stephanie inside.

He was sitting up in bed. He smiled and held out his arms to her. "Steffie," he said faintly, "come here, Princess." She saw that he was connected to several monitoring devices.

She walked into his hold, careful to stay clear of the wires and tubes, astonished at his weak embrace after the bone-crushing hugs she was accustomed to receiving. Her sisters had said the spark was back in his eyes. They'd talked about how well he looked.

Stephanie disagreed.

She was shocked by his paleness, by the gaunt-
ness of his appearance. If he was so much better *now,*
she hated to think what he must have looked like a
week ago.

"It's so good to see you," her father said, his voice
cracking with emotion. "I've missed you, Princess."

"I've missed you, too," Steffie said, wiping a tear
from the corner of her eye as she straightened.

"You're home to stay?"

Steffie wasn't sure how to answer. Home repre-
sented so much to her, much more than she'd realized,
but she loved Italy, too. Still, just gazing out on the
orchards this morning had reminded her how much
she'd missed her life in Orchard Valley.

She'd left bruised and vulnerable; she'd returned
strong and sure of herself. Being in Italy had helped
her heal. But there was no longer any reason to stay
away. She was ready to come home.

She'd been trying to decide what to do next when
she'd received word of her father's heart attack. Her
courses were completed, but remaining in Italy had a
strong appeal. She could travel for a while, continue
her studies, perhaps do some teaching herself. She
could move to some place like Boston or New York.
Or she could return to Orchard Valley. Steffie hadn't
known what she wanted.

"I'm home for as long as you need me."

"You'll stay," her father insisted with unshakable
confidence.

"What makes you so sure?"

He smiled mysteriously and his voice dropped to a whisper. "Your mother told me."

"Mom?" Steffie was beginning to appreciate Valerie's concerns.

"Yup. I suppose you're going to act like your sister and suggest I see some fancy doctor with a couch in his office. I did talk to your mother. She sends her love, by the way."

Steffie didn't know how to respond. Should she ask him to convey a message for her? "What did Mom... tell you?" she ventured instead.

"Quite a bit, but mainly she said I had quite a few years left in me. She promised they'd be good ones, too." He paused, chuckling softly. "Your mother always did know I had a soft spot for babies. And there's going to be a passel of them born in this family within the next few years."

"Babies?"

"An even dozen." The first sign of color crept into his cheeks. "Can you believe it? My little girls are going to make me a grandfather twelve times over."

"Uh..."

"I know it sounds like I've got a screw loose, but..."

"Daddy, you think whatever you like if it makes you happy."

"It's more than thinking, Princess. It's a fact, sure as I'm lying here. But never mind that now. Let me get a look at you. My goodness," he said, grinning proudly, "you're even lovelier than I remembered."

Steffie beamed with pleasure. She knew very well that she was no raving beauty, but her looks were nothing to be ashamed of, either. Her dark hair was straight as a clothespin, reaching to the middle of her back. She wore it pulled away from her face, using combs, a style that accentuated her prominent cheekbones and the strong lines of her face. Her eyes were deep brown.

Steffie had just started to regale her father with the adventures of the past week when the same nurse who'd escorted her in to see him reappeared, ready to lead her back to the waiting area.

Steffie wanted to argue. They'd barely had five minutes together! But she forced back her objections; she wouldn't do anything that might upset her father. She kissed his leathery cheek and promised to return soon.

Valerie was waiting for her, but Norah was nowhere in sight.

"Well?" Valerie asked, glancing up from her magazine. "Did he say anything about talking to Mom?"

Steffie nodded, secretly a little amused. "He seems downright excited about the prospect of grandchildren. I hate to see him disappointed, don't you?"

"Hmm?" Valerie muttered.

"Since you're the oldest, it makes sense you should be the first," she teased, enjoying her sister's blank look.

"For what?" Valerie asked.

"To produce a grandchild for Dad. The last time you wrote, I seem to remember you had quite a lot to say about Rowdy Cassidy. Might as well aim high— marry a multimillionaire—even if he is your boss."

"Rowdy," Valerie repeated as though she'd never

heard the name before. "Oh... Rowdy. Of course there's always Rowdy. Why didn't I think of him?" With that, Valerie returned to her magazine.

Baffled, Steffie shook her head.

She wandered over to the coffeemaker, poured herself a fresh cup and sat down near her sister. She picked up the newspaper she'd brought with her and opened it to the front page, reading each article in turn. She was relieved to recognize several names; obviously not much had changed while she was away.

Folding back the second page of the weekly paper, she found that her eyes were automatically drawn to the small black-and-white photograph of Charles Tomaselli. For a wild second her heart seemed to stop.

He looked the same. Still as attractive as sin. No man had the right to be that good-looking. Dark hair, gleaming dark eyes. But what bothered her the most was the impact his picture had on her. It wasn't supposed to be like this. She should be free of any emotional entanglement. She should be able to stare at that photograph and feel nothing. Instead she was swamped by so many confused, uncomfortable emotions that she could hardly breathe.

Determined to focus her attention elsewhere, she started on an article with Charles's byline. He'd written an investigative feature, clearly one of a series, about the unhealthy and often unsafe conditions under which many of the migrant workers lived and worked in the community's apple orchards.

Two paragraphs into the piece, Steffie had to stop reading. She'd come to her father's name, along with the name of their orchard. Obviously Charles hadn't done his research! Steffie knew how hard her parents had worked to ease the plight of the migrant workers. Her mother had set up a medical clinic. And unlike certain other orchard owners, her father had built them decent housing and seen to it that they were properly fed and fairly paid.

Steffie tried to continue reading, but the red haze of anger made it impossible. Her stomach twisted in painful knots as she rose to her feet, tucking the paper under her arm.

"Valerie," she demanded. "What was Dad doing when he suffered his heart attack?"

"I think Norah said he was sitting on the porch. What makes you ask?"

"He was reading the newspaper, wasn't he?"

"I wouldn't know for sure, but I don't think so."

"He must have been!" Steffie declared, walking toward the elevator. She stabbed the button with her thumb, seething at the sense of betrayal she felt. All the evidence pointed to one thing. She'd found the paper spread open in his den. Her father had picked up the *Orchard Valley Clarion,* read the article and then in shock and dismay had wandered onto the porch.

"Steffie, what is it?"

"Have you *read* this?" she asked, thrusting the newspaper in front of her sister. "Did you see what Charles Tomaselli wrote about our father?"

"Well, I skimmed it, but—"

"Look at the date," she said, folding back the front page.

"Yes?" Valerie asked, still sounding confused.

"Isn't that the day of Dad's heart attack?"

"Yes, but—"

"You'd be upset, too, if you'd worked half your life improving the conditions of migrant workers only to have your efforts ridiculed before the entire community!"

"Steffie," Valerie said, gently pressing Steffie's arm. "Charles is Dad's friend. He's called several times to ask about him. Why, he was even here the night of Dad's surgery."

"He was probably feeling a large dose of guilt." It seemed perfectly obvious that Charles knew what he'd done. Her father's heart attack had happened the same day the article was published. So Charles *must* have known, must have figured it out himself. And that was why he'd come calling—she was sure of it.

But it was going to take a whole lot more than a few words of concern to smooth over what he'd done. Once Steffie had confronted Charles, she intended to stop at Joan Lind's office. Joan might be as old as a sand dune, but she was a damn good attorney and Steffie meant to sue Tomaselli for everything he ever hoped to have.

The elevator arrived and she stepped briskly inside.

"Where are you going?" Valerie asked as the doors started to close.

"To give Tomaselli a piece of my mind."

The doors blocked Valerie from view, but her sister's words came through loud and clear. "A piece of your mind? Are you sure you have any to spare?"

* * *

By the time Steffie reached Main Street and located a parking spot, the anger and hurt actually made her feel ill. Her cheeks were feverishly hot. Her stomach churned.

Charles disliked her, and he was taking it out on her father. Well, she couldn't let him do it.

She entered the newspaper office, then hesitated. There was a reception desk and a polished wooden railing; it separated the public area from the work space, with its computer terminals and ringing phones. Beyond it several desks occupied by reporters and other staff lined each side of the room, creating a wide center aisle that led directly to the editor's desk.

She noticed Charles immediately. As the *Clarion*'s editor, he had a work area that took up the entire end of the room. He was on the phone, but his eyes locked instantly with hers. There'd been a time when she would have swooned to have him look at her like this—with admiration, with surprise, with a hint of pleasure. But that time was long past.

Undaunted, she opened the low gate and walked purposefully down the center aisle until she got to his desk. She could hear the gate swinging back and forth behind her, keeping time with her steps. By now, Charles clearly understood that this wasn't a social call.

"Brent, let me get back to you." He abruptly replaced the receiver. "Well, well, if it isn't Stephanie Bloomfield. To what do I owe this visit?"

His casual insouciance infuriated her. Steffie

slapped the newspaper down on his desk. "Did you really think you'd get away with this?" she asked, astonished by the calmness of her own voice.

Charles's eyes steadily held hers. "I don't know what you're talking about."

"You published this…piece, didn't you?"

"What piece do you mean? I publish lots of pieces."

His attitude didn't fool her. "The one about living conditions among migrant orchard workers. Now, I ask you, who owns the largest apple orchard in three counties? The first paragraph is filled with innuendo, but then you get right down to brass tacks, don't you—by naming my father!"

"Stephanie—"

"I'm not finished yet!" she shouted. In fact, she was just warming up to her subject. "You didn't think any of us would notice, did you?"

"Notice what?" He crossed his arms over his chest as though he'd grown bored with her tirade.

"The date of the article," she said, gaining momentum. "It's the same day as my father's heart attack. The very same day—"

"Stephanie—"

"Don't call me that!" Tears rolled down her face. "Everyone calls me Steffie." Roughly, she wiped them away, hating this display of weakness, especially in front of Charles. "I—don't know how you can live with yourself."

"If you want the truth, I don't have much of a problem."

"I didn't think your sort would," she muttered contemptuously. "Well, you'll be hearing from Joan Lind."

"Joan Lind retired last year."

"Then I'll hire someone else," she said, turning on her heel. She marched through the office, slamming the low gate, which had only recently recovered from her entrance.

To her surprise, confronting Charles hadn't eased her pain.

When she pulled out of the parking space, the tires spun and squealed. She felt suddenly embarrassed. She hadn't meant to make such a dramatic exit. Nor was she pleased when she glanced in her rearview mirror to find that Charles had followed her outside.

Two

With the hurt propelling her, Steffie raced home. In her present frame of mind, she didn't dare go back to the hospital. Now wasn't the time to make polite conversation with her sisters, or to meet her father's doctor. Not when she desperately needed to vent this terrible sense of frustration and betrayal.

Charles's treachery cut deep. They'd had their differences, but Steffie had never once believed he would purposely set out to hurt her or her family. She'd been wrong. Charles was both vindictive and unforgiving, and that was more painful than the things he'd said to her that last day they'd been together. That horrible day when he'd laughed at her.

She was shocked he still had the power to make her feel like this, but apparently his grip on her heart was as strong now as it had been three years earlier. The time she'd spent away from home, the time she'd given herself to heal, might never have existed. She was no less vulnerable to him now.

From the moment Steffie first met Charles, she'd been fascinated with him. Infatuated. In the beginning, she hoped he returned her feelings. She'd been attending the University of Portland, making the fifty-mile commute into the city every day. Her mother had died a few months earlier, so Steffie had decided against moving into a dorm, as she'd originally planned.

In her sorrow, she'd craved the comfort of familiar people and places. She was worried, too, about her father, who seemed to be walking around in a fog of grief.

Valerie was already living in Texas at that point, and although she'd come home often while their mother was ill, her work schedule had kept her from visiting much since.

Norah, who was in the university's nursing program, used to drive to Portland with her. But Steffie would have made the hour's drive twice a day by herself if she'd had to, simply so she could see Charles more often.

It mortified her now, looking back. Her excuses to see him had been embarrassingly transparent. She'd been so wide-eyed with adoration that she'd repeatedly made a fool of herself.

Her cheeks flamed as she recalled the times she'd followed him around like a lost puppy. The way she'd studied every word, every line, he'd written. The way she'd worshiped him from afar, until her love had burned fiercely within her, impossible to contain or control....

She didn't want to remember, and as she so often

had in the past, she blocked the memories from her mind rather than relive the humiliation she'd suffered because of him.

Her anger had cooled by the time she'd finished the ten-mile drive out of Orchard Valley to the family home. Once she arrived, the thought of going inside held no appeal. She needed to do something physically demanding to work off her frustration.

The stables were located behind the house. Valerie and Norah had never really taken to riding, but Steffie, who was the family daredevil, had loved it. The sense of freedom and power had been addictive to a young girl struggling to discover her own identity. Some of the happiest memories of her childhood were the times she'd gone horseback riding with her father.

She knew from Norah's letters that he hadn't ridden much lately and had left exercising the horses to the hired help.

The stable held six stalls, four of them empty, and a tack room at the rear. Both Fury and Princess raised their sleek heads when she entered the barn. Princess was the gentle mare her father had purchased and named for her several years earlier; Fury was her father's gelding, large and black, notoriously temperamental. He pawed the ground vigorously as she approached.

"How're you doing, big boy?" she asked, rubbing his soft muzzle. "I'm not ignoring you, Princess," she told the mare across the aisle. "It's just that I'm in the mood for a really hard workout."

After allowing Fury to refamiliarize himself with

her, Steffie collected saddle and bridle from the tack room. She slipped on Fury's bridle, then opened the stall gate and led him out. The gelding seemed to be as eager to run as she was to ride, and he shifted his weight impatiently as she tightened the girth and adjusted the stirrups.

Leading him out of the stable, she'd set her foot in the stirrup, ready to mount, when she noticed a small red sports car racing down the driveway. It didn't take her two seconds to recognize Charles.

Steffie had no intention of speaking to a man she considered a traitor. In fact, she didn't want to ever see him again. She planned to talk to her sisters, then seek legal counsel. Charles would pay for what he'd done to her father, and she'd make sure he paid dearly. Even if he retained bitter feelings about her, that was no reason to take vengeance on her family.

Reaching for the saddle horn, she hoisted herself onto Fury's back. She hadn't used a Western saddle since she'd left home and needed a moment to get used to it again. Fury scampered in a side trot as Steffie changed her position, leaning slightly forward.

"It's all right, boy," she assured him in a calm, quiet voice that belied her eagerness to escape—and leave Charles behind.

She ignored his honk and although it was childish, she derived a certain amount of pleasure from turning her back on him. She nudged Fury's sides and with her chin at a haughty angle, trotted away.

She'd only gone a short distance when she became aware that Charles was following her. Fury didn't need any encouragement to increase his steady trot to a full gallop. Although she was an experienced horsewoman, Steffie wasn't prepared for the sudden burst of speed. Fury raced as though fire was licking at his heels.

Holding on to the reins, Steffie adjusted as well as she could, bouncing and jolting uncomfortably, unable to adapt to Fury's rhythm. She'd ridden in Italy, but not nearly as often as she would've liked and always with an English-style saddle. Not only was she out of practice, she didn't have the strength to control a horse of Fury's size and power—especially one who hadn't been exercised lately. She should've thought of that, she groaned. Thank goodness he was familiar with the terrain. He galloped first along the dirt road, bordered on both sides by apple trees. He kicked up a cloud of dust in his wake, which made it impossible for Steffie to tell whether Charles had continued after her. She prayed he hadn't.

Only when Fury took a sharp turn to the left, through a rough patch of ground, did Steffie see that Charles was indeed behind her. She tried to pull in the reins, to slow Fury down to a more comfortable trot, but the gelding had a mind of his own. She tried to talk to him but her hair flew about her face, the long ends slapping her cheeks, blinding her. Between her bouncing in the saddle and the hair flapping in her face, she couldn't manage a single intelligible word.

By now she had a lot more than Charles to worry about. She was about to lose what little control she had of the horse. And on this rough ground, she feared for the animal's safety, not to mention her own.

Steffie remembered the land well enough to realize they were headed for a bluff that overlooked the valley. It was at the farthest reach of her family's property, and a place Steffie had often gone when she needed to be alone. She approved of Fury's choice, if not his means of getting there.

Her one consolation was that it would be virtually impossible for Charles to follow her any farther. His vehicle would never make it over the rock-strewn landscape. With no other option, he'd be forced to turn back. Or wait. And if he chose to wait by the side of the dirt road, he'd be out of luck—she'd simply take another route home, connecting with the road at a different point.

Once they reached their destination, Fury slowed to a canter. Steffie pulled back on the reins, slid out of the saddle and commanded her trembling legs to keep her upright. She wiped the sweat from the gelding's neck and rubbed him down with a handful of long dry grass, then led him to a nearby stream. She was loosely holding the reins, allowing him to drink the clear, cool water, when she saw a whirl of dust. Thinking at first that it might be a dust devil, she only glanced in that direction. Her heart sank all the way to her knees when she made out the form of a red sports car.

It wasn't possible. The terrain was far too uneven and rocky. Charles must be insane to risk the undercarriage of his car by racing after her.

Squaring her shoulders, she turned to face him, refusing to give one quarter. Charles bounded out of the small car like a spring being released. She nearly flinched at the hard, angry set of his face.

"What do you think you're doing?" he demanded— as though he had a right to ask.

Steffie didn't acknowledge him but resumed her rubdown of the horse.

"You might have been killed, you idiot! And you might have killed that horse, too."

She was about to tell him she was no idiot, but she refused to become involved in a shouting match. And she *did* feel guilty about taking out a horse she couldn't control—her father's horse, yet. But Charles was a traitor, and worse. The next time she spoke to him, Steffie thought angrily, it would be through an attorney.

It looked for a moment as though he intended to grab her by the shoulders; in fact, what she heard him mutter sounded like a threat to "shake some sense" into her. He raised his hands, then briefly closed his eyes and spun away from her.

"You haven't changed a bit, have you?" he cried, jerking one hand through his hair as he stalked toward his car.

Still Steffie remained silent, although she had to bite her tongue in an effort not to lash back at him. He'd purposely hurt her family, hurt her. There was nothing left to be said.

He yanked his car door open, and Steffie blinked at the unexpectedness of his withdrawal. She wasn't sure what he'd planned to do, but this swift capitulation came as a surprise.

Not wanting him to assume she cared about his actions one way or the other, she tried to ignore him. She looped Fury's reins around a low branch and walked away. Her legs were trembling so badly that she decided to climb onto a boulder. Perched there, she gazed out at the sweeping view of the valley below, jewel-like in its green lushness.

Charles's footsteps behind her announced that he hadn't left, after all.

"Read it!" he shouted, slapping the very newspaper she'd given him against her thigh. "*This* time finish the article."

Steffie gasped, then pressed her lips together, tilting her head to avoid looking at him.

"Fine, be stubborn. That's nothing new. But if you won't read the article, I'll do it for you." He opened the paper.

Steffie wanted to blot out every word, but she wouldn't resort to anything quite as juvenile as plugging her ears. She cringed inwardly as his strong voice read the opening paragraph. On hearing it a second time, she felt the piece sounded even more hostile to her father than she'd believed earlier. It was as though Charles had taken the very heart of David Bloomfield's accomplishments and crushed it with falsehoods and accusations.

By the time he reached the spot where Steffie had stopped reading, where her father's name was mentioned, the anger inside her had rekindled. She closed her eyes to the wave of pain that threatened to overwhelm her.

He read on, and she waited with foreboding for

the attack she knew was coming. But it didn't happen. As Charles continued, she suddenly realized how wrong she'd been. How *terribly* wrong. Her heart in her throat, she turned toward him. Charles went on, reading a direct quote from David Bloomfield in which he told of the changes he'd made over the years to aid migrant workers.

At first Steffie was convinced she'd misunderstood. Nor was she entirely sure she could believe Charles. He might be making it up as he went along, she thought wildly, instead of actually reading the article. She reached for the newspaper and snatched it away from him.

It only took her a moment to locate the paragraph he'd just read. He hadn't made it up! There, bold as could be, was the quote from her father, followed by two long paragraphs that reported the progressive measures Bloomfield Orchards had implemented over the years.

Her stomach plummeted, and she began to feel as though she were sitting in a deck chair on the *Titanic*. That feeling intensified as she finished reading the article. Because she soon discovered that not only was her father quoted—approvingly—several times, but their family orchard was used as a model for other local orchards to follow.

Steffie drew in a deep breath before she looked up at Charles. Once again, she'd made a fool of herself in front of him. She cringed in acute embarrassment and self-contempt. What a jerk she'd been. What a total jerk.

She'd known that meeting Charles again was inevitable. She'd hoped that on her return he'd view her—from afar, of course—as mature. Sophisticated. She'd wanted him to see her as cosmopolitan and cultured, unlike the lovesick twenty-two-year-old who'd left Orchard Valley three years before.

She'd imagined their first meeting. She'd step forward, a serene smile on her face, and hold out her hand politely. She'd murmur ever so sweetly that it was lovely to see him again, but unfortunately she couldn't quite recall his name. Charles Something-or-other, wasn't it?

"It looks like I owe you an apology," she said instead, her voice quavering a bit despite her efforts to keep it even.

"Yeah, I'd say you owe me an apology!" he flung back. "I'd assumed you might have changed in three years. Instead you're an even bigger…nuisance."

His words felt like a slap across the face, and she flinched involuntarily. There wasn't a thing she could say in her own defense, nothing that would take away the shame of what she'd done. No words would erase the way she'd stomped into his office and created a scene in front of his entire staff.

"So it seems," she said as steadily as her crumbling poise would allow.

"You scared me, taking off like that," he raged. "You might have killed yourself."

Again, there was nothing she could say. Had she been in any other frame of mind, she would have recognized that with a horse like Fury, she was heading for trouble.

"You're a crazy woman!" he shouted, his anger fully ignited now. "How do you think I would've felt if you'd been hurt? What about your father? You accuse *me* of causing his heart attack! What do you think would've happened to him if you'd killed yourself?"

"I—I..." Hating the telltale action, she bit her lip to stop its trembling.

To Steffie's dismay, he reached down and pulled her to her feet. His hands clasped her shoulders and he drew her into his arms.

Before she had a chance to react, she was completely caught in his embrace, her hands trapped against his heaving chest.

One hand left her shoulder and slid into her long, tangled hair.

"Do you even have a clue what I was thinking?" he whispered. "Do you have any idea what was going through my mind?"

Her heart thundered. She should fight her way out of his embrace. She should demand that he release her, tell him he had no right to take her in his arms. But Steffie couldn't make herself move, couldn't make herself speak.

She didn't try to stop him even when it became obvious that he was going to kiss her. Mentally she braced herself, closing her eyes.

When his mouth found hers, it was a gentle brushing of lips. Her eyes opened in wonder and surprise.

Charles kissed her again, longer this time, his

mouth gliding over hers. Before she realized what she was doing, she moved her arms upward and timidly locked them behind his neck. Her lips parted to his and he pressed her closer.

But only for a moment. "No, Steffie," he said in a raw whisper, clasping both wrists and breaking her hold. He stepped back. Their eyes met for several seconds before he turned and hurried away.

He left as abruptly as he'd arrived, his sports car spitting dirt and small stones as he roared off. She sighed and prepared to mount Fury for the long journey home.

Steffie took a nap that afternoon, waking sometime in the early evening. The sun was setting, dousing the orchards in a lovely shade of pink. Not knowing what time it was, she came downstairs to find Norah in the kitchen, emptying the dishwasher.

"Hi," Norah greeted her, smiling brightly when she saw Steffie. "I was beginning to wonder if you'd ever wake up. You must've been exhausted."

Steffie nodded.

"There's a plate for you in the oven. I bet you're famished."

The last thing she'd eaten had been that banana at breakfast. Murmuring her thanks, she walked across the room and removed the plate. Her sister had always been a good cook and Steffie gazed longingly at the broiled chicken breast, red new potatoes and fresh green beans.

"Where'd you go this morning?" Norah asked

cheerfully, continuing to put the dishes away. "Valerie said you seemed upset about Charles Tomaselli."

Steffie pulled out a stool at the counter and sat down to eat. "I needed to ask him something."

"Did you get everything settled?"

Steffie lowered her gaze. "Everything's clear now."

"Good. He really has been wonderful through all this. Dad's pleased with how well the article on migrant workers was received. You read it, didn't you? The two of them spent weeks collecting facts, and Dad actually did a bit of undercover work. It was the first time since Mom died that he showed much interest in anything. I don't think even Charles knows how much Dad put into that piece. He must've gone over every detail a dozen times."

Steffie, who was just about to begin her meal, promptly lost her appetite. "I—I didn't realize that."

"I was planning to mail you the article, but then Dad had the heart attack and everything else fell by the wayside," Norah explained conversationally, leaning against the counter.

"Where's Val?"

"In the den. She's working. You know Val. She's got a mobile office set up there. Although I have to admit her mind hasn't been on the job lately."

"Oh?" Steffie made an effort to taste her meal. The chicken was tender and delicious. She took a second bite.

Norah wiggled her eyebrows playfully. "In case you hadn't noticed, there's a romance brewing between Val and Dr. Winston."

"There is?" Steffie asked, fork poised in midair. "What about Valerie's boss? Every time I got a letter from her it was Rowdy this and Rowdy that."

"I don't know about Rowdy, but I do know what I saw the night of Dad's surgery."

"Which was?" Steffie asked anxiously.

"Valerie fell apart after we were allowed to go in and see Dad. She didn't realize I knew how upset she was, but I figured she needed a few minutes alone. I hadn't seen Dad myself, and when I did, I could understand Valerie's concern. He was very close to death. I don't know how much anyone's told you about Dad's condition, but it's a miracle he survived the open-heart surgery. Anyway," she said with a sigh, "when I went in to see Dad I wondered if he'd last the night. I know Colby didn't think he would. Neither did any of the others on the surgical team. Naturally, they didn't say that, but I could tell what they were thinking. I've worked in surgery often enough myself to know who's likely to survive and who isn't. One look told me we'd be lucky if Dad lasted another few hours, although I was encouraged because he'd survived the surgery itself. There were plenty of complications, with the fluid in his lungs and all."

"Tell me about Valerie," Steffie urged.

"Oh, yeah, Valerie. Well, after she'd been with Dad she went out onto the patio outside the surgical waiting room. She was crying, which we both know is rare for Val. I could tell she needed someone. When I got back from seeing Dad, I started to go out to her, thinking we'd be able to comfort each other, but I stopped when I saw that Colby was with her."

Steffie had heard wonderful things about Dr. Winston already, but his compassion for her sister confirmed everything she'd come to know of him. She said so to Norah, who nodded.

"They were sitting together and he was holding her in his arms. I don't know how to explain it, but he had this...look. As though he would've done anything within his power to take away her pain. I thought right then that he had the look of a man who's just discovered he's fallen in love."

"And Valerie?"

"I think she might have realized they were in love with each other before Colby did. You know how strong Valerie is, how she never wants to let anyone do anything for her. Well, for the first time since I can remember, she needed someone and Colby's the person she turned to."

"Valerie and Dr. Winston," Steffie said slowly. She'd often wondered what it would be like when her oldest sister fell in love. Valerie had always been so pragmatic, much too sensible to get involved in a relationship while she was in college. She was there to be educated, not to find a husband, she'd told Steffie.

"Then Dad began to improve," Norah went on, "and he started all this talk about the three of us marrying and having kids. I'm afraid Valerie's taking it much too seriously, worrying about it too much. But then, she's in love for the first time in her life and she's frightened half to death that Colby's the wrong man for her. Or more to the point, that *she's* the wrong woman for him."

"Love is love, and if they both feel so strongly, what's the problem?"

Norah's smile was sad and a bit hesitant. "Colby's as traditional as they come. I think he wants a woman straight out of the 1950s."

"Valerie knows this?"

"Of course she does. Colby's well aware of what Valerie's like, too. Her calling isn't the kitchen, it's the boardroom."

"I say more power to her." In Steffie's opinion, Colby Winston should appreciate her sister's God-given talents.

"Exactly!" Norah agreed. "But if Valerie marries Colby she'd probably have to quit her job. For one thing, CHIPS doesn't have an office in this part of the country. And she's worked too hard and too long to let go of her career."

"In other words, they'd both have to compromise— and they can't?"

"Exactly," Norah said again. She sighed. "No one ever told me love could be so complicated. I feel sorry for them both. They couldn't be more miserable."

Steffie finished off the last of the small red potatoes, not wanting her sister to guess how curious she was about her father's "chat" with her mother. "What do you think of all this talk about Dad's…experience?"

Norah pulled up a stool and sat across from her. "I don't know. *He* believes he talked with Mom and that's what's important, don't you think?"

Steffie wasn't sure of anything anymore. She'd once been confident that she knew what she wanted in life. Then everything had fallen apart. But the time she'd spent in Italy had helped her regain a perspective on her own life...hadn't it?

It suddenly occurred to Steffie with a sense of horror that she'd spent three years studying and traveling in Italy, and her primary purpose had been *to impress Charles Tomaselli* when she returned.

She'd impressed him, all right, by making an even bigger fool of herself than before.

"Dad's been talking about his grandchildren all afternoon," Norah continued, breaking into Steffie's thoughts. Steffie was grateful for the intrusion.

"Grandchildren," she repeated softly. "From you, naturally?" She couldn't imagine Valerie as a mother, and she herself had no intention of marrying. When her father was well enough to come home, Steffie intended to find herself an apartment in Portland and to apply for a fellowship and begin her doctorate. She'd completed her master's in Italy after an intensive language program, and in her last year there, she'd also taken several advanced courses. It was hard to believe someone so well educated could be so dismally unaware of her own motives, she mused unhappily.

"Dad claims I'm going to present him with six grandchildren," Norah said, barely restraining a smile. "Can you imagine me with *six* children?"

"Which means Valerie's going to be responsible for another six."

"No, three. According to Dad's ramblings, you're going to have three of the little darlings yourself."

Steffie grinned, in spite of her depression. The picture of her married and with a brood of children was somewhat amusing. She'd only loved one man in her life and the experience had been so painful that she was determined never to repeat the mistake.

"I guess we'll see," Steffie said, sliding off her stool to carry her now-empty plate to the sink.

"I guess we will," Norah concurred.

Although she'd slept for a good part of the afternoon, two hours later Steffie was yawning. Making her excuses, she returned to her bedroom, showered and got into bed, savoring the crisp, clean sheets.

Sitting up, her knees tucked under her chin, she pondered her conversation with Norah. In the years since she'd moved away, a number of her friends had married. She'd gotten wedding invitations, passed on by Norah, every few months. And several of her high school and college friends were already mothers, some two times over.

While she was in Italy, Steffie hadn't allowed herself to think about anything more pressing than her studies, which had occupied most of her time. She'd traveled and studied and worked hard. But at odd moments, when she received a wedding invitation or a birth announcement, she'd occasionally taken a moment to wonder if her life was missing something. Or when she was with Mario, the adorable young son of her landlady in Rome, she'd imagined, more than once, how it would feel to have a family of her own…. She'd usually managed to suppress the yearning quickly.

And now she was experiencing it again, and more sharply than ever before. All this talk of weddings and children troubled her. She felt excluded, somehow. In the end, Valerie would probably marry her Dr. Winston, and there'd be a wonderful man for Norah, she was sure of it.

But for her? She found she couldn't believe in the same kind of happy ending.

Three

Although she was exhausted, Steffie couldn't sleep. After tossing about restlessly and tangling her sheets, she sat on the edge of the bed and pushed the long hair away from her face.

She'd prefer to think the nap she'd taken that afternoon was responsible for this inability to sleep.

But she knew better.

She couldn't sleep because her thoughts wouldn't leave her alone. The memory of what a fool she'd made of herself with Charles hounded her until she wanted to scream.

With graphic clarity she recalled the first time she'd heard of Charles Tomaselli. She'd read his introductory column in the *Clarion* and had loved his wit. No matter what she thought of him now, she could never fault his talent as a writer. Charles had a way of turning a phrase that gave a reader pause. He chose his words carefully, writing in a clear, economical manner that managed to be both clever and precise. And he had a wide range of subjects, covering everything from social trends to the local political scene.

When she'd read his first few columns, she'd assumed he was much older, because the confidence of his observations and his style suggested a man of considerable experience. It wasn't until several weeks later that she'd actually met him. At the time she'd been so dumbstruck she could barely put two words together.

She'd tried to tell him how much she enjoyed his editor's column, but the words had twisted on the end of her tongue and came out sounding jerky and odd, like something a preschooler might say.

She'd been terribly embarrassed, but Charles had responded graciously, thanking her for the compliment.

It wasn't just the fact that he was in his late twenties—and not his fifties—that had taken Steffie by surprise. Nor was it the fact that he was strikingly handsome, although he was. What struck Steffie like a fist to the stomach was the instant and powerful attraction she felt for him.

Unlike Valerie, who'd gone out on only a handful of dates through high school and college, Steffie had had an active social calendar. She'd always been well liked by both sexes—popular enough to be voted Prom Queen her senior year of high school. But although she had lots of friends who happened to be boys, Steffie had never been in love. She'd thought, more than once, that she was, but she'd been wise enough to realize she was only infatuated, or in love with the idea of being in love.

Although she was twenty-one, going on twenty-two, she'd never been involved in a serious relationship. She hadn't considered herself ready for one—until she met the newly hired editor of the *Orchard Valley Clarion*.

When she met Charles, she knew immediately that she was going to love this man. How she could be so certain was unclear, even to her, but to the very depths of her young heart, she was absolutely convinced of it.

After that initial meeting, Steffie had driven home in a daze. She didn't tell anyone, including her sisters, what she felt. She didn't know how she could possibly explain her feelings without sounding silly. Love at first sight was something reserved for movies and romance novels.

She'd been filled with questions, wondering if Charles had felt it, too; she soon persuaded herself that he had.

He was older—twenty-seven, she discovered— amazingly mature and sophisticated, while she was an inexperienced third-year college student.

Steffie lived for the next edition of the *Clarion,* ripping open the newspaper until she found his column, and devoured each word Charles had written. Occasionally he wrote a feature article, and she read those just as avidly. She soon discovered that other people were equally taken with his work. He'd been in town for less than two months and had already become a source of pride and pleasure to the entire community.

Steffie straightened and reached over to turn on her bedside lamp. Obviously she wouldn't be able to sleep, and sitting in her room, dredging up memories of Charles, wasn't helping.

The house was dark and silent, which meant Valerie and Norah were both asleep. Not wanting to wake either of her sisters, Steffie slipped quietly down the dimly lit stairs.

She thought about making herself a cup of tea, then decided against it. Instead, she tiptoed into her father's den. She turned on a soft light and reached for *Sonnets from the Portuguese*—an especially lovely edition her father had given her mother years ago, before they were married. Steffie cuddled up in his reading chair, already comforted.

The leather felt cool against her skin. An afghan her mother had knitted when the girls were still young lay neatly folded on the ottoman. Valerie must have brought it in with her, since it hadn't been there the night before.

Steffie reached for the rose-colored afghan and tucked it around her, then turned to one of her favorite poems.

She made it through two pages before her mind drifted back to Charles. Back to that first year...

He hadn't noticed her. Hadn't shared the instant attraction. In fact, he hadn't even remembered her name. Steffie was stunned. She'd dreamed of him every night since the day they met. Wonderful dreams of laughing and loving, of strolling hand in hand through the apple orchard, sharing secrets and planning the rest of their lives. Her heart was so full of love that it was all she could do not to tell him outright.

Getting a man to notice her was a new challenge for Steffie. Until then, it had always been the other way around. The men—no, *boys*—had been the ones to seek her out. For the first time in her life, Steffie found herself at a disadvantage in a relationship. Clearly the only option open to her was to let Charles know as subtly as possible that she was interested. It shouldn't be such a difficult task for a former Prom Queen.

Except that it was...

The first thing Steffie did was to write him a letter commending his writing ability and his opinions. She'd agonized over every word, then waited nearly two weeks for a reply.

There hadn't been one.

Charles hadn't printed her letter and didn't respond, either. Steffie had been crushed. Never one to quit, though, she'd visited the newspaper office with suggestions for a wide variety of stories. As she recalled, she'd managed to come up with 150 such ideas. Admittedly some were better than others.

Charles had been polite, but had made it plain that although he appreciated her suggestions, he already had an enthusiastic staff whose job it was to come up with regional stories.

Her plan had been for Charles to be so awed by her concern about local issues and her invaluable ideas that he'd invite her to dinner to discuss her interest. Although, in retrospect, it sounded terribly naive, she'd actually believed this would happen.

Apparently, she spent more time than she realized hanging around the newspaper office over the next

few months because Charles unexpectedly asked her
out for coffee one morning.

Steffie had been so excited that she could barely
sit still. She was further encouraged when Charles
chose a booth in the farthest, most private corner of
the local coffee shop.

Even now, more than three years afterward, Steffie
could recall how thrilled she'd been. She'd slid into
the red vinyl seat across from him, sure he could read
all the love and adoration in her eyes.

The encounter, however, proved to be a bitter disappointment for Steffie. Charles had been kind, but
firm. He couldn't help noticing, he'd said, how much
time she spent at the newspaper office, and was sure
her studies must have been suffering. He'd also gotten her letter and the other notes she'd sent him, and
although he was flattered by her attention, he was
much too busy with the paper to become involved in
a relationship.

When Steffie had pressed him for more of an explanation, he'd told her without a second's pause that
he considered her too young for him. Furthermore, he
felt she was…too innocent.

Steffie was aghast at his lack of foresight. She was
a mature woman, and six years' difference in their
ages was unimportant. If she didn't object, then he
shouldn't, either.

As an active member of her high school debating
team, Steffie had learned how to argue, and now she'd
used every skill at her disposal.

It didn't work.

He'd finally told her she was a nice *kid* but he simply wasn't interested. That he was a busy man and didn't have the time or patience to be a babysitter. A babysitter! He wasn't exactly impolite, but it was clear he had no intention of asking her out. Ever.

Their coffee had just been served, and Charles hadn't taken more than a sip before he tossed some money on the table and left.

Steffie had remained there, too hurt to breathe, too numb to feel anything more than a painful disappointment. She couldn't remember how long she'd sat in the booth. Long after her coffee had cooled, she knew.

Obviously she'd sat there much *too* long because she'd decided that Charles Tomaselli was clearly lying.

"Steff."

The gentle voice was followed by a warm hand on her shoulder.

"What are you doing sleeping down here?"

Steffie raised her head and blinked. Valerie, dressed in a housecoat, stood beside her.

"What time is it?"

"Morning," Valerie said with a smile. "How long have you been here?"

Moving her legs, Steffie winced at the unexpected discomfort. Her legs were stiff and sore and the book still lay open on her lap.

"I was going to fix myself coffee and toast before heading to the hospital. Do you want some?"

"Please." She worked one shoulder and then the other and rotated her neck, hoping to ease the crick.

Her thoughts had been so full of what had happened between her and Charles in those early days that she couldn't remember falling asleep. It surprised her that she had. She wondered if her musings had followed her into her dreams, then felt it would be better if they hadn't.

"I can't tell you how good Dad looks compared to a week ago," Valerie said when Steffie joined her in the kitchen.

"I'm sorry I wasn't there." She paused, shaking her head. "It was so crazy being stuck in Italy like that."

"You know—" Valerie paused, clutching a large earthenware mug "—in a way I'm grateful you couldn't get home for a while. It might be the one thing that kept Dad alive. He was determined to see you before he died."

Steffie wasn't sure she understood. "Do you mean to say Dad had a means of controlling the timing of his…demise?"

"Sort of. Death was what he wanted. If I've learned anything through all this, it's that the human will is incredibly powerful."

Steffie began making toast, taking the butter and Norah's homemade strawberry jam out of the refrigerator. "I'm not totally clear on what you mean about the human will."

"I don't know if I can explain it," Valerie said after a moment, her look distant and thoughtful. "All I know is that Dad was on the brink of death for days. When I first arrived, Colby told us Dad would require open-heart surgery. He wanted to perform the operation immediately but couldn't because of various complications Dad was experiencing. If you want the medical terms for all this you can ask Norah or Colby, but basically it boiled down to one thing. Dad had lost the will to fight for his life. He's been miserable without Mom. We both know that, but I don't think anyone fully appreciated exactly how *lonely* he's been."

"I shouldn't have left him." Despite Valerie's reassurances, Steffie partially blamed herself for her father's failing health. She'd known when he came to visit her in Italy last year that something was wrong. He'd taken the trip to Europe not out of any desire to travel but because Valerie and Norah had thought it would help revive his spirits. The fact that Steffie was living in Italy had been a convenient excuse.

Steffie had enjoyed the time with her father, and had been excited about showing him the country she'd come to love and introducing him to her new friends. She'd carefully avoided any conversation having to do with Orchard Valley or her mother. Her father had urged her to come home, but she'd already registered for new courses and paid her rent in advance and planned another trip. All excuses. Because it really came down to one thing: she'd been afraid to go home.

Steffie Bloomfield afraid! The family daredevil. Dauntless, reckless Steffie Bloomfield was afraid of a mere man. More precisely, she was terrified of having to speak to Charles again, of looking him in the eye and pretending it didn't hurt anymore. Pretending she didn't love him. Pretending she didn't feel humiliated.

She was incapable of shrugging off the past, especially when it was much simpler just to stay in Europe. She loved her art history courses, she enjoyed traveling throughout Italy, she was fond of her landlady's family, she had lots of friends and acquaintances. She'd discovered, too, that she had a real aptitude for languages; besides being proficient in Italian, she'd picked up some French and German and hoped to continue learning them. No, she'd decided, there were too many good reasons to remain in Europe. And so she'd stayed.

"Do you want to ride to the hospital with me?" Valerie asked, apparently deep in her own thoughts.

"Sure."

"I might need to do a few errands later, but you might be able to get a ride home with Norah if I'm not back."

"I'm not worried. I haven't been able to spend much time with Dad yet." Steffie felt guilty about rushing out of the hospital the day before without returning to see him.

As it turned out, Steffie couldn't have chosen a better morning to be with her father. It was the day he was being transferred out of the Surgical Intensive Care Unit and onto the surgical ward. His time in the SICU was only four days, his recovery nothing short of remarkable. Even Dr. Winston seemed to think so.

"I can't get over how beautiful you've become," her father said when he woke from a brief nap. Steffie was sitting at his bedside, doing the *New York Times* crossword puzzle and feeling downright pleased with herself that she'd managed to fill in a good half of the answers.

"I'll tell you what I've become," Steffie said with a laugh, "and that's Italian. The first day after I left Rome I slipped from English to Italian and then back again without noticing. I think I spent twice as long clearing customs as anyone else, simply because the agent didn't know what to make of me."

"So can you cook me some real Italian spaghetti?" her father asked.

"I certainly can, and I promise it'll be so good you'll dream about it the rest of your life."

"With plenty of garlic?"

Steffie raised the tips of her fingers to her lips and made a loud smacking sound. "With enough garlic to ward off vampires for the next hundred years. Besides, I hear garlic's good for your heart."

"But lousy for your love life."

"I don't think either of us needs to worry about that," she teased.

"Ah." David Bloomfield shook his head. "That's where you're wrong, Princess. You, my darling Stephanie, are about to discover what it means to be in love."

Steffie didn't want to say she already knew all she cared to on that subject. *Thanks, Dad—but no thanks,* she told him silently. Falling in love wasn't an experience she wanted to repeat.

"You aren't going to argue with me like Valerie did, are you?"

"Would there be any point?"

"No," he said, smiling broadly.

"I didn't think so."

"You don't believe I really talked to your mother, do you?"

"Uh…" It wasn't that she disbelieved him exactly. *He* was convinced that something had happened, so her opinion was irrelevant. He claimed to have enjoyed a lengthy conversation with her mother while strolling around some celestial lake. Valerie had mentioned it soon after Steffie's arrival. Norah had talked about it, too. Steffie found their accounts fascinating. Did she believe it had happened? She didn't know. She was inclined to think he'd experienced some kind of revelation—but whether it was spiritual, as he thought, or a dream, or a fantasy of his own making, she had no idea. And it didn't matter.

"You won't be the only one who doesn't believe my talk with your mother was real."

"It isn't that, Dad."

"Don't you worry about it. Time will prove me right."

"Prove you right about what?" a distinctive male voice asked from behind her. Steffie froze and the dread washed over her.

Charles Tomaselli.

He was the last person she'd expected to meet here. The last person she wanted to see again.

"How're you feeling, David?" he asked.

"I've been better."

"I'll bet you have," Charles said wryly.

Steffie was on her feet immediately. "I'll leave you

two to chat," she said with a cheery lilt, anxious to leave the room.

"There's no reason for you to go," her father countered, holding out his hand to her. "Your smile is the brightest sunshine I've seen in days. Isn't that so, Charles?"

Steffie cringed inwardly, and not giving Charles time to comment, quickly squeezed her father's hand. "I don't think it's a good idea for you to have too much company all at once."

"That's probably true," Charles agreed. "Besides, I've got some business to discuss with you. I thought you'd be interested in hearing what happened as a result of that article we did on the migrant-worker situation."

Steffie's breath caught in her throat until she realized Charles wasn't referring to the stunt she'd pulled in his office the day before. She went weak with relief when she heard him mention something about Commissioner O'Dell initiating an inspection program.

Steffie still hadn't looked at Charles, still hadn't turned to face him. She delayed it as long as possible, leaning forward to kiss her father's cheek. "I'll get a ride back to the house with Valerie or Norah, but I'll be in again this evening and we can finish our...discussion."

"I'll see you then, Princess."

Steffie nodded and mentally braced herself as she turned away from her father's bed. She looked shyly at Charles. To her astonishment, their eyes met instantly. They seemed drawn to gaze at each other, as though neither could resist the pull of mutual attraction. Her own heart gave a small burst of joy and she wondered if, deep within, his did, too.

"Hello, Steffie."

"Charles." Her voice was low and wispy. "I'll see you later, Dad."

"Bye, Princess."

Her eyes skidded past Charles as she hurried from the room, eager now to make her escape. By the time she reached the end of the corridor, she heard a roaring in her ears and she was breathless—all because of a casual encounter with Charles. Obviously she'd need to prepare herself mentally for even such minor confrontations.

She hadn't been nearly as shy with him that summer evening three years earlier, she remembered with chagrin. It mortified her now to think of her brazen behavior....

If Charles considered her a *kid* when he'd invited her for coffee, then Steffie decided she owed it to herself to show him he was wrong. Without difficulty, she'd been able to discover where Charles lived. Crime had never been much of a problem in Orchard Valley, and Charles had been kind enough to leave his front door unlocked.

When he appeared several hours later, there were scented candles lit throughout the living room and a bottle of champagne chilling in the kitchen.

"Is that you, darling?" Steffie had called out from the bathroom. She'd been sitting in a bubble-filled tub for the better part of an hour, and her skin had started to shrivel. She was also worried about the candles dripping and the champagne getting warm, but she dared not leave, fearing she'd never be able to get the bubbles just right again. It was important that he think she was completely nude, though in reality she wore a skimpy bikini.

Charles didn't answer. He stalked into the room, stopping abruptly in the doorway as his shocked gaze fell on her.

"What the hell are you doing here?" he demanded.

"I thought you should know I'm not a child."

"Then what are you—a mermaid?"

She forced a soft laugh and said in what she hoped was a sultry, adult voice, "No, silly man, I'm a *woman* and if you'll come here, I'll prove it to you."

"Get out."

"Out? But…but I was hoping you'd join me."

"No way, sweetheart. Now either you remove yourself from my home or I'm calling the police."

She pushed her big toe under the water tap. "I think my toe might be stuck."

"Fine, I'll call the plumber."

"But, Charles, darling…"

"Charles, nothing," he snapped. Marching into the bathroom and gripping her by the upper arm, he lifted her halfway out of the tub. She screeched, stumbling to find her balance. As soon as she was upright, Charles tossed a towel at her and told her she had five minutes to leave before he called the police.

Steffie had fled, but she'd seen the gleam of male admiration in Charles's eyes, seen the way he'd looked at her for a second or two. And, fool that she was, she hadn't been the least bit discouraged. Instead, she'd devised yet another plan.

Steffie wandered into the waiting area searching for Valerie. One of the orderlies mentioned that her sister had gone to pick up office supplies. Steffie remembered hearing something about an errand, but she hadn't been paying enough attention to recall whether Valerie was returning to the hospital or going straight home.

Oh, well, there was always Norah.

Tracking down her youngest sister didn't take long. Within five minutes, Steffie found her in the emergency room—preparing to go on duty. The hospital was understaffed, and now that their father was beginning to recover, Norah had returned to work. Steffie didn't bother to ask for a ride.

Hoping Charles would be gone, she went back to the surgical ward. Her luck hadn't improved, and they met at the elevator.

"I thought you were headed home?"

"I'll have to wait for Valerie," she said, trying to edge past him. "Or get a cab."

His arm blocked her escape. "There's no need to do that. I'll drop you off at the house."

"No, thanks," she returned stiffly.

"I want to talk to you, anyway," he said, none too gently guiding her into the elevator. "And as they say, there's no time like the present."

"This really isn't necessary, Charles."

"Oh, but it is."

She noticed, when he led her out of the hospital to the parking lot, that he was driving the same red sports car she'd seen the day before. It eased her conscience a bit that it hadn't been damaged during his race across the countryside.

He opened the door for her, and Steffie climbed inside. She was adjusting the seat belt when Charles joined her. The space seemed to shrink like silk pressed against a hot iron. Their shoulders touched, their thighs, their arms. For a moment, Steffie held her breath.

"You said you wanted to talk to me?" she said after he'd pulled out of the hospital parking lot. She was leaning as close to the passenger door as she could.

"I thought we'd discuss it over a glass of iced tea. You *are* inviting me inside, aren't you?" He turned and grinned at her, that boyish, slightly skewed grin she'd always found so appealing.

She'd planned to tell him she had no intention of letting him in; instead she cleared her throat and said, "If you'd like."

"I would."

The ten-mile drive to the house generally took fifteen minutes. Steffie could have sworn Charles was purposely dragging out the time, driving well below the speed limit. They were so close in the small cramped car that she couldn't avoid brushing against him, even though she tried not to. She was trying to forget that he'd kissed her the day before, and this didn't make it any easier.

Steffie closed her eyes. It was all she could do not to shout at him to hurry. Why was he prolonging these moments alone? The least he could do was make polite conversation.

"My father seems cheerful, doesn't he?" If Charles wasn't going to say something, then she would. Anything to ease this terrible awareness.

"He certainly does."

"He's got a reason to live now, and that's made all the difference in the world. I'm not sure what to think about his dream, but—"

"What dream?"

"Uh...nothing... It's not important." Steffie couldn't believe what she'd done. In her nervousness, in her desperation to fill the silence, she'd blurted out what should never have been shared.

She relaxed when Charles finally turned off the road onto the mile-long family driveway. He parked in front of the house.

Steffie didn't wait for him, but threw open her door and jumped out, her keys already in hand. She had the front door open by the time he caught up with her and, tossing her purse onto the hall table, led him briskly into the kitchen.

Norah had made some iced tea that morning. Steffie silently thanked her sister for her thoughtfulness as she took out the cold pitcher. A minute later, she'd found two tall glasses, added ice and sliced a fresh lemon. Another minute, and the drinks were ready.

"What was it you wanted to say?" Steffie reluctantly asked. She hadn't realized how warm she was and held the glass between both hands, enjoying the coolness against her palms.

"It's about what happened yesterday," Charles said, walking away from her. He paused at the bay window that overlooked the backyard. Just beyond his view was the stable. "Or more appropriately, what *shouldn't* have happened."

Four

"I'd rather not discuss it," Steffie said adamantly. She didn't want to hear any more about her irresponsible accusations and rash actions. Nor did she wish to hear how much Charles regretted kissing her.

"If anyone needs to apologize, it's me," she said quickly. "Why don't we just leave it at that? I was wrong."

Charles's back was to her as he stared outside toward the stables. "I don't think anyone's ever infuriated me this much," he said quietly. He turned, set his glass of iced tea aside and thrust his hands into his pockets. "I've never met a woman who manages to irritate me the way you do."

Steffie stiffened. "I've already apologized for leaping to conclusions. I admitted I was wrong." She shrugged elaborately. "My only excuse is that I spent a hellish week trying to get home and I haven't slept properly in days and I—"

"This isn't necessary," he said, interrupting her.

"I'm not looking for an apology.... Actually I'm here to make my own. I want you to know I'm sorry about chasing after you. It was a dangerous thing to do. I might have spooked Fury into throwing you."

"Not to mention damaging your car."

"True enough."

"Let's put it behind us," Steffie suggested with a weak smile. "I was wrong to run away. It was…childish."

"You were angry, too."

"I've never met a *man* who manages to irritate me the way you do," she said, consciously echoing his words.

"We always seem to get on each other's nerves, don't we?" His grin was warm and gentle, just as his kiss had been. Strangely, Steffie found his smile no less devastating.

"We certainly have a history of annoying each other." It took her more courage than he'd ever know to refer to the past. But suddenly she hoped they could put that behind them, too.

"I'd never be able to forgive myself if anything had happened to you," he said.

"I wasn't really in any danger of Fury throwing me." Okay, so that was a slight exaggeration, but she *had* stayed in the saddle.

"It was, shall we say, a memorable way for us to meet again." Charles's voice was husky. He moved closer to her and she lowered her eyes, but not before she noticed how his attention seemed to center on her mouth. "There's one thing I'm not sorry about."

He took another step toward her and raised his hand to touch her cheek. His fingers brushed aside a stray lock of hair. Steffie couldn't move. She couldn't think coherently. She could barely breathe.

"I don't regret kissing you," Charles whispered.

Then she did move. Trembling, she stepped backward and bolted to the other side of the room.

"Stephanie?"

"Call—call me Steffie," she stuttered. Her hands were shaking so badly that she jerked them behind her.

"I prefer to call you Stephanie. You're not a little girl anymore."

She smiled brightly. Now was the perfect time to convince him how sophisticated she'd become after three years in Europe—sophisticated and *experienced.* She was sure that was the type of woman he expected, the type of woman he wanted.

"As kisses go, it was very nice," she agreed in an offhand manner. Was she overdoing it? she wondered. "Yours had a gentleness, and that was unusual. Most men aren't like that, you know? When they kiss a woman it's hot and sweaty. They leave a girl breathless."

"I see," Charles said, raising one eyebrow.

She placed her hands on her hips, fashion-model style, and tilted back her head, letting her long brown hair swing lightly. "I'm not the same person I was three years ago. You're right about that. I'm all grownup now."

"So it seems."

"I appreciate the ride home," she said, walking out

of the kitchen. She hoped Charles would follow her because she wasn't sure how much longer she could maintain this performance.

"Is there anything else these…hot, sweaty men taught you?" he asked in a dispassionate voice. He reached for his iced tea, apparently disinclined to leave quite so soon.

She turned around and smiled serenely. "You'd be surprised." Deciding to give him the answer he deserved, she rashly went on. "As you might imagine, I met men of all nationalities—students from all over Europe—and I sampled my fair share of kisses." Mostly chaste kisses of greeting or farewell, but he didn't have to know that. And then there were Mario's exuberant hugs…. Mario was only four years old, but Charles didn't have to know that, either.

Charles scowled, and set his glass down on the counter hard enough to slosh liquid over the edges. He stalked past her. "Goodbye, *Steffie,*" he said coldly, throwing the words over his shoulder.

It wasn't until he'd slammed the front door that she understood his words had been meant as an insult. He was telling her he'd changed his mind, reconsidered. He'd seen through her little dramatization and decided he'd been wrong: she wasn't an adult. She remained a silly, immature girl.

Steffie wandered between two rows of budding apple trees, contemplating her latest disaster with Charles. The setting sun cast a rosy splendor over the orchard. All her life, Steffie had come out here when she needed to think. This was where she found peace, and a tranquillity that eased her burdens. Since her last meeting with Charles, there'd been plenty of those. And regrets. She hadn't seen him in several days and that helped. But it also hurt. There were so many unanswered questions between them, so many unspoken words.

Hearing footsteps behind her, Steffie turned to see Norah walking toward her.

"You've got to do something!" Norah moaned.

"About what?" she asked when Norah moved three agitated paces ahead of her.

"You've got to help Valerie. You can give her advice. You've had more experience with men."

Steffie suppressed the urge to laugh at the irony of this statement, considering her ludicrous performance in front of Charles. She reached up to run her fingers along the smooth bark of a branch. "What's wrong with her?"

"She's making the biggest mistake of her life," Norah said dramatically. It wasn't often that her sister sounded so distraught. Unfortunately Steffie was hardly the ideal person to advise Valerie on romance.

"I told you before that Valerie and Dr. Winston are in love," Norah continued. "Everyone around them can see it. And whenever Valerie and Colby are together, they can't keep their eyes off each other."

"So what's the problem?"

"They aren't seeing each other anymore."

"What do you mean?"

"They're avoiding each other. I don't think they've talked in days."

Norah's words struck a chord in Steffie. She knew exactly what Valerie was doing, because she was guilty of the same thing herself. She hadn't seen Charles since the day he'd driven her home from the hospital. They were obviously taking pains to avoid each other—just like Valerie and Dr. Winston.

"I don't see what I can do," Steffie muttered.

"Talk to Val," Norah argued. "She might listen to you."

"What am I supposed to say?"

Norah hesitated, frowning. "I don't know, but you'll think of something. I've given it my best shot and I just wasn't getting through to her. Maybe you can."

"I'm glad you have so much faith in my abilities," Steffie said lightly.

"I do have faith in you," Norah said, her blue eyes serious. "You're different now than before you left."

"Three years in Italy will do that to a girl." As she had with Charles, Steffie strived to seem flippant and worldly.

"I don't mean that. You're more thoughtful. More— I don't know—mature, I guess. Before you left Orchard Valley you acted like you had to prove yourself to the world, but it isn't like that now. I can't see you doing some of the crazy things you used to do."

Just as well that Norah didn't know about some of her "mature" behavior these past few days. And thank heaven no one in the family had any idea of the embarrassing stunts she'd pulled trying to attract Charles's attention three years ago.

"I remember the time you stood on Princess bareback and rode around the yard. You were lucky you didn't break your neck."

Steffie remembered the incident well. It had been shortly before their mother died. She'd been grieving so terribly, and doing something utterly dangerous had helped vent some of her pain and grief. But Norah was completely right. She shouldn't have done it.

"Okay, I'll talk to Valerie," Steffie promised, "but I don't know how much good it'll do."

Steffie tried. But the conversation with her sister hadn't gone as planned. One look at Valerie told her how much her sister was suffering. Valerie tried to hide it, but Steffie knew the signs from her own limited experience with love.

They'd become involved in a lengthy discussion about love, then decided neither one of them was qualified to advise the other. They'd thought of bringing Norah in on the conversation but that suggestion had resulted in a bout of unexpected giggles. They couldn't ask Norah about falling in love because she was too busy dating.

One interesting detail that emerged from their talk was something Valerie mentioned almost casually. While Steffie was struggling to find a way home, Charles had seemed very concerned about her. He'd even pulled a few strings in an effort to help when she didn't arrive on schedule.

Although they'd never openly discussed her relationship with Charles, Valerie seemed to know how Steffie felt. It wasn't that Steffie had tried to conceal it; with one breath, she admitted she'd made a fool of herself over the newspaper article and with the next, she'd asked her sister about falling in love. Valerie was certainly astute enough to figure out Steffie's feelings for Charles.

David Bloomfield was now recuperating at home and doing well. Steffie still hadn't seen Charles. She'd thought maybe he'd be stopping by the house to visit her father, whose release from the hospital had been a festive event.

Steffie was pleased to see that Valerie and Colby were able to steal a few moments alone that afternoon, but she didn't think their time together had gone well. They'd gone for a walk in the orchard; Valerie had looked pale and sad when they returned, and Colby had remained silent throughout the celebration dinner that followed.

Knowing it was inevitable that she'd see Charles again, Steffie tried to mentally brace herself for their next meeting.

She couldn't have guessed it would be at the local gas station.

"Why, Steffie Bloomfield," Del of Del's Gas-and-Go greeted her when she went inside to pay for her fill-up and buy a bottle of soda. "I swear you're a sight for sore eyes."

She laughed. Del was potbellied and at least sixty,

but he had to be the biggest flirt in town. "It's good to see you again, too. What do I owe you for the gas?"

"If I were a rich man, I'd say the gas was free. Looking at your pretty face is payment enough. Right, Charles?"

It always happened when she was least prepared, when seeing him was the last thing she expected.

"Yeah, right," Charles answered from behind her with a decided lack of enthusiasm.

"Hello, Charles," she said, turning around to greet him, trying to sound casual and slightly aloof. She pasted a smile on her face, determined not to let him fluster her as he had every single time they'd encountered each other.

"Stephanie."

"I don't know if you heard, but Dad's home now."

"I got word of that the other day." Charles took his wallet out of his hip pocket and paid for his gas.

Steffie twisted the top off her soda and took a deep swallow. It tasted cool and sweet, bringing welcome relief to her suddenly parched throat. "I was thinking you might stop by and visit." *Hoping* more aptly described her thoughts, but she couldn't admit that.

He didn't answer as he followed her outside. The service-station attendant was washing her windshield and Steffie lingered, wanting to say something, anything, to make a fresh start with Charles.

"As I recall, you wrote one of your first columns about Del's, didn't you?"

"You've got a good memory," Charles said, his words a bit less stiff.

The boy had finished with her windows and there was no further excuse to dawdle. Reluctantly she opened her car door. "It was good seeing you. Oh, by the way, Valerie told me you made several efforts to find me when I was trying to get home from Italy. I appreciate all the help you gave my family."

He shrugged. She set one foot inside the car, then paused and glanced back at Charles. She *had* to speak up—now. "Charles." He turned around again, a surprised expression on his face. "There's something you should know."

"What is it?"

"I'm very grateful for your friendship to my family—and to me." With that she ducked inside her car, heart racing, and drove off without looking back.

Unfortunately dinner that evening was a strained affair. Norah had come to Steffie an hour before with the news that Colby had dated another nurse, a friend of Norah's, three nights running. Norah didn't know whether to tell Valerie, and had asked Steffie's advice.

Steffie thought it best not to say anything to their sister until Norah had slept on the matter.

But Steffie suspected that Valerie was already aware of it, suspected that Valerie knew it in her heart. Although her sister hadn't said anything to the family, Steffie believed she'd quietly made arrangements to return to Texas and her job as vice president of CHIPS, a software company based in Houston.

Everyone could feel something was wrong, but no one said a word during dinner. Everyone was terribly polite—as though the others were strangers—which only heightened the tension.

Their father had made his excuses, claiming to be especially tired, and with Norah's help retired to his room almost immediately after dinner.

Apparently Valerie wasn't in the mood for company either, because she excused herself and retreated to her bedroom, leaving Steffie and Norah to their own devices.

After they'd finished clearing up after dinner, Norah left to attend a wedding shower for a friend.

Feeling at loose ends, Steffie inspected the kitchen. On impulse, she decided to make the spaghetti sauce she'd promised her father. She dragged out the largest pot she could find and began to assemble ingredients. Fresh tomatoes, onions, tomato paste, garlic. No fresh herbs, so dried would have to do. Oh, good, a bottle of nice California red...

Humming to herself, she put on a CD of Verdi's *Aida* and turned up the volume until the music echoed against the kitchen walls. The emotional intensity and dramatic characterizations of the Italian composer suited her mood.

She found an old white apron her father had used years before whenever he barbecued. Wrapping it around her waist, she drew the long strings around to the front and tied them.

Half an hour later, she was stirring the last of the tomato paste into the pot. She added a generous amount of red wine, all the while singing at the top of her lungs. The sound of someone pounding at the back door jolted her back to reality.

Running barefoot across the kitchen, she pulled open the door and saw Charles standing there, holding a pot of purple azaleas.

"Charles! What are you doing here?"

"No one answered the front door," he remarked dryly.

"Oh. Sorry." She walked to the counter to turn off her CD player. "Come in." The silence was nearly deafening.

"I thought you said your father was home from the hospital?" As though self-conscious about holding a flowerpot, he handed it to Steffie.

"He is," she said, setting the plant aside. "How thoughtful. I'm sure Dad will love this."

"It isn't for David."

"It isn't?"

"No, I was...we just got a full-page ad from How Green Is My Thumb Nursery and I felt it might be a gesture of good faith to buy something. I thought you'd appreciate an azalea more than your father would."

Steffie wasn't quite sure what to say other than a soft "Thank you."

He shrugged, apparently eager to leave. He stepped toward the door and she desperately tried to think of something to keep him there, with her.

"Have you eaten?" she asked quickly, even though the sauce was only just starting to simmer and wouldn't be properly ready until the following day.

"What makes you ask?"

"I was just putting together a pot of spaghetti sauce for tomorrow. Dad asked me to cook him an Italian meal and...well, if you wouldn't mind waiting a bit, I'll be happy to fix you a plate. It really needs to simmer longer, but I know from experience that it's perfectly edible after an hour." She sounded breathless by the time she'd finished.

"I've already had dinner, but thanks, anyway," Charles told her. "I could do with a cup of coffee, though." He nodded toward the half-full pot sitting beside the stove.

"Sure...great. Me, too. I'd get Dad but he's sleeping," she explained as she poured him a cup, then one for herself.

"Through that?" Charles motioned toward the CD player.

"Sure. He loves listening to the same music I do. Besides, he's way over on the other side of the house. I doubt he could even hear it." She didn't mention that a tragic love story might suit Valerie's mood, however. And since her sister's bedroom was directly above the kitchen she was the one most likely to have been serenaded.

Charles held the mug in both hands and walked over to examine her efforts. "So you learned to cook while you were away?"

"A little," she admitted.

"I wouldn't have guessed you were the domestic type." He stirred the sauce with a wooden spoon, lifted it out of the pot and tasted it, using one finger. His brows rose. "This is good."

"Don't sound so surprised."

"There must've been some Italian man you were hoping to impress."

The only man she'd ever wanted to impress was the one standing in the kitchen at that very moment.

"I was too busy with my studies to date much," she said, dumping the empty tomato-paste cans in the recycling bin.

"That isn't the impression you gave me the other day."

She hesitated, her back to him. "I know. I certainly seem to make a habit of playing the fool when I'm with you."

Charles's voice was rueful. "I've occasionally suffered from the same problem."

The unexpectedness of his admission caught her off balance, and she twisted around to face him. For a long, unguarded moment she soaked in the sight of him.

"There wasn't anyone I dated very often," she told him in a raw whisper.

"Surely there was someone?"

She shook her head. They gazed silently into each other's eyes, and Steffie seemed to lose all sense of time.

Charles was the one who broke the trance. "Uh, your pot seems to be boiling."

"Oh, darn, I forgot to turn down the burner." She raced across the kitchen, flipped the knob on the stove and stirred the sauce briskly, praying it hadn't burned.

While she stood at the stove, Steffie basked in a

glow of unfamiliar contentment. It felt so wonderful to be with Charles—not fighting or defensive, not acting like a love-struck adolescent. For the first time, she was truly comfortable with him.

"I'm sure the sauce will be fine," she murmured, picking up her coffee mug.

He pulled out a chair and sat.

As she was getting cream, sugar and teaspoons, she thought she heard some noise from upstairs. Glancing at the ceiling, she frowned.

"What's wrong?"

Steffie joined him at the table, adding only cream to her own coffee and pushing the sugar bowl toward Charles. "I'm worried about Valerie," she said frankly. "So is Norah. Everyone is, except Dad, which is for the best—I mean, he's got enough on his mind healing from the surgery. He shouldn't be worrying about any of us."

Charles added a level teaspoon of sugar to his coffee, then paused, the spoon held above his cup. "How'd you know I take sugar?"

Her gaze skirted away from his. "We had coffee together once before, remember?"

"No" came his automatic response.

Steffie preferred not to dredge up the unhappy memory again, especially since *he* didn't even seem to recall it. She stared down at the table. "It was the first time you asked me to—you know, leave you alone."

He scowled. "The first time," he repeated, then shook his head in apparent confusion. Just as well, Steffie thought to herself, astounded that he had absolutely no recollection of an incident she remembered in such complete and painful detail.

She decided to change the subject. "Norah baked cookies the other day, if you'd like some."

Charles declined. "Tell me what's going on with your sister." His eyes darted to the ceiling.

Steffie wondered how much of Valerie's dilemma she should confide in him, but then remembered Norah's telling her that Charles had been with them the night of her father's surgery. More than likely he knew how Colby and Valerie felt about each other.

"She's in love," she said after a moment.

"It's Doc Winston, isn't it?"

Steffie nodded. "They both seem to have fallen hard."

"So what's wrong?"

Steffie wasn't sure she could explain, when she didn't entirely understand it herself. So she shrugged and said, "I think Colby wants her to be something she can't. Valerie's an incredibly gifted businesswoman. But I gather he wants a woman who'd be happy to stay home and be a housewife—there's nothing wrong with that, of course, but it just isn't right for Valerie. It doesn't look like either one of them is going to compromise."

"If she loves him, maybe she should be willing to compromise first," Charles said, then sipped his coffee. "Take the first step."

"What about Colby? Why does it always have to be the woman who compromises? Don't answer that, I already know. Women have been forced to adapt to men's fickle natures for so many generations that it comes to us naturally," she said with heavy sarcasm. "Right?"

Charles was silent. "I didn't come here to argue about your sister," he finally said.

"I know, it's just that I found your statement so—" She stopped in midsentence because she didn't want to fight with him, either. They'd done so much of that. And she didn't want this encounter to end the way all the others had.

"I'm sorry," she said. "I'm concerned about her, and I can't help feeling a bit defensive. I'm pretty sure she's making arrangements to return to Texas—and I wish she wouldn't."

"You haven't had much time with her, have you?"

Steffie tapped the mug with her spoon, staring into the dregs of her coffee. "That's not the whole reason I wish she'd stay." She was silent for a moment. "Leaving your problems behind simply doesn't work. Not unless you've exhausted every possibility of reaching a compromise. In fact, I think leaving can make everything much worse. The problem is, I can't tell Valerie that. It's one of those painful realities we each need to discover on our own, I guess. I'm going to talk to her, but I doubt it'll make any difference."

Charles's dark eyes were sympathetic. "I hope she listens."

Steffie thanked him with a smile. "I hope she does, too, but the three of us seem to share a wide streak of stubbornness."

Charles rubbed his eyes, and she realized he must

be exhausted. "You won't get an argument out of me," he said with a tired grin.

"Are you still working as many hours?"

He nodded. "Fifty to sixty a week. We publish twice weekly now and eventually we're looking to go daily. Some days I feel like I'm married to that paper."

The word "married" seemed to hang in the air. At one time Steffie had been convinced beyond any doubt that *they'd* be married, she and Charles. It was this unshakable resolve that had created so many difficulties in her relationship with him. Naively, she'd assumed that all she had to do was *show* him they were meant to love each other and after a few short object lessons, he'd agree. Now she knew that life—and love—didn't work that way.

"Are you still a jack-of-all-trades at the paper?" she asked, remembering that his job meant he had a hand in every aspect of publishing the newspaper—from writing, editing and layout to distribution.

"Everything except the classifieds."

"Do you still have an intern?"

Charles relaxed against the back of his chair and nodded. "Wendy. She's a recent graduate from the University of Portland."

He smiled as he spoke, and a red light went on in front of Steffie's eyes. "What happened to Larry? I thought you were working with him?" The idea of Charles spending long hours with an attractive college student filled her with a sense of dread.

"No, he moved on to an internet news service. So, Wendy's with me now."

Wendy's with me now? Then it came to her. She didn't need to worry about competing for Charles anymore.

She was out of the running.

Five

"Is someone here?" Steffie heard her father even before he entered the kitchen. He was wearing his plaid housecoat, cinched at the waist, which emphasized the weight he'd recently lost. His white hair was rumpled from sleep.

"David, hello," Charles said, standing to shake hands with him. Her father slowly made his way to the table, declining Charles's gesture of assistance.

"I thought you were still asleep," Steffie said with a loving smile. She'd missed the worst of the crisis, but her sisters had repeatedly told her how close they'd come to losing their father. Now, every time she was with him, she felt a sense of renewed love and gratitude that his life had been spared.

"How do you expect a man to sleep with such delicious smells coming from the kitchen?" David grumbled good-naturedly. "I swear it's driving me to distraction."

"It's my Italian spaghetti sauce."

Her father squinted. "But we already ate dinner."

"I know. The sauce needs to simmer for several hours and it's even better if you let it sit overnight. I was hoping to surprise you tomorrow evening."

Her father nodded approvingly. "Sounds great, Princess." Then he grinned at Charles. "Good to see you, boy."

"You, too, old man."

She could tell that they'd often bantered like this. The atmosphere was relaxed, one of shared affection and camaraderie.

"You were in the neighborhood and decided to stop by?" David inquired. It wasn't likely Charles would come this way except to visit the Bloomfields, and they all knew it.

"I stopped in to check up on you," Charles said, but his gaze drifted involuntarily toward Steffie. Their eyes met briefly before she looked away.

"That's the *only* reason?" her father pressed.

"I, uh, brought that for Stephanie," he said and pointed in the direction of the potted azalea.

"You wouldn't by any chance happen to be sweet on my little girl, would you?"

"Dad," Steffie broke in urgently, "how about something to drink? Coffee, tea, a glass of water?"

"Nothing, thanks. I just came to see if I was dreaming about garlic and basil or if this was for real. I'll leave the two of you to yourselves now." He stood awkwardly, as though he wasn't quite steady on his feet. Steffie's instincts were to help him, but she knew it was important that he do as much as possible on his own. She stepped back, ready to assist him if necessary.

Charles must have been thinking the same thing because he stood beside her, a concerned look on his face.

"I'll see you to your room," she said. The effort of rising from his chair and walking a few paces seemed to deplete her father's strength.

"Nonsense," he objected. "You've got company. Charles isn't here to visit me. I heard him say so himself. That was just an excuse so he could bring you that pretty flower."

"Don't argue with me, Daddy."

Her father grumbled, but allowed her to wrap her arm around his waist to support him. She looked over her shoulder at Charles. "I'll be back in a minute."

"Take your time."

No sooner were they out of the kitchen than David came to a halt, wearing the most delighted grin Steffie had ever seen. "What's so amusing?" she asked.

"Nothing," he said. Then he started chuckling softly. "It's just that your mother was right about this, too. Surprises me, but it shouldn't."

"What? Right about what?"

"You and Charles."

"Daddy, there's nothing between us! We're hardly even friends."

"Perhaps, but all that's about to change. Soon, too. Very soon."

Her father continued to mutter under his breath, as pleased as ever. Steffie closed her ears to his remarks, knowing that he had to be referring to his dream—the time he'd supposedly spent tiptoeing around the afterlife, gathering information. It hadn't bothered her nearly as much when he was going on about Valerie and Colby, but now that it was her turn, she felt decidedly uneasy.

"Charles isn't here to see me," she insisted. "Bringing me the azalea didn't mean anything. He got a new advertising account, that's all. I'm sure he intended to give it to you, but you were sleeping."

"Whatever you say, Princess."

Arguing wouldn't get her anywhere, and besides, she didn't want to keep Charles waiting. She suspected he'd be leaving soon, anyway. Her father sat on the edge of his bed, his eyes curious as he smiled up at her. "I might have guessed. I wasn't sure what to think when your mother mentioned you and Charles. She told me you've been in love with him for quite some time. She's right, isn't she?"

Steffie kissed his brow and ignored his question. "Do you want me to tuck you in?"

"Good heavens, no! You hurry back to your young man. He's waiting for you. Has been for years."

"Good night, Dad," she said pointedly.

Her father's grin broadened. "By golly, your mother was right," she heard him mutter again. "I should've known. Forgive me, Grace, for doubting."

Outside the bedroom door, Steffie started to tremble. Without directly saying so, her father was telling her what she'd most dreaded hearing, and at the same time what she desired above all.

Whether it was the result of fantasy, intuition or, as he believed, spiritual intervention, he'd become convinced that she'd be marrying Charles. The same way he was so certain about what would happen between Valerie and Colby Winston. And Steffie wasn't any more confident about her older sister's relationship than she was about her own with Charles.

"You look like you've seen a ghost," Charles told her when she rejoined him in the kitchen.

She raised her eyes to his, dismayed that he'd noticed. She needed to sit down. He was right, it *had* been a scare, listening to her father talk like that about the two of them, making marriage sound imminent.

"What is it? Is your father okay?"

She nodded. "Oh, he's fine, growing stronger every day..."

"It's good to see him smile again."

Steffie nodded and glanced at the simmering pot of sauce. Anything to keep her eyes away from Charles.

"What's really wrong?" he asked her. His concern was gentle and undemanding, and it touched her heart. This was the man she'd always known him to be. The man she'd fallen in love with—the man she'd never been able to forget.

Had it been anyone else, she would have laughed off her father's words. She would have joked with her "destined" husband-to-be about how her father was bent on playing matchmaker.

She couldn't do that with Charles, not when she'd so blatantly played the role herself. He'd assume, and not without justification, that she was up to her old tricks.

"It's nothing," she said, forcing herself to smile brightly. "I can't help thinking how lucky we are to have him with us again."

Charles studied her intently. "You're *sure* there's nothing wrong?"

"Of course." She looked at him in what she hoped was a reassuring manner.

"If there's anything I can do…"

"There isn't." She smiled, to take the sting from her words. "You've already done so much. We're all indebted to you…you've been wonderful."

"You make me sound like some saint. Trust me, Stephanie, no one's going to canonize me—especially with the things I'm thinking right now." He was behind her before she even realized he'd moved. His hands were on her shoulders and he drew her back and slipped his arms around her waist. He nuzzled her neck and breathed in deeply, as though to inhale her scent.

Deluged with warm sensation, Steffie closed her eyes and savored the moment. She'd never believed this could happen. She dared not believe it even now.

It would be so easy to turn into his arms, to bury herself in the comfort he offered. She'd dreamed of this for so long. But now that it was here, she was afraid.

Her hands folded over his, which were joined at her middle. "I—the flowers are…"

"A gesture of good faith."

His words confused her. He must have sensed her uncertainty because he spoke again in a low voice.

"Let's start all over again, shall we? From the beginning."

"I— I'm not sure I know what you mean."

He softly kissed the side of her neck, then released her and turned her around so they were face-to-face. "Hello there, my name's Charles Tomaselli. I understand you're Stephanie Bloomfield. It's a real pleasure to meet you." He held out his hand to her, which she took. If his eyes hadn't been so serious, she would have burst into peals of laughter.

"Charles, you say? Anyone call you Charlie?"

"Hardly ever. Anyone call you Steffie?"

"Only when I was much younger," she teased. "A mere kid."

"I understand you're recently back in town. I don't suppose you've had time to notice, but there've been a few changes in Orchard Valley. How about if I drive you around, show you the place?"

She hesitated. "When?"

"No time like the present."

"But we've just met."

"I'm hoping that won't stand in your way. It shouldn't. I'm completely trustworthy."

"Then I'll accept your kind invitation."

"Do you want to bring a sweater?" he asked.

She shook her head.

He reached for her hand, his fingers entwined with hers as he led her toward the front door. It felt like the most natural thing in the world for them to be together.

They bounded down the steps, carefree and laughing. Charles opened the car door for her, helped her inside and without warning leaned forward to kiss her. Their lips met briefly, then lingered. When he broke away, Charles seemed surprised himself. Steffie glanced up at him, thinking she might read some sign of regret in his eyes, but there was none. Only a free-flowing happiness that reflected her own feelings exactly.

"Where were you last night?" Norah asked late the next morning. "I came home from Julie's wedding shower and you were nowhere to be found."

Steffie spread a thin layer of her sister's strawberry jam across her English muffin. "I went out for a while." She didn't add any details because her father was sitting at the table, lingering over his cup of coffee and the paper. He'd make all the wrong assumptions if he knew she'd been with Charles.

They'd spent nearly two hours driving around the area. Charles had taken her past several new businesses, including fast-food restaurants and some specialty boutiques. He'd shown her the recently constructed six-plex movie theater, a new housing complex and a brand-new mall on the outskirts of town. The drive had been highlighted by an ongoing commentary that included the latest gossip.

Steffie hadn't enjoyed herself so much in ages. Charles had been entertaining and fun, and he seemed to take pains never to refer to their past differences.

It was late when they'd gotten back to the house, but they sat in the car for another thirty minutes, talking, before Steffie went inside.

She'd fully expected to lie awake half the night savoring the time she'd spent with him, but to her astonishment, she'd fallen asleep immediately.

"Steffie was out with Charles," their father announced without looking up from his paper. "She didn't get home until late."

Steffie feverishly worked the knife back and forth across the muffin, spreading the already thin layer of jam even thinner.

"Charles Tomaselli?" Norah repeated as though she wasn't sure she'd heard correctly.

"Two girls and a boy," David returned cheerfully.

"I beg your pardon?" Steffie asked.

"You and Charles," he answered. "You're going to get married and within the next few years have your own family."

Rather than argue with her father or listen to more of this, Steffie glanced at her sister. "I need to do a few errands around town, but then I'm driving to Portland. Does anyone need anything?"

"Portland?" her father echoed. "Whatever for?"

"I thought it was time I applied for my doctorate and a part-time teaching position at the university. I *am* qualified, Dad, as you well know since you paid dearly for my education."

"But you can't worry about finding work now."

"I realize the country's in a recession, but—"

"I'm not talking about the economy," he said. "You're going to be married before the end of the summer, so don't go complicating everything with a job."

Steffie could feel the heat leap into her face. He

seemed so certain of a marriage between her and Charles, and that exasperated her no end. "Dad, *please* listen—"

"It doesn't make sense for you to be starting a job or a course and then taking time off for a honeymoon."

Steffie wasn't sure if it was a good idea to humor him anymore. This had gone on long enough, but she didn't know what to say. She was aware that her father claimed everything would work out between Valerie and Colby, too. After seeing her older sister's pale, drawn features that morning, Steffie had no faith in her father's words. Not that she'd really ever believed him…

"I don't actually expect to make a lot of contacts, since most of the offices won't be open on a Saturday, but I'm hoping to look around, check out the library, get a few names. Obtaining a teaching position now might be difficult, anyway, especially for the fall session. But I'd like to get started on a thesis soon."

"In other words you're going to Portland, no matter what I say?"

"Exactly."

"Then go shopping when you're done," her father suggested. "Try on a few wedding dresses. Both you and your sister are going to need 'em. Soon."

Norah was watching Steffie closely and spoke the moment their father had left the kitchen.

"What are we going to do?" Norah pleaded.

"I don't have a clue," Steffie said, fully agreeing with her sister's concern. "If Dad insists on believing—"

"Not Dad," Norah blurted out impatiently. "I'm talking about Valerie."

Steffie's exasperation with her father was quelled by her compassion for Valerie. "What *can* we do?"

Norah's face was pinched with worry. "That's the problem. I don't know, but we can't let her leave town like this. She came down early this morning.... I decided I had to tell her about Colby dating Sherry Waterman."

"How'd Valerie take it?"

"I don't know. She's so hard to read sometimes. It was as if she already knew, which is impossible." Norah frowned. "I wish you'd talk to her again. She's in her room now and, Steffie, I'm really worried about her. She's in love with Colby—she admitted it—but she seems resigned to losing him."

Steffie thought she understood her older sister's feelings.

"To complicate matters," Norah went on, "Valerie and I started talking and...arguing, and Dad heard us. He asked what we were fighting about."

"What did you say to him?"

"I didn't get a chance to say anything. Dad did all the talking. At least he and I agree. Dad believes Valerie should go talk this out with Colby, too. But I don't think she will."

"Where's Valerie now?" Steffie asked.

Norah looked away. "She's upstairs."

"Doing what?" Her sister had been spending a lot of time alone in her room lately.

"I don't know, but I think you should go to her.

Someone's got to. Valerie needs us, only she's so in-dependent she doesn't know how to ask."

Steffie disagreed. Her sister was getting—and ap-parently ignoring—advice from just about everyone, when what she needed to do was listen to her own heart.

"What's all this about you and Charles?" Norah asked with open curiosity. "I didn't know you even liked him."

In light of their recent confrontation over the news-paper article, it was natural for her sister to assume that.

"We're just friends."

"Which is definitely an improvement," Norah mut-tered.

Eager to leave before Norah asked more questions, Steffie went upstairs to her room. She toyed with the idea of talking to her sister, of telling her that seeking a long-distance cure for a broken heart didn't work.

But Valerie was intelligent enough to make her own decisions, and Steffie didn't feel qualified to say or do any more than she already had.

She dressed in a bright blue suit for her trip to Port-land, one Valerie would have approved of had she been home. Her sister had mysteriously disappeared with-out saying where she was headed.

Steffie was on her way out the door when her fa-ther stopped her. "Sit on the porch with me awhile, will you, Princess?"

"Of course." The wicker chair beside her father had belonged to her mother. Steffie sat next to him and gazed out over the sun-bright orchard she loved so much.

"Are you serious about this—getting a teaching position and all?"

"Yes. I can't stay home and do nothing. It'd be a waste of my education."

"Wait, Princess."

All his talk of marriage was beginning to annoy her. "But, Dad—"

"Just for a couple of weeks. You've been home such a short while— I don't want you to move away just yet. All I ask is that you delay a bit longer."

"I won't be moving out right away..." She hesitated. She couldn't deny her father anything, and he knew it. "Two weeks," she promised reluctantly. "We'll visit, catch up, make some plans. Then I'll start looking for an apartment."

"Is Charles coming for dinner tonight?"

"No." She'd invited him, but he had a late-afternoon meeting and doubted he'd be back in time.

"He's going to miss out on your Italian dinner."

"There'll be others."

"You should fix a plate and take it into town for him. A bachelor like Charles doesn't often get the opportunity to enjoy a home-cooked dinner."

"He seems to be doing just fine on his own," Steffie said, hiding a smile. Her father wasn't even trying to be subtle.

"He's a fine young man."

"Yes, I know. I think he's probably one of the most talented newsmen I've ever read. To be honest, I'm surprised he's still in Orchard Valley. I thought one of the big-city newspapers would've lured him away long before now."

"They've tried, but Charles likes living here. He's turned down several job offers."

"How do you know?" That he'd received other offers didn't surprise Steffie, but that her father was privy to the information did. Then she remembered he and Charles had worked together on the farmworker article.

"I know Charles quite well," her father answered. "We've become good friends the past few years."

Steffie crossed her legs. "I'd forgotten the two of you wrote that article."

Her father shook his head. "Charles wrote nearly every word of that story. All I did was get a few of the details for him and add a comment now and then, but that was it."

"He credits you with doing a lot more."

Her father was silent for a few minutes, reflective. Steffie wondered if he was worrying about Valerie the way Norah had been. She was about to say something when her father spoke.

"Charles is going to make me a fine son-in-law."

Steffie closed her eyes, trying to control the burst of impatience his words produced.

"Daddy, don't, please," she murmured.

"Don't what?"

"Talk about Charles marrying me."

"Why ever not?" he asked, sounding almost offended. "Why, Princess, he's loved you for years, only

I was too blind to notice. I guess I had my head in the clouds, because it's as clear as rainwater to me now. Soon after you left for Italy, he started coming around, asking about you. Only…he was so subtle about it I didn't realize what he was doing until I saw the two of you together last night."

"I know, but—"

"You don't have a clue, do you?" her father said, chuckling and shaking his head. "Can't say I blame you since I didn't guess it myself."

The way her father made it sound, Charles had spent the past three years pining away for her. Steffie knew that couldn't be true. He was the reason she'd left. He'd humiliated her, laughed at her.

"When your mother said you'd be marrying Charles—"

"Dad, *please*." Steffie felt close to tears. "I'm not marrying Charles."

He studied her, eyes narrowed in concern. "What's wrong, Princess? You love him, don't you?"

"I did…but that was a long time ago when I was young and very foolish." Her father had no way of knowing just *how* foolish she'd been.

Even after the incident in Charles's home, when she'd soaked in his tub until her skin resembled a raisin, she hadn't stopped. Some odd quirk of her nature refused to let her believe he didn't want her, not when she loved him so desperately.

Oh, no, she hadn't been willing to leave well enough alone. So she'd plotted and planned his downfall.

Literally.

Leaving a message at the newspaper office that her father needed to see him right away, Steffie had waited in the stable for Charles's arrival. She'd spread fresh hay in the first stall.

No one was home and she tacked a note on the front door directing Charles to the stable.

He'd arrived right on time. She had to say that for him; he was punctual to a fault. He hesitated when he saw she was there alone, then asked to talk to her father. He kept his distance—which might have had something to do with the pitchfork in her hand.

Steffie had planned this meeting right down to the minutest detail. She'd worn tight jeans and a checkered shirt, half unbuttoned and tied at her waist.

She remembered Charles repeating that he was anxious to talk to her father. Among other things, he'd told her, he wanted to clear the air about what was happening between him and Steffie.

At the time she'd nearly laughed out loud. *Nothing* was happening, despite her best efforts.

Steffie remembered again how perfect her timing had been. As she was chatting with him, explaining that she wasn't sure where her father had gone, she set aside the pitchfork and started up the ladder that led to the loft. At precisely the right moment, she lost her balance, just as she'd planned. After teetering for a second, she dropped into Charles's arms.

He broke her fall, but the impact of her weight slamming against him had taken them both to the floor, and into the fresh hay. For a moment, neither said a word.

"Are you all right?" He spoke first, his voice low and angry.

Steffie had never been more "all right" in her life. For the first time she was in Charles's arms and he held on to her as though he never intended to let her go, as though this was exactly where he'd always wanted her to be.

Steffie had gazed down on him and slowly shaken her head. His gaze had gone to her parted lips and then his hands were in her hair and with a groan he'd guided her mouth to his. The kiss was wild, crazily intense. No man had ever kissed her with such hunger or need. Steffie didn't understand what she was feeling; all she knew was that she wanted Charles more than she'd ever wanted anything. So she'd done what came instinctively. She'd kissed him back with the same searing hunger, until it seemed neither of them would be able to endure the intensity any longer.

Steffie would never forget how he'd rolled away from her, bounding effortlessly to his feet, breathing hard.

At first he'd said nothing. Steffie knew she'd have to speak first. So she'd looked up at him and said what had been on her heart from the moment they'd met. She'd told him simply, honestly, how much she loved him.

Steffie would forever remember what happened next.

Charles had stared down at her in silence for several heart-stopping seconds, and then he'd begun to laugh.

Deep belly laughs, as though she'd said the funniest thing he'd ever heard.

She was exactly what he needed, he'd said with a twinge of sarcasm—a lovesick girl running after him. How many times did he have to tell her he wasn't interested? When he was ready for a woman in his life, he wanted exactly that, a *woman,* not a child. Especially not one as immature as she was.

He'd said more, but by then Steffie was running toward the house, tears streaking her face. The sound of his laughter had followed her, taunting her, ridiculing her.

"Charles has loved you all these years," her father said now. He spoke confidently, crashing into her memories and dragging her back to the present. The past was so painful that Steffie was content to leave it behind.

"He's never loved me," she whispered through a haze of remembered pain.

"Ah, my sweet Princess," her father countered. "That's where you're wrong."

Six

"Dad, listen to me." Steffie stood, turning her head for fear her father would see the tears glistening in her eyes. "Whatever you do, please don't say anything to Charles about—you know?"

"Being in love with you?"

"That, too," she pleaded, "but I'm particularly concerned about this marriage thing."

"That worries you?"

"Yes, Dad, it worries me a great deal."

"You don't understand, do you?" he asked softly.

"Oh, Dad, you're the one who doesn't understand."

"Steffie, my Princess, don't limit yourself to the things you understand," her father said in the gentlest voice imaginable, "otherwise you'll miss half of what life has to offer."

She had to leave, had to escape before she dissolved into an emotional storm of tears. Not until she was in the car, heading she didn't know where, did she realize her father hadn't promised one way or the other. He might well blurt everything to Charles.

By the time Steffie had reached Orchard Valley, she'd composed herself. She'd do her errands—pick up dry cleaning, visit the small local library, mail a birthday card to little Mario in Italy—before she drove to Portland. Because it was Saturday, Main Street was busy and she was fortunate to find a parking spot. Not so fortunate as she would have liked, however, since the only available space was directly in front of the newspaper office.

For at least ten minutes, Steffie sat in the family station wagon, considering whether to talk to Charles herself. *Should* she warn him about her father's crazy dream, his matchmaking hopes?

She was still debating the issue when she saw him, talking to the girl at the front desk. Her heart gladdened at the mere sight of him. He'd removed his suit jacket and the sleeves of his white shirt were rolled halfway up his arms. He was so attractive, so compelling. For several minutes she watched him, mesmerized.

At first glance, Steffie thought Charles might have been talking to Norah, but that was impossible. The resemblance was there, though. This young woman was blonde and exceptionally pretty. Even from inside her car, Steffie could see how she gazed up at Charles with wide, adoring eyes.

The dread that went through her was immediate and unstoppable. She was jealous, and she hated it. The blonde was probably Wendy, the apprentice Charles had mentioned, and Steffie didn't doubt for an instant that she was in love with him. Not that Steffie blamed her; she'd once played the role of doting female herself. Was playing it even now, despite her most strenuous efforts.

Charles was still talking to his intern, his hand resting against the back of her chair. He leaned forward as the two of them reviewed something, their heads close together. The blonde laughed at some remark of his and smiled up at him, her heart in her eyes.

Steffie couldn't watch any more. It was like looking back several years and seeing what a fool she'd made of herself. Hurriedly she got out of the car and swung her purse over her shoulder. Forcing her eyes away from the newspaper office, she locked the car door. She was about to walk down the street when Charles stepped onto the sidewalk.

"Stephanie, hello." He sounded surprised to see her. More than that, he sounded pleased.

"Hi," she returned awkwardly, feeling guilty, although she wasn't sure why. It wasn't as if she'd actually been spying on him.

"Where are you headed?" he asked, giving her business suit an appreciative glance.

"I—I was thinking about driving into Portland and visiting the university after I do some errands here. I plan eventually to rent an apartment in the city, but Dad…" She hesitated.

Charles grinned knowingly. "But your father wasn't delighted with the idea."

"Exactly. I promised him I'd wait another couple of weeks."

"Why two weeks?"

"Uh…" For a few seconds, she panicked, wondering if Charles had guessed, wondering if her father had mentioned his dream, praying he hadn't. "It seemed like a reasonable compromise."

"Have you got a moment? I'd like you to meet Wendy. She's the intern I was telling you about. Bart's here, as well. You remember Bart, don't you?"

Steffie bit her lip, feeling reluctant. The last time she'd been to the newspaper office she'd come bent on vengeance, with threats of a lawsuit burning in her eyes.

"Tell you what, I'll throw in lunch. I've got an appointment at one, but it's barely twelve now."

She was still caught in the throes of indecision, when Charles took her firmly by the elbow and escorted her inside. She felt a wave of relief; after all, the opportunity to spend time with him, even a few minutes squeezed in between appointments, was too precious to decline.

It might have been Steffie's imagination, but the people in the newspaper office seemed delighted to see her. She wondered what Charles could possibly have said to salvage her reputation.

A couple of the reporters, one of whom she remembered from high school, welcomed her back to Orchard Valley. Bart, the pressman, inquired about her father's health. Even Wendy seemed inclined to like her, which raised Steffie's guilt by several uncomfortable notches.

"I'll be back at one," Charles said as he guided Steffie out the front door.

"But—" Bart stopped abruptly when Charles cut him off with a glare.

"I'll be here in plenty of time," he promised. "What's your pleasure?" he asked, smiling down at her.

"Whatever's most convenient for you."

"The Half Moon's serving sandwiches now. How does that sound?"

"Great." When Steffie left for Italy, the Half Moon, just down the street from the *Clarion,* had been a small coffee shop.

Now she saw that it had been expanded and modernized. While Charles placed their order, Steffie found them a table. Several customers, old acquaintances, greeted her and asked about her father, and before she realized it, she was completely at ease, laughing and joking with the people around her.

When Charles returned with their turkey-and-tomato sandwiches and coffee, she smiled at him happily, content to shed the troubled thoughts she'd carried into town with her. At least for the moment...

"How's your father this morning?" Charles asked, holding his sandwich with both hands to keep bits of tomato and lettuce from escaping.

"Cantankerous as ever." Opinionated, too, and occasionally illogical, but she didn't say any of that. Even if she decided to warn Charles, now didn't seem to be the time. Not when they were sitting across from each other, relaxed and lighthearted, and all the world felt right.

The hour passed quickly. This kind of pure, simple happiness never lasted, she told herself. But, oh, how she wished it could. Charles seemed equally reluctant for their visit to end.

Steffie walked back to work with him. "Thanks for lunch," she said, standing on the sidewalk in front of the office.

"I'll call you," Charles promised as Bart came out, looking anxiously at his watch. "I'll be right there," Charles told him, a bit impatiently. He turned back to Steffie. "Sometime tomorrow?"

"Sure." She nodded eagerly.

Sometime tomorrow. A few short hours and yet it felt like a lifetime away.

Valerie was leaving.

Steffie did try talking to her. She'd tried to explain that running away from love wouldn't help; it would just follow her wherever she went. Her sister had listened, then quietly packed her bags.

Sunday morning, when Valerie was about to go, Colby showed up unexpectedly. Steffie was thrilled; it was as if everything she'd read about the power of love, everything she'd always secretly believed, was true. Colby would prove it. He'd come to declare his love and sweep Valerie off her feet.

It soon became clear, however, that Colby wasn't there because of Valerie. He hadn't known she was catching a flight that afternoon, and when he heard, he seemed to accept it as inevitable. Furthermore, he had no intention of stopping her. No intention of asking her to stay. If anything, he seemed almost relieved at her imminent departure.

When the moment came for Valerie to go, Steffie thought she might burst into tears herself. She'd so desperately wanted to believe in the power of love, in its ability to knock down barriers and leap over obstacles.

Valerie hugged them all farewell, and with shoulders held stiff and straight, walked from the porch to her rental car. Then, just before she left, she turned and looked at Colby.

Steffie would always remember the tenderness she saw in her sister's eyes. It was as though she'd reached back, one last time, to say goodbye…and to thank him. At least, that was how it seemed to Steffie. She'd never been so affected by a mere glance. That look of Valerie's was full of love, but it also expressed dignity and a gracious acceptance.

Steffie was trying to sort out her mingled emotions of anger and pain as Valerie drove away. She turned to Colby, who still stared after her sister's car. It took every ounce of self-control she had not to scream at him. Only the anguish in his eyes prevented her from lashing out, and when she recognized the intensity of his pain, her own anger was replaced by a bleak hopelessness.

"She's gone," he whispered.

"She'll be back," her father said with the same unquestioning confidence that had driven Steffie nearly mad with frustration.

"No," she insisted, her voice quavering. "She won't. Not for a very long time."

Then, unable to face either Colby or her father, she dashed back into the house. Norah followed soon afterward, and Steffie realized that her younger sister was crying.

"She's going to marry Rowdy Cassidy," Norah wailed. "What's so terrible is that she doesn't even *love* him."

"Then what makes you think Valerie would do anything so foolish?" Steffie asked calmly. Valerie might be unhappy about losing Colby Winston, but she was too sensible to enter into a loveless marriage.

"You don't understand," Norah said as she continued to sob. "*He's* in love with her. He's called nearly every day and sent flowers and…and Valerie's so vulnerable right now. I just know she's going to make a terrible mistake."

"Val's not going to do anything stupid," Steffie reassured her sister. Valerie wouldn't marry her boss on the rebound—Steffie was confident of that. Deep down, she knew exactly what her sister would be doing for the next three years—if not longer. She knew because she'd done it herself. Valerie would try to escape into her work, to the exclusion of everything else. Because then she wouldn't have time to hurt, time to deal with regrets and might-have-beens. She wouldn't have time to look back or relive the memories.

An hour later, Steffie took a glass of iced tea out to

her father, who stubbornly refused to leave the porch. He sat in his rocking chair, anxiously studying the road. "They'll both be back," he said again.

Steffie didn't try to disillusion him. By nightfall he'd be forced to accept the truth without her prompting.

Within ten minutes of Valerie's departure, Colby had left, too. He hadn't raced down the driveway in hot pursuit or given the slightest indication that he was going anywhere but back to town.

"Mark my words," her father said confidently. "Valerie and Colby will be married before the end of June."

"Dad…"

"And you and Charles will follow a few weeks later. All three of my daughters are going to be married this summer. I know it in my heart, as surely as I know my own name."

Although she nearly choked, Steffie swallowed her words of argument.

Needing some physical activity to vent her frustrations, she saddled Princess. She knew better than to try her luck with Fury again. But the mare, who was generally docile, seemed to sense Steffie's mood and galloped down the long pasture road and across the rocky field until they reached the bluff. The same place Fury had taken her.

Holding the reins, Steffie slid off the mare's back and sat on the very rock she had before. She lost track of time as she sat looking out on the valley, thinking about Valerie. And Colby. Remembering her own disastrous relationship with Charles, and how her willful behavior had destroyed any chance they'd had three years ago. Now there seemed to be a fresh beginning for her and Charles, however fragile it might be. Not for Valerie, though… Life wasn't fair, she thought, and love didn't make everything perfect.

She rode slowly back and had just finished rubbing down Princess and leading her into her stall when Charles appeared. "I thought I heard someone here." He stood by the stable door, hands on his hips, smiling.

"Charles." She shouldn't have been so surprised to see him. After all, he'd made a point of telling her he'd be in touch.

"Your dad figured you'd gone out riding, but he seemed to think you'd be home soon."

"Have you been waiting long?"

"Not really. Your father's kept me entertained."

"Is he still on the front porch?"

"He hasn't moved since I got here."

Dispirited, Steffie looked away. "That's what I was afraid of. Valerie's gone, and he seems to believe she'll come back if he sits there long enough."

Charles frowned heavily. "Is something going on? A problem?"

"No," she answered quickly, perhaps too quickly because Charles's eyes narrowed suspiciously. "I mean, nothing you need to worry about. Dad desperately wants to believe Colby and Val will kiss and make up—that's the reason he's being so stubborn. By dinnertime he'll have to recognize that it simply isn't going to happen."

It might've been because she was nervous and flustered, or maybe she just wasn't watching where she was going, but Steffie tripped over a bale of hay.

Although she threw out her arms in an effort to right herself, it was too late. She fell forward, but before she completely lost her balance, Charles caught her around the waist. He twisted his body so that when they went down, he took the brunt of the fall.

It was as though the years had evaporated. They'd been in virtually the same position on that previous occasion, with Steffie sprawled over him, her heart pounding. Only this time she hadn't manipulated the circumstances. This time she wasn't in control.

They were both breathing hard. A tumult of confused emotions raged within her, and she braced her arms against him, ready to get up and move away. Instead, his arms, which were around her waist, held her firmly in place.

"It seems we've been here before," he said, his eyes gazing into hers.

"I—" She stopped abruptly and nodded.

"Do you remember what happened that day?"

Incapable of speaking, she nodded again.

"Do you remember the way we kissed?"

She couldn't look at him, couldn't allow him to read the answer in her eyes.

He held her fast for another long moment before he gradually eased his hold. "Let's talk about that time."

"No!" she cried. The instant she was free, she rushed to her feet, not realizing she must have sprained her ankle. But when she placed her weight on her left foot she experienced a sharp stabbing pain. She couldn't suppress a whimper as she leaned against the stall door for support.

"You're hurt," Charles said, immediately getting to his feet. He slipped his arm around her waist.

"I'm sure it's nothing. I've just twisted my ankle—it hardly hurts at all," she lied.

Without another word, Charles effortlessly scooped her into his arms.

"Charles, please," she said, growing angry. "I'm perfectly fine. It's a minor sprain, nothing more. There's no need for this."

He didn't reply but began to carry her out of the stable.

"Where are you taking me?" she demanded.

"The kitchen. You should put ice on it right away."

"I want you to know I don't appreciate these cave-man tactics."

"That's too bad." He was short of breath by the time he reached the back door, which infuriated Steffie even more. "Put me down this instant," she snapped.

"In a minute." He managed, after some difficulty, to open the door, then deposited her unceremoniously in a chair—like a sack of flour, she thought with irritation. He was pulling open the freezer section of the refrigerator and removing the ice-cube tray.

She rested her sore foot on her opposite knee and was about to remove her shoe when he stopped her. "I'll do that."

"Charles, you're being ridiculous."

He didn't answer, but carefully drew off her shoe and sock. His fingers were tender as he examined her ankle, and it felt strangely intimate to have him touch her like this.

"I told you already—it doesn't hurt anymore," she argued. "I might have gotten up too fast or put my foot down wrong. I don't feel a thing now."

"Try standing up."

Cautiously she did. His arm circled her waist as she gingerly placed her weight on the foot. "See," she said, feeling both triumphant and foolish. "There doesn't seem to be any damage."

"I wouldn't be so sure. Try walking."

The floor felt cool against her bare foot as she took a guarded first step. There was barely a twinge. She tried again. Same result. "See?" she said. "I'm fine." And she proceeded to prove it by marching around the kitchen.

"Good." Charles replaced the ice-cube tray in the freezer, but he was frowning.

"Don't look so disappointed," she teased as she pulled on her sock and shoe.

He glanced at her, then smiled slowly, sensually. "I've heard of some inventive ways to avoid kissing a man, but..." He let the rest fade as he sat down beside her, then pulled her chair toward him until they sat face-to-face, so close their knees touched.

Steffie shut her eyes as his hands came to rest on her shoulders. His breathing grew ragged and he whispered her name. "Stephanie," he said, leaning forward to touch her lips with his own.

Steffie was afraid—of his kiss and of her own response. But she felt a thrill of excitement, too. He must have sensed that, because the quality of his kiss changed from gentle caress to fierce desire.

Charles groaned, and she slid her hands up his chest, delighting in the feel of hard, smooth muscles as she gave herself fully to his kiss.

Suddenly he broke away, his shoulders heaving. Steffie let her eyes flutter open and for a long silent moment they stared at each other.

His hand reached out to touch her hair, a small, intimate gesture that moved her unbearably.

Then he stretched out his arms, clasping her by the waist and lifting her from the chair to set her securely in his lap. She wasn't given the opportunity to protest before his mouth claimed hers once more.

This time his kiss was slow and gentle, as tender as the earlier kiss had been hungry and demanding. She felt herself melting in his arms, surrendering the last of her resistance.

"I want to talk about what happened," he whispered.

She knew what he meant, and she wanted none of it. That scene in the stable—the fall she'd faked—was much too embarrassing to examine even now. "That was in the past."

"It has to be settled between us."

"No," she said, trying to change his mind with a deep, hungry kiss.

His voice was rough when she finished. "Steff, we have to clear the past before we can talk about the future."

"We only just met, remember?" He was the one

who'd suggested they start over. He couldn't bury the past and then ask that they exhume it.

"Just listen to me…"

"Not yet," she pleaded. Maybe never, her heart whispered, balking at the idea of reliving a time that had been so painful for her.

"Soon." He tangled his fingers in her hair and spread kisses across her face.

"Maybe," she agreed reluctantly.

The sound of laughter broke into the haze of her pleasure. At least Steffie assumed it was laughter. It took her a wild moment to realize the sound was coming from the porch, and that it must be her father. Not knowing what to think, she slowly broke away from Charles.

"Is that David laughing?" he asked.

Steffie shrugged. "I'd better find out if something's wrong."

He nodded, and they walked hand in hand to the porch.

"Dad?" she asked softly when she saw her father, rocking contentedly. His smile broadened when he noticed her and Charles. His gaze fell to their hands, which were still clasped tightly together, and his eyes fairly twinkled. "Check the freezer, will you? By heaven, I wish I'd thought of this sooner."

"The freezer?" she repeated, glancing at Charles, wondering if her father had lost his wits. "Why do you want me to check it?"

"We need something special to fix for dinner tonight. We're going to have a celebration!"

Steffie frowned in puzzlement. "What kind of celebration?"

"There's going to be a wedding in the family."

Steffie groaned inwardly. "Dad…"

"Don't argue with me, Princess, there isn't time."

"But, Dad…"

"See there?" he said, pointing toward the long stretch of driveway. "What did I tell you?"

Steffie looked, but she couldn't see anything except a small puff of dust, barely discernible against the skyline.

"I was about to give up on those two," he said with a wry chuckle. "They're both too stubborn for their own good. I have to admit they gave me pause, but your mother was right. Guess I shouldn't have doubted her."

"Dad, what are you talking about?"

"Your sister and Colby. They're on their way back to the house now."

Steffie glanced up again, and this time the make and color of the car was unmistakable. Colby was returning to the house. And although she couldn't clearly tell who the passenger was, she knew it had to be her sister.

Seven

"Even now I can't believe it," Valerie said wistfully, sitting cross-legged on her bed. Steffie and Norah lounged on the opposite end, listening.

"Colby actually chased you down on the freeway?" Norah wanted to know.

Valerie's smile lit up her whole face as she nodded. "It really was romantic to have him race after me. He told me he didn't realize he was planning to do it until he was on the interstate."

"You've got everything worked out?" Steffie asked. From what Norah had told her, and from remarks Valerie herself had made, she knew there were a lot of obstacles standing in the way of this marriage.

"We've talked things out the best we can. It's been a struggle to come up with the right compromises. I've got a call in to Rowdy Cassidy at CHIPS. I think I can talk him into letting me open a branch of the company in Oregon. He's already done a feasibility study for the Pacific Northwest. He was just waiting until he could find the right person to head it up. He didn't originally have me in mind, but I don't think he'll have a problem giving it to me. Then again—" she paused thoughtfully "—it may be better to discuss this in person."

"Colby doesn't mind if you continue working?" Norah's voice was tinged with disbelief.

"No. Because it's what I need. Naturally he'd rather I was there to pamper him when he gets home from the hospital every night, but this way we'll learn to pamper each other."

"I'm so happy for you." Steffie leaned forward to hug her sister. Valerie's eyes reflected an inner joy that Steffie had never seen in her before. This was what love—real love—did for a person. When two people cared this deeply for each other, it couldn't help but show.

"Now that we've decided to go ahead with the wedding, Colby wants to do it as soon as possible," Valerie went on to say. "I hope everyone's willing to work fast and hard because we've got a wedding to plan for next month."

"Next month!" Norah's blue eyes widened incredulously.

"I was lucky to get him to wait *that* long. Colby would rather we flew to Vegas tonight and—"

"No way!" was Norah's and Steffie's automatic response.

"I never thought I'd be the sentimental sort," Valerie admitted sheepishly, "but I actually want a large fancy wedding. Colby loves me enough to agree, as long as I organize it quickly. Once that man makes a decision, there's no holding him back."

Steffie smiled to herself. Dr. Colby Winston was in for a real surprise. Valerie was talented enough in the organizational department to manage the United Nations. If he gave her a month to arrange their wedding, she'd do a beautiful job of it with time to spare.

A wedding so soon meant the family was about to be caught up in a whirlwind of activity, but that suited Steffie. It was time for them to celebrate. The grieving, the anxiety, were over.

"You've been seeing a lot of Charles lately, haven't you?" Norah asked, looking expectantly at Steffie. "Do you think we could make this a double wedding?"

Valerie smiled broadly at Steffie, as though she'd be in favor of the idea, too.

"I haven't been seeing *that* much of Charles," Steffie answered, thrusting out her chin. She realized she sounded defensive. "Well, I—I suppose we have been together quite a bit lately, but there's certainly never been any talk of marriage."

"I've always liked Charles," Norah said, studying Steffie closely. "I mean, I could go for this guy, given the least bit of encouragement. First Valerie falls in love and now you. You know, it's a little unfair. I'm the one who lives at home and you two fly in and within a few weeks nab the two most eligible men in town."

"Me?" Steffie argued. "You make it sound like a done deal. Trust me, it isn't."

"You're in love with him," Valerie said quietly. "Aren't you?"

Steffie didn't reply. She was unwilling to openly admit her feelings for Charles. It would be so easy to fool herself into believing he held the same tenderness for her. But he'd never said so, and other than a few shared kisses he hadn't given her any indication he cared.

But he had, something inside her said.

Steffie refused to listen. She couldn't, wouldn't, forget that she'd made a fool of herself over him, not once but three times. Because she'd cared, and he hadn't.

"I don't know how Charles feels about me," Steffie said in a soft steady voice.

"You're joking!" Norah exclaimed.

And Valerie added, "Steffie, it's obvious how he feels."

Steffie discounted their assurances with a shrug. "For all I know, he could be hanging around me in order to get close to Norah."

"Charles? No way." Both Valerie and Norah burst into loud peals of laughter.

"Are you saying you wouldn't mind me dating him?" Norah teased, winking at Valerie.

"Feel free." In fact, Steffie would throttle Norah if she went within ten feet of Charles, though she could hardly say so.

"I hope you're joking," Norah said, shaking her head. "I should've seen what was going on a long time ago. I don't know how I could've been so dense. Charles and Dad became friends shortly after you left—good friends."

"That doesn't mean a thing," Steffie insisted. She

didn't need anyone else building up her hopes, and although her sisters meant well, their encouragement would only make her disappointment harder to bear.

"It wouldn't mean much if Charles hadn't made a point of asking about you every time he stopped by," Norah was saying. "I have to hand it to the guy, though—he was always subtle about his questions."

"Now that you mention it, whenever I talked to Charles, Steffie's name cropped up in the conversation," Valerie reported thoughtfully. "I should have guessed myself."

"You were too involved with Colby to see anything else," Norah teased and then sighed. She crossed her arms and rested them atop her bent knees. "Don't get me wrong, I'm happy for you two, but I wish I'd fall in love. Don't you think it's my turn?"

"Aren't you leaping to conclusions here?" Steffie asked. She wasn't exactly sporting an engagement ring the way Valerie was. She and Charles hadn't arrived at that stage of commitment—and probably never would. Besides, her past mistakes with him had been the result of leaping to certain incorrect conclusions about his feelings, and she wasn't ready for a repeat performance.

Steffie didn't see Charles again until Tuesday afternoon. She wasn't surprised not to hear from him, knowing how involved he was with the production of the paper during the first part of every week.

Valerie and Steffie had driven into town to visit The Petal Pusher, the local flower shop. Valerie had decided on a spring color theme for her wedding and had already chosen material for Steffie's and Norah's gowns in a pale shade of green and a delicate rose.

Valerie angled the car into the slot closest to the flower shop. Since the newspaper office was almost directly across the street, it was natural for her to glance curiously in that direction.

"You haven't talked to Charles in a couple of days, have you?"

"He's busy with the paper."

"There's time to stop in now and say hello if you want. I'll be talking to the florist, so you might as well."

Steffie was tempted, but felt uncomfortable about interrupting Charles at work. "Some other time," she said with a feigned lack of interest, though in actuality she was starving for the sight of him. Helping Valerie plan her wedding had forced some long-buried emotions to the surface. Steffie hadn't admitted until these past few weeks how deeply she longed for marriage herself. A family of her own. A husband to love and live with her whole life.

A husband.

Her mind stumbled over the word. There'd only ever been one man she could imagine as her husband, and that was Charles. Even though Steffie knew it was unwise, she'd started dreaming again. She found herself fantasizing what her life would be like if she was married…to Charles. She wanted to blame her sisters for putting such thoughts in her head, but she couldn't. Those dreams and fantasies had been there for years. The problem was that she couldn't suppress them anymore.

An hour later, at the same moment as Steffie and Valerie were leaving the flower shop, Charles happened to step out of the *Clarion* office.

Steffie instinctively looked across the street, where he was walking with Wendy, deep in conversation. Something must have told him she was there because he glanced in her direction. He grinned warmly.

Steffie relaxed and waved. He returned the gesture, then spoke to Wendy before jogging across the street to join Steffie and her sister.

"Hello," he said, but his eyes lingered on Steffie. He barely seemed to notice Valerie's presence.

"Hi." It was ridiculous to feel so shy with him. "I'd have stopped in to say hello, but I knew you'd be busy."

"I'm never too busy for you." His eyes were affectionate and welcoming.

"See," Valerie hissed close to Steffie's ear. Then, more loudly, "I've got a couple of errands to run, if you two would like a chance to talk."

Charles checked his watch. "Come back to the office with me?"

"Sure." If he'd suggested they stand on their heads in the middle of Main Street, Steffie would have willingly agreed.

Valerie cast a quick glance at the clock tower. "How about if I meet you back at the car in—"

"Half an hour," Charles supplied, reaching for Steffie's hand. "There's something I'd like to show you," he told her.

"Fine, I'll see you then, Steff," Valerie said cheerfully. She set off at a brisk walk, without looking back.

Their fingers entwined, Charles led Steffie across the street to the newspaper office. "I was going to save this for later, but now's as good a time as any." He ushered her in and guided her down the center aisle, past the obviously busy staff, to his desk.

Steffie wasn't sure what to expect, but a mock-up of the *Clarion*'s second page wasn't it. As far as she could see, it was the same as any other inside page she'd read over the years.

"Clearly I'm missing something," she said after a moment. "Is the type different?"

"Nope, we've used the same fonts as always." He crossed his arms and leaned against the desk, looking exceptionally pleased with himself.

"How about a hint?" she asked, a bit puzzled.

"I might suggest you read the masthead," he said next, his dark eyes gleaming.

"The masthead," she repeated as she scanned the listings of the newspaper's personnel and the duties they performed.

"All right, I will. Charles Tomaselli, editor and publisher. Roger Simons—"

"Stop right there," he said, holding up his hand.

"Publisher," she said again. "That's new. What exactly does it mean?"

His smile could have lit up a Christmas tree. "It means, my beautiful Stephanie, that I now own the *Orchard Valley Clarion*."

"Charles, that's wonderful!" She resisted the urge to throw her arms around him, but it was difficult.

"My dream's got a mortgage attached," he told her wryly. "A lot of folks think I'm an idiot to risk so much of my future on a medium that's said to be dying. Newspapers are folding all over the country."

"The *Clarion* won't."

"Not if I can help it."

Her heart seemed to spill over with joy. She knew how much Charles loved his work, how committed he was to the community. "I'm so excited about this."

"Me, too," he said, his smile boyishly proud. "I'd say this calls for a celebration, wouldn't you?"

"Most definitely."

"Dinner?"

She nodded eagerly and they set the date for Thursday evening, deciding on a restaurant that overlooked the Columbia River Gorge, about an hour's drive north.

Steffie felt as if her feet didn't touch the pavement as she hurried across the street thirty minutes later to meet her sister. Never, in all the time she'd known Charles, had she seen him happier. And she was happy with him, and *for* him. That was what loving someone meant. It was a truth she hadn't really understood before, not until today. This intense new feeling had taught her that real love wasn't prideful or selfish. Real love meant sharing the happiness—and the sorrows—of the person you loved. Yes, she understood that now. She realized that her past obsession with Charles had focused more on her own desires than on his. Her love had matured.

Charles had wakened within her emotions she hadn't known it was possible to experience. Emotions—and sensations. When she was with him, especially when he kissed her, she felt vibrant and alive.

"You look like you're about to cry, you're so happy," Valerie said when Steffie joined her in the car. "I don't suppose Charles popped the question."

"No," she said with a sigh. "But he asked me to dinner to help him celebrate. Guess what? Charles is the new owner of the *Clarion*."

Valerie didn't seem nearly as excited as Steffie. "He's going to be working a lot of extra hours then, isn't he?"

"He didn't say." If he spent as much time at the newspaper as he had three years earlier, there wouldn't be any extra hours left.

"I suppose his eating habits are atrocious."

Steffie suspected they were, but she shrugged. "I wouldn't know."

"I bet he'd enjoy a home-cooked meal every now and then, don't you?"

Steffie eyed her sister suspiciously. "Is there a point to this conversation?"

"Of course," she answered with a sly grin. "I think you should heat up some of that fabulous spaghetti sauce and take it to him later. You know what they say about the way to a man's heart, don't you?"

"Funny, that sounds exactly like a suggestion of Dad's. What's your interest in this?"

"Well," Valerie said coyly, "that way I wouldn't feel guilty about asking you if I could take some to Colby's. If he tasted your spaghetti sauce and happened to assume, through no error of mine, that I'd cooked this fabulous dinner—" she paused to inhale deeply "—he'd be so overcome by the idea of marrying such a fabulous cook that he'd go over the wedding list with me and not put it off for the third time."

"There's method in your madness, Valerie Bloomfield."

"Naturally. Colby doesn't know that I can't tell one side of a cookie sheet from the other. I don't want to disillusion him quite so soon. He suggested I make dinner tonight and, well, you get the picture."

"I do indeed. I'll be happy to share the spaghetti sauce with you."

"I'll hang around the kitchen to be sure some of the aroma sticks to me."

"I'll give you the recipe if you want."

"I want, but if I have trouble cooking with a microwave, heaven only knows what I'll do once I'm around a stove. One with burners and a real oven."

Steffie chuckled. She certainly had no objection to helping her sister prepare dinner for Colby, but she wasn't sure taking a plate over to Charles's house was such a good plan.

Valerie and Norah convinced her otherwise.

"Charles never did get to sample your cooking," Norah reminded her. "He stopped by and you offered him dinner, but he'd already eaten. Remember?"

"How'd you know that?"

Norah looked mildly surprised, as though everyone must be aware of what went on between Steffie and Charles. "Dad told me."

Her dear, matchmaking father. Steffie should have known.

"It isn't going to hurt anything," Valerie reminded her. "If you want, you can ride into town with me. I'll go over to Charles's house with you and we can drop off the meal, then I'll drive you home."

Steffie still wasn't sure, but Norah and Valerie believed it was a romantic thing to do. They both seemed to think Charles was serious about their relationship.

As for Steffie, she didn't know what to think anymore. In fact, she preferred not to think about their relationship at all. And yet...

She remained hesitant about this project of delivering him a surprise dinner but Valerie and Norah were so certain it would be a success that she went ahead with it.

They were apparently right.

She'd found his door open—that hadn't changed, she thought with a twinge of embarrassment—and had left a container of the sauce, some noodles with instructions and a couple of last-minute extras on his kitchen table.

Steffie was propped up in her bed reading a new mystery novel at ten-thirty that night. Her bedroom window was open and a breeze whispered through the orchard. The house was quiet; her father had gone to bed an hour earlier, and her sisters were both out for the evening.

When the phone chimed, she answered on the first ring, not wanting it to wake her father.

"How'd you do it?" Charles asked, sounding thoroughly delighted. "I came home exhausted and hungry, thinking I was going to have to throw something in the microwave for dinner. The minute I walked into the house, I smelled this heavenly scent of basil and garlic. I followed my nose to the table and found your note."

"You should thank Valerie and Norah. The whole thing was their idea." Had he been furious, Steffie would gladly have shifted the blame, so she figured it was only right to share the credit.

"I haven't tasted spaghetti that good since my grandmother died. I'd forgotten how delicious homemade sauce can be."

Steffie was warmed by the compliment. "I'm glad you enjoyed it."

"Enjoyed it! You have no idea. It was like stepping back into my childhood to spend the evening with my grandmother. She was a fabulous cook, and so are you."

Steffie leaned against the heap of pillows and closed her eyes, savoring these precious moments.

"The bottle of red wine and the small loaf of French bread were a nice touch," he told her.

"I'm glad," she said again. A dozen unnamed emotions whirled inside her.

"I wish you didn't live so far out of town," Charles said next. "Otherwise I'd come over right now—to thank you."

"I wish I didn't live so far out, too."

"Since we're both making wishes, there are a few other things I'd like, as well," he added in tones as smooth as velvet.

"You're limited to three." How raspy her own voice sounded.

Charles chuckled. "Only three? What happens if I want four?"

"I'm not sure, but I seem to remember reading about a handsome young newsman who was turned into a frog because he got greedy about wishes."

"How many have I got left?"

"Two."

"All right, I'll choose carefully. I wish we were together in your father's stable right now."

"You're wasting one of your wishes on the stable?"

"That's what I said. It seems as though every time I'm there, you end up in my arms. In fact, I'm looking forward to visiting your father's horses again soon."

"That can be arranged. Fury and Princess will be thrilled."

"I'm glad to hear it," he murmured. Steffie could picture him sprawled comfortably on his sofa, talking to her, a glass of wine in his hand.

"Be warned, you have only one wish left."

"Give me a moment—I want to make this good. I've had two glasses of wine and in case you haven't noticed, I'm feeling kind of mellow."

"I noticed." She smiled to herself.

"Know what I'd like?"

"You tell me," she teased.

"With my last wish, I'd like to wipe out the past."

"That one's easy," she said, and even though he couldn't see her, she made a sweeping motion with her hand. "There. It's gone, forgotten, never to be discussed again."

"Uh-oh. I think I made a mistake."

"Why's that?"

"We can't sweep it away."

"Why not?" she asked, striving for a flippant air. "It was one of your wishes, and it's in my power to grant it, so I have."

"But I don't want it wiped out *completely.* Let's talk about it now, Stephanie, get this over with once and for all."

Steffie's heart jolted. "Sorry, it's gone, vanished. I haven't a clue what you're talking about." Willfully she lowered her voice, half pleading with him, not wanting anything to ruin these moments.

The silence stretched between them. "You're right, this isn't something we can discuss over the phone. Certainly not when I'm half drunk and you're so far away."

"You're tired."

"It's funny," Charles told her, and she could hear the satisfaction in his voice. "I'm so exhausted I'm dead on my feet, and at the same time I feel so elated I want to take you in my arms and whirl you around the room."

"You never once mentioned buying the paper." She didn't mean it as a criticism. But he'd managed to keep it a secret not only from her, but from just about everyone in town. When Steffie had mentioned Charles's news to her father, he'd been as pleasantly surprised as she.

"I couldn't, but believe me, I was dying to tell you. Negotiations can be tricky. I was prohibited from saying anything until I'd reached an agreement with Dalton Publishing and the financing had been arranged."

Steffie snuggled down against her pillows. "So much is happening in our lives. First there was Dad's heart attack, and now Valerie's wedding. Oh, Charles, I wish you were here to see Valerie. I didn't know anything in the world could fluster my sister, but I was wrong. Being in love flusters her.

"I was with her Monday when she tried on wedding dresses. My practical, levelheaded older sister would stand in front of a mirror with huge tears running down her cheeks."

"She was crying?"

Steffie smiled at the memory. "Yes, but these were tears of joy. She never allowed herself to believe that Colby loved her enough to work through the things that stood between them. The two of them are so different, and that's been the problem all along. But neither of them seems to understand, even now, that it was those very differences that attracted them to each other."

"*We're* different."

His words gave Steffie pause. "I know but—"

"And I'm attracted to you, Stephanie. Very attracted."

It was ironic that she'd told him how love had completely unsettled her sister, only to be sitting on her own bed a few minutes later with the phone pressed against her ear and the tears sliding down her cheeks.

"Aren't you going to say anything?"

"Yes," she whispered in a trembling voice.

"Stephanie? What's wrong? You sound like you're crying."

"That's the silliest thing I ever heard," she rallied, rubbing her eyes with one hand.

"I wish I was there."

"Sorry," she said, laughing and crying at once, "you're flat out of wishes."

Eight

"More wine?" Charles asked, reaching for the bottle of Chablis in its silver bucket.

"No, thanks," Steffie said, smiling her appreciation. Their dinner had been delectable. It was one meal she wouldn't soon forget, although it was Charles's company that would linger in her mind more than the excellent halibut topped with bay shrimp.

"How about dessert?"

Steffie pressed her hands to her stomach and slowly shook her head. "I couldn't."

"Me neither." He leaned against the back of his chair and gazed out the window to the Columbia River below. The gorge was in one of the most scenic parts of Oregon. Steffie had always loved this view of the mighty river coursing through a rock-bound corridor.

"I've looked forward to this evening for a long time," Charles said, turning back to her.

"I have, too." Until tonight, Steffie had only

dreamed of being with Charles like this. As his equal, an adult...a woman in love.

"I don't think I've ever seen you look more beautiful, Stephanie."

His words brought a flush of color to her cheeks. Steffie had dressed carefully, choosing an elegant Italian knit dress in a subdued shade of turquoise. Valerie had lent Steffie her pearl necklace and earrings, and Norah had contributed a splash of her most expensive perfume.

Her sisters and her father, too, had put a good deal of stock in this evening's date. Steffie wasn't sure what her family was expecting. No doubt some miracle. For herself, she was content just to spend the evening with Charles.

"You look wonderful yourself." She wasn't echoing his compliment, but was stating a fact. He'd worn a dark suit with a silk tie of swirling colors against a pale blue shirt.

"Then we must make an attractive couple tonight," Charles commented, rotating the wine goblet between his fingers.

"We must," Steffie agreed.

Charles finished off the last of his wine and set the glass aside. "You were generous enough to grant me three wishes the other night, remember?"

Steffie wasn't likely to forget. She felt warm and shivery inside whenever she thought about their late-night telephone conversation.

"Being the honorable gentleman I am, not to mention talented and handsome, as you so aptly pointed out, it seems only fair that I return the favor. You, my lady, are hereby granted three wishes."

"Anything I want?" Steffie cocked her head.

"Within reason. I'd be willing to drive you to Multnomah Falls to watch the water by moonlight, but I might have a bit of trouble if you decide you want world peace."

"The falls by moonlight?"

"I was hoping you'd ask for that one."

She blinked at the way he'd turned her question into a pre-approved wish. "Charles," she said, "you're a romantic."

"Don't sound so shocked."

"But I am. I'd never have guessed it."

She was teasing him, and enjoying it and was surprised when he frowned briefly. "That's because we've never discussed what happened—"

"Not tonight," she said, holding a finger to his lips. "It's one of my wishes. We'll discuss nothing unpleasant."

His frown deepened. "I think we should. There's a lot we—"

"You're the one who granted me three wishes," she reminded him solemnly.

He nodded, his expression somewhat disgruntled. "You're right, I did, and if you want to squander one of your wishes, then far be it from me to stop you."

"It's too lovely a night to dredge up the past, especially when it's so embarrassing. Let's just look forward—"

"Fine," Charles agreed quickly and turned to thank

their waiter when he brought two cups of steaming coffee to the table. "We'll just look ahead. Now, remember you have one remaining wish."

Steffie hesitated. "Do I have to claim it now?"

"No, but the wishes expire at midnight."

Steffie laughed softly. "You make me feel like Cinderella."

"Perhaps that's because I'd like to be your prince."

His gaze was dark and unguarded. Steffie lowered her eyes, for fear he'd read all the love that was stored in her heart.

"Do I frighten you?" he asked after a moment.

Steffie's eyes flew back to his. "No. I thought I frightened you!"

He laughed outright at that. "Not likely."

They drank their coffee in silence, as though afraid words would destroy the mood. After Charles had paid the bill, he drove toward Multnomah Falls, managing the twisting narrow highway with ease. Steffie had visited the Falls many times, but had always been a bit scared of the drive. However, Charles took the sharp turns in slow, controlled moves, and she relaxed, enjoying the trip.

The rock walls along the road were built of local basalt more than seventy years earlier, during the Depression.

"I love this place," Charles said as they reached the parking area across the roadway from the waterfall. Because it was a weeknight, there were only a few cars in the lot.

Dusk was settling, and the tall, stately firs border-

ing the falls were silhouetted against the backdrop of
a cloud-dappled sky. The forested slopes were already
dark as Steffie and Charles began the gradual, wind-
ing ascent to the visitors' viewpoint.

A chill raced down her arms and Steffie was grateful she'd brought a thin coat with her. Multnomah Falls
was Oregon's highest waterfall, plummeting more than
six hundred feet into a swirling pool, then slipping
downward in a second, shorter descent. The force of
the falling water misted the night.

With his hand at her elbow, Charles guided them to
the walkway that wove up the trail. When they got to
the footbridge that spanned the falls, Steffie stopped
to gaze at the magnificence around her. The sound of
falling water roared in her ears.

"If we wait a few minutes, the moon will hit the
water," Charles told her. He stood behind her, shield-
ing her from the wind that whipped across the water's
churning surface.

Steffie closed her eyes. Not to the beauty of the
scene before her, but to the sensation she experienced
in Charles's protective embrace.

"I've dreamed of holding you like this," he whispered. "Of wrapping my arms around you and feeling you next to me. I love the way your hair smells. It
reminds me of wildflowers and sunshine."

Steffie couldn't speak. She couldn't get even one
word past the knot in her throat. She swallowed and
slowed her breathing, hoping that might help, because
there was so much she longed to say, so many things
she yearned to tell him.

"I don't ever want to be separated from you again," Charles told her, his voice raw.

She didn't understand. Charles had all but sent her away. He'd all but cast her out of his life. She turned in his arms until they faced each other and raised her hands to his face.

Charles smiled then and gently gripped her wrists. He moved his head until his mouth met the sensitive skin of her palm, and he kissed her there.

"You know, three years ago there was so much I couldn't tell you," he began.

"I have one wish left," she reminded him. "I want you to kiss me. Now."

"With pleasure." She could hear the smile in his voice.

They'd kissed before, but they'd never shared what they did in those moments. Charles's lips found hers in the sweetest, most loving exchange she'd ever experienced, and Steffie's emotions exploded to life.

Steffie wanted this, wanted it more than anything she'd ever known, yet at the same time she felt overwhelmed by confusion. Charles had ordered her out of his life, laughed at her declaration of love, humiliated her until she couldn't bear to live in the same town. Now, he seemed to be suggesting that he *hadn't* wanted her to go, and that he never wanted her to leave again.

Steffie wasn't sure what to believe. With all her heart she longed to lose herself in Charles's kiss, to savor all the sensations that flooded her. And yet the uncertainty remained. Did he merely desire her, or did he, too, feel a forever kind of love?

But his kiss wiped out all thought as the joy rushed through her, replacing fear and doubt.

"Someone's coming," Charles whispered suddenly. He broke away, still holding her shoulders, and brushed his mouth against her forehead. Then he released her.

Steffie's father was sitting by the fireplace in his den when she let herself into the house later that night. She saw the lamplight spilling into the entryway and decided to check on him.

"Dad?" David was sitting in the wingback leather chair beside the fireplace, her mother's afghan tucked around his legs. His head drooped and his lips were slightly parted.

Steffie had spoken before she realized he was asleep. But just as she turned to tiptoe from the room, he stirred.

"Steffie?"

"I didn't mean to wake you," she told him quietly.

"Good thing you did. I was waiting up for you." He ran one hand through his hair and sat up straighter. "How was your dinner with Charles?"

Steffie sank onto the ottoman, angling her legs to one side. She knew her eyes had a dreamy look, but she didn't care. "Wonderful."

"Did Charles ask you anything?"

"Ask me anything?" she repeated, feigning ignorance. "What could he possibly have to ask me?"

David Bloomfield frowned. "Plenty. I thought—I hoped he was going to mention…an upcoming event."

"Oh, that!" she said with a light disinterested laugh. If the evening hadn't been so wonderful, she would've felt irritated with his pressure tactics. But she found it impossible to complain when she was this happy.

"He did, you mean? And what did you tell him? Don't keep me in suspense, Princess."

Steffie splayed her fingers and studied the smoothly polished nails before sighing. "I told him we'll see about it on Sunday."

"Sunday? You're going to keep that boy in agony until Sunday?"

She nodded, affecting a complete lack of concern. "He wanted to know if we could go horseback riding, and I said we could probably do it on Sunday. That's the question you're referring to, isn't it?"

"No," came his disappointed reply. "And well you know it. I expected that boy to ask you to marry him."

"Well, he didn't and even if he had—"

"Even if he had, what?" The frown slid back into place. "I tell you, Stephanie, you're as stubborn as your mother when it comes to this sort of thing. You can't fool me—you've been in love with Charles for years. If he asks you to marry him—"

"But he hasn't and from what I could see, he doesn't have any intention of doing so."

"I don't agree."

"You're free to think what you want, Dad, but keep in mind that this is *my* life and I won't take kindly to your interfering in it. And remember that Charles values his privacy, too."

"He didn't ask you to marry him," her father muttered under his breath. "You don't think he intends to, either?" he demanded, louder now.

"Not to my knowledge."

A look of righteous indignation came over him. "Then I'd better have a talk with that boy. I won't allow him to trifle with your affections."

"Dad!" Steffie had trouble not laughing over the old-fashioned terms he used. She was sure Charles would find it humorous, too, if she suggested he was "trifling" with her heart.

"I mean it, Steffie. I refuse to let that young man hurt you again."

"He only has that power if I give it to him—which I won't. You're looking at a woman of the twenty-first century, Dad, and we're too smart to let a man *trifle* with us."

"Nevertheless, I'm having a talk with him."

Her expression might have been outwardly serene, but Steffie's insides were dancing a wild jig. "You'll do no such thing," she insisted.

"Apparently Charles Tomaselli doesn't know what's good for him."

"Dad! We talked about this before, remember?" Her good mood was quickly evaporating. "Now I want you to promise you're not going to interfere with Charles and me."

Her father refused to answer.

"I'll be mortified if you even bring up the subject of marriage to him."

"But—"

"I'm trusting you, Dad. Now good night." She stood and kissed his forehead before hurrying up the stairs to her own bedroom.

"I appreciate the ride to the airport," Valerie said as they drove out of town early Saturday afternoon. Her sister's flight was scheduled to leave at six, which gave them plenty of time for a leisurely trip into Portland. Valerie was going to meet with Rowdy Cassidy to tell him about her engagement and request a job transfer.

"I'm glad to do it," Steffie assured her older sister. Now that Valerie had set the preparations for her wedding in motion, she was free to return to Texas. There were several tasks, besides the discussion with Cassidy, that she needed to take care of. She had to pack her personal things, deal with her furniture and put her condo on the market.

"Colby wanted to come with me, but his schedule's full," she explained wistfully. "That's something we'll both have to adjust to."

"Heavy schedules?"

Valerie nodded. "I'll talk to Rowdy about that while I'm in Houston."

"Do you think he'll agree to let you head up the West Coast branch of CHIPS?"

"It's hard to say.... I don't think he's going to be pleased about my wanting to leave Houston, but he hasn't got a choice." Steffie noticed a hesitancy in her sister that she hadn't seen earlier. "Rowdy can be hard to predict," Valerie added. "He might be absolutely delighted for me and Colby. But there's also a chance that he'll be angry I took an extended leave of absence to plan my wedding." She sighed. "I didn't tell him the whole truth about why I didn't return the day I said I would."

"Why not?" Steffie prodded, briefly taking her eyes from the road when Valerie didn't immediately offer the information.

"I know I should have, but it just didn't seem right to do it over the phone. Besides, I'm afraid Rowdy might be…have been interested in me himself. At one point, I even thought I was interested in him! Good heavens, I didn't know a thing about love until I met Colby. I don't mean to hurt Rowdy's feelings but I can't give him any hope."

"Do you want me to fly back with you?"

"Oh, no. Rowdy's really a gentleman beneath that cowboy exterior."

Steffie's suspicions were raised. "Does the good doctor know how Rowdy feels about you?"

"I think he might. Then again, we've never really discussed Rowdy, and why should we? If you want the truth, I think Colby would rather forget about him."

"Maybe he should take his head out of the sand."

"Don't you go saying anything to him," Valerie said vehemently. "I mean it, Steff. What happens between Rowdy and me is between Rowdy and me."

"Is Colby the jealous type?" Steffie remembered how she'd felt the day she saw Charles standing next to Wendy, the intern at the *Clarion*. Until that moment, she'd never thought of herself as jealous. Even now the blood simmered in her veins when she recalled how the little blonde had gazed up at Charles, her blue eyes wide with open admiration.

"I don't know if Colby is or not. I only know how I'd feel if the situation was reversed." Valerie seemed to consider her next words. "Before Colby and I became engaged he was dating a nurse named Sherry Waterman, a friend of Norah's. Apparently he'd been going out with her for quite a while. Everyone was expecting them to announce their engagement. Norah seemed to feel otherwise, but that's another story."

"I swear Norah's got a sixth sense about these things."

Valerie nodded. "I think she does, too. At any rate, Colby and I decided that although we were attracted to each other, a long-term relationship was out of the question. Colby...asked me to hurry up and leave because my staying made everything so much more painful for us both."

"He didn't!" Steffie was outraged. "It's a good thing he didn't say that around me."

Valerie laughed. "He didn't really mean it. Oh, maybe he did at the time, but I didn't make falling in love easy for either of us."

Valerie's stubbornness was a trait the three Bloomfield sisters shared, Steffie thought with a small, rueful grin.

"After we talked, Colby started dating Sherry again. I think they went out four or five nights in a row. I didn't know about it, but in a way, I guess I did. I certainly wasn't surprised when I heard.

"Poor Norah felt she had to let me know what was happening. I think it was harder on her than on me."

"Were you jealous?"

"That's the funny part," Valerie said pensively. "At first I was so jealous I wanted to scratch Sherry's eyes out. I fantasized about hunting down Colby Winston and making him suffer."

"You should've asked me to help you. I'd gladly have volunteered."

Valerie smiled and patted Steffie's forearm. "Spoken like a true sister, but as I said that was my *first* reaction. What I found interesting was that it didn't last.

"I sat down and thought about it and realized how selfish and unfair I was being to Colby. If I truly loved him, I should want him to have whatever made him happy. If that meant marriage to Sherry Waterman, then so be it."

"In other words you were willing to let him go."

"Yes. And that was a turning point for me. Don't misunderstand me, it hurt more than anything I've ever done. Remember the day I was supposed to fly back to Houston?"

Steffie wasn't likely to forget it. "Of course."

"When I got ready to leave, I really had to work at controlling myself. I wasn't sure I could make it down the front steps without bursting into tears."

"I knew you were upset…."

"Naturally, Colby would have to choose right then to stop in for a visit. That man's sense of timing is going to be a problem." Valerie shook her head in mock exasperation.

Steffie laughed. Give Valerie a week and she'd have Colby's life completely reorganized.

"Somehow I managed to pull it off," Valerie continued. "I remember sitting in the car and—this is odd—I felt a sense of peace. I don't know if I can explain it. I felt this incredible...nobility. Don't you dare laugh, Steffie, I'm serious. I didn't stop loving Colby—if anything, I loved him more. Here I was, willingly walking away from the first man I'd ever loved."

"I wanted to throttle Colby about then."

Valerie grinned. "I remember learning about the tragic hero in my college literature courses. In some ways, I felt like I qualified for the tragic heroine."

"You weren't sorry you'd fallen in love with him, were you?"

"No, I was grateful. I was leaving him and at the same time I was giving him permission to find his own joy. And like I said, that somehow...ennobled me."

Steffie recalled the farewell scene on her front porch when she'd been so angry with Colby. "I...don't know if I could be that noble about Charles."

"What's happening with the two of you?"

"I'm not sure." Steffie was being entirely honest. "We had a wonderful dinner on Thursday, then we drove to Multnomah Falls and watched the moonlight on the water."

"That sounds so romantic."

"It was. We walked up to the footbridge and... talked."

"I'll bet!" Valerie laughed.

"We did—only we did more kissing than talking."

Steffie knew that Charles had wanted to talk, wanted to discuss the past with her. She hated the thought of reliving all that pain. But more than anything she dreaded examining her utterly ridiculous behavior. Every time she recalled the scene in his bathroom, with her playing the role of waterlogged enchantress, she burned with humiliation. Someday they'd talk about it, but not now. It was too soon.

"Dad seems to think you two will get married."

This discussion was a repeat of the one she'd had with her father every day for the past two weeks. "You know Dad when he's got a bee in his bonnet. I've had to make him promise not to say a word about marriage to Charles."

"Do you really believe he listened to you?" Valerie asked.

"I hope so," she muttered.

Valerie frowned as she turned to stare out the car window. Steffie's hands tightened on the steering wheel and she glanced around her. Wild rhododendrons blossomed along the side of the road, their bright pink flowers a colorful contrast to the lush green foliage.

"I'm worried about Dad."

Valerie's words surprised Steffie. "Why? He's getting stronger every day. His recovery is nothing short of miraculous. I've heard you say so yourself, at least a dozen times."

"All right, I'll rephrase that. I'm worried for you."

"Me? Whatever for?" As far as Steffie was concerned, her life had rarely been better. She'd applied for late admission to the Ph.D. program and planned to begin researching thesis topics soon. As for Charles... well, things were wonderful. Yes, she still had a lot of murky ground to cover with him, but there'd be time for that later.

"Dad's riding high on success," Valerie reminded her. "He seems to think that because everything fell into place with Colby and me, it should for you and Charles, as well. Remember he's supposed to have dreamed all this."

"I know. We've had our go-arounds on that issue. He's told me at least twice a day for the past two weeks that I'm going to marry Charles by the end of the summer. Now I just smile and nod and let him think what he wants."

"It doesn't bother you?"

"It drives me nuts." Possibly because she wanted to believe it so badly...

"Aren't you nervous that Dad's going to get impatient and say something to Charles?"

"No," Steffie answered automatically. "Dad and I've been over this. He knows better than to say anything to Charles."

Valerie nodded. "I wish I shared your confidence."

Steffie put on a good front for the remainder of the drive, but she was growing more and more concerned. She knew one thing; she didn't have the personality to take on the role of tragic heroine. She'd leave that to her older, wiser sister.

As soon as Valerie had checked in for her flight to Texas, Steffie headed back to Orchard Valley. As the minutes ticked away, she became increasingly anxious to get home.

It was just like Valerie to plant the seeds of doubt and then fly off, leaving Steffie to deal with the result—a garden full of weeds!

When she pulled into the driveway, Steffie experienced an immediate sense of relief. Her world was in order; her fears shrank to nothing. All was well. Her father was rocking on the front porch, the way he did every evening. He smiled and waved when he saw her.

"Hello, good-lookin'," she said as she climbed out of the car. "How was your day?"

"I had a great afternoon. Every day's wonderful now that I've got all these reasons to live. Oh, before I forget, Charles stopped by to see you. Guess he must've been in the neighborhood again." A smile twinkled from her father's eyes. "You might want to call him. I suspect he's waiting to hear from you."

Steffie froze. Doubt sprang to new life. "You didn't say anything to him about…what we discussed, did you?"

"Princess, I didn't say a word you wouldn't want me to."

"You're sure?"

"As positive as I'm sitting here."

Steffie went inside the house, reassured by her father's words. Norah was busy in the kitchen, kneading bread dough on a lightly floured countertop.

"Did you happen to see Charles?" Steffie asked in passing. She opened the refrigerator and removed a cold soda.

"He stopped by earlier and sat on the porch with Dad. I think he was here for about fifteen minutes."

Steffie swallowed a long cool drink. "I'll give him a call."

"Good idea."

She waited until she was in her room, then sat on her bed and reached for the phone. Although it had been several years since she'd called Charles, she still remembered his number. The same way she remembered everything else about him.

He must have been sitting by the phone, because he answered even before the first ring was finished.

"Charles, hello," she said happily. "Dad said you came by."

"Yes, I did."

His voice was cool, and Steffie paused as the dread took hold inside her. "Is something wrong?"

"Not wrong, exactly. I guess you could say I'm disappointed. I thought you'd changed, Steffie. I thought you'd grown up and stopped your naive tricks. But I was wrong, wasn't I?"

Nine

"Dad!" Steffie struggled to keep the anger and distress from her voice. She hurried to the porch, her fists clenched against her sides. "You told me...you promised..." She hesitated. "What *exactly* did you say to Charles?"

Her father glanced upward momentarily, clearly puzzled. "Nothing drastic, I assure you. Is it important?"

"Yes, it's important! I need to know." She had to call on every ounce of self-control not to shout at him and demand an explanation. She longed to chastise him for doing the very thing she'd begged him not to.

"You look upset, Princess."

"I am upset and I'm sure you know why... Just tell me what you said to Charles."

"Sit down a bit and we'll talk."

Steffie did as her father requested, sitting on the top porch step near his chair and leaning back against the white pillar. "Charles stopped in this afternoon, right?"

"Yes, and we had a nice chat. He tried to make me think he was here to visit me, but I saw through that." Her father's smile told Steffie all she needed to know. For one angry second, she thought he resembled a spider, waiting patiently for someone to step into his web.

"Obviously I was the subject under discussion, wasn't I?" She forced herself not to yell, not to rant and rave at a man so recently released from the hospital.

Her father rocked back and forth a few times, then nodded. "We talked about you."

Steffie closed her eyes, her frustration mounting. "I see. And what did the two of you come up with?"

"Let me tell you what Charles said first."

She balled her hands into fists again, praying for patience. *"What did he say?"*

"Well, Charles stopped by, as I said, pretending it was me he was here to visit, when we both knew he was coming to see you. I went along with it for a while, then asked him flat out what his intentions were toward you. I fully expected you to be wearing an engagement ring by now, and I let him know it."

"Dad!" Without meaning to, Steffie sprang to her feet. "You breached a trust! I trusted you to keep your word, not to talk to Charles about this. And now you pass it off as…as nothing. Don't you realize what you've done?"

For the first time he looked chagrined. "I did it because I love you, Princess."

"Oh, Dad…you've made everything so much more difficult."

"Aren't you interested in what he had to say?" His smile was bright and cocky again. "Well, aren't you? Now sit back down and I'll tell you."

"Oh, all right." She sighed, lowering herself onto the porch step, her legs barely able to support her. She was shaking with trepidation.

"Charles seemed more concerned with the fact that I'd asked than with answering the question. To be perfectly honest, Princess, he wasn't overly pleased with me."

"I can't believe he even answered you."

"Of course he did. He said if the subject of marriage did come up, then it was between the two of you, and not the three of us. It was a good response."

"You never should've said *anything* about us marrying."

"Well, Princess, the way I figured it, he was going to pop the question, anyway. Besides, I don't want Charles leading you on, or hurting you again."

"Dad, you've made it nearly impossible for me now and—"

"Let me finish, because there's more to tell you." But after silencing her, he went strangely quiet himself.

"Go on," she urged, clenching her jaw.

"I'm just trying to think of a way to tell you this without annoying you even more. I told Charles something you didn't want me to tell him."

"The dream?" The question came out a whisper. "But you said you hadn't told Charles anything I wouldn't want you to. And before—you *promised* you wouldn't mention marriage!"

"No, Princess, I never did promise. I took it under consideration, but not once did I actually say I wouldn't discuss this with Charles. Now don't look so worried. I didn't tell him a thing about talking to your mother or about the three precious children the two of you are going to have someday."

"What did Charles say? No," she amended quickly, "tell me *exactly* what you said first."

"Well, like I already told you, we were chatting—"

"Get to the part where you brought up marriage."

"All right, all right. But I want you to know I didn't say anything about the dream. Not because you didn't want me to, but because when it came right down to it, I didn't think he'd believe me. You three girls are having trouble enough, so I can hardly expect someone outside the family to listen."

"You told Colby about it."

"Of course I did. He's my doctor. He had a right to know."

"Great. In other words you blurted out that you expected Charles to marry me—because you didn't want him trifling with my heart?" Spoken aloud, it sounded so ludicrous. Not to mention insulting. No wonder Charles was cool toward her.

"Not exactly. I asked his intentions. He said that was between the two of you. As I already explained."

"Good." Steffie relaxed a little. "And that was the end of it?" she murmured hopefully.

"Not entirely."

"What else is there?"

"I told him you were anticipating a proposal of marriage, and for that matter so was I."

Steffie ground her teeth to keep from screaming. It was worse than she'd feared. Sagging against the pillar, she covered her face with both hands. It would've been far better had he told Charles about the dream. That way, Charles might have understood that she'd had nothing to do with this. Instead, her father had made everything ten times worse by *not* mentioning it.

Charles was angry with her; that was obvious from their telephone conversation. He'd refused to discuss it in any detail, just repeating that he was "disappointed." He seemed to believe she'd manipulated her father into approaching him with this marriage business. He wasn't likely to change his mind unless she could convince him of the truth.

"Where are you going?" her father asked when she left him and returned a moment later with her purse and a sweater.

"To talk to Charles—to explain things, if I can."

"Good." David's grin was full. "All that boy needs is a bit of prompting. You'll see. Once you get back, you'll thank me for taking matters into my own hands. There's something about making a commitment to the right woman that fixes everything."

Steffie was drained from the emotion. She found she couldn't remain angry with her father. He'd talked to Charles with the best of motives. And he didn't know what had gone on between her and Charles in the past—the tricks she'd played. So he couldn't possibly understand why Charles would react with such anger to being pressed on the issue of marriage.

"I'll wait up for you and when you get home we'll celebrate together," he suggested.

Steffie grinned weakly and nodded, but she doubted there'd be anything to celebrate.

She took her time driving into town, using those minutes to organize her thoughts. She hoped Charles would be open-minded enough to accept her explanation. Mostly, she wanted to reassure him that she hadn't talked her father into interrogating him about marriage. They'd come so far in the past few weeks, she and Charles, and Steffie didn't want anything to spoil that.

Charles was waiting for her, or he seemed to be. She'd barely rung his doorbell when he answered.

"Hello." His immediate appearance took her by surprise. "I—I thought it might be a good idea if the two of us sat down and talked."

"Fine." He didn't smile, didn't show any sign of pleasure at seeing her.

"Dad told me he talked to you about…the two of us marrying." The words felt awkward on her tongue.

"He did mention something along those lines," Charles returned stiffly.

He hadn't asked her to make herself comfortable or invited her to sit down. It didn't matter, though, since she couldn't stand still, anyway. She paced from one side of his living room to the other. She felt strangely chilled, despite the warm spring weather.

"You think I put Dad up to it, don't you?"

"Yes," he said frankly.

He stood rooted to the same spot while she drifted, apparently aimlessly, around the room. His look, everything about him, wasn't encouraging. Perhaps she should have delayed this, let them both sleep on it, instead of forcing the issue. Perhaps she should've dropped the whole thing, and let this misunderstanding sort itself out. Perhaps she should go home now before the situation got even worse.

"I didn't ask Dad to say anything to you," she told him simply.

"I wish I could believe that."

"Why can't you? This is ridiculous! If you intend to drag the past into every disagreement, punish me for something that happened three years ago, then—"

"I'm not talking about three years ago. I'm talking about here and now."

"What do you mean?"

"I'll say this for you, Steffie, you've gotten a lot more subtle."

"How...do you mean?"

"First, you park in front of the newspaper office just as I happen to—"

"When?"

"Last week. I was talking to Wendy, and when I looked up, I saw you sitting in your car, staring at us. Just how long had you been there?"

"I...don't know."

"Now that I think about it, I realize what a fool I've been. You've been spying on me for weeks, haven't you?"

The idea was so outlandish that Steffie found herself laughing incredulously. Nothing she said would make any difference, not if he believed what he was saying. Because if he did, there was nothing of their relationship left to salvage.

"There's no fooling you, is there?" she threw out sarcastically. "You're much too smart for me, Charles. I've been hiding around town for days, following you with binoculars, charting your activities. It's amazing you didn't catch on sooner."

He ignored her scornful remarks. "Very convenient the way you twisted your ankle the other day, too, wasn't it? Somehow you managed to fall directly into my arms."

"The timing was perfect, wasn't it?" she said with a short, humorless laugh. "You're right, I couldn't have planned that any better."

He frowned. "Then there was the dinner waiting for me at the house the other night. Italian, too, just the way my grandmother used to make it."

"Interesting how I knew that, huh?"

"All of this adds up to one thing."

"And what might that be?" she asked scathingly, folding her arms. She'd assumed far too much in this relationship. She'd lowered her guard and actually believed Charles loved her, because she loved him so deeply. Now she understood how wrong she'd been.

"It adds up to the fact that you're playing games again."

"Don't forget the moonlight the evening we were at Multnomah Falls. I arranged that, too. I have to admit it took some doing."

"There's no need to be sarcastic."

"I don't agree," she returned defiantly.

Charles frowned and muttered something she couldn't hear.

"I must say I'm surprised you caught on so quickly, what with me being so subtle and all."

"Let's clear the air once and—"

"But the air *is* clear," she said, waving her arms wildly. She knew she was going too far with this, but the momentum was building and she couldn't seem to stop. "I've been found out, and now it's all over."

"Over?"

"Of course. There's no need to pretend anymore."

"What are you talking about?"

"Revenge. It's supposed to be sweet, and it would've been if you hadn't caught on when you did."

"Just what did you intend to do?" he demanded.

"You mean you don't have that figured out, as well?"

"Tell me, Stephanie." His voice was hard as ice and just as cold.

"Fine, if you must know. Once I got you to the point of proposing—" she paused dramatically "—I was going to laugh and reject you. It seems only fair after the way you humiliated me. You laughed at me,

Charles, and it was going to be my turn to laugh at you. Only you found me out first...."

His frown deepened into a scowl. "Your father—"

"Oh, don't worry, he didn't know anything about that part. Getting him to shame you into a marriage proposal was tricky, but I managed it by telling him I was afraid you were...trifling with my affections." She gave a deep exaggerated sigh, astonished that he seemed to believe all this.

"I see."

"Oh, you're too clever for me, Charles. What can I possibly say?"

"Perhaps it would be best if you left now."

"I think you're right. Well, at least you know what it feels like to have someone laugh at you."

Charles walked to his front door and held it open for her. With a jaunty step, Steffie walked out of his house. "Well, I'll see you around, but you don't need to worry—I won't be spying on you anymore."

His jaw was clamped tightly shut, and Steffie realized she'd succeeded beyond all her expectations. Charles was disgusted with her. And furious. So furious that he couldn't get her out of his home fast enough.

"You can't blame a girl for trying," she said with a shrug once she'd slipped past him.

In response, Charles slammed his door.

By the time Steffie was inside the car, she was shaking so badly that she could hardly insert the key into the ignition. Her breath seemed to be trapped in her chest, creating a painful need to exhale.

Like Charles, she was angry, angrier than she'd ever been in her life. In one rational corner of her mind, she knew—had known all along—that it was a mistake to goad him with all those ridiculous lies.

But the shocking thing, the sad thing, was that he'd believed them. To his way of thinking, apparently, it all fit. And as far as Steffie was concerned, there was nothing more to say.

In time, she'd regret her outburst, but she didn't then. At that moment, she was far too infuriated to care. In time, she'd regret the lies, the squandered hopes—but it wouldn't be soon.

"Well?" her father asked, his expression pleased and expectant as she let herself into the house an hour later. "Are you two going to look for an engagement ring in the next few days?"

"Not exactly," Steffie said, moving into his den. As he'd promised earlier, her father was waiting up for her, reading in his favorite chair.

His face fell with disappointment. "But you did talk about getting married, didn't you?"

"Not really. We, uh, got sidetracked."

"You didn't argue, did you?"

"Not really." Steffie was unsure how much to tell him. She worried that if he knew the extent of the rift between her and Charles, he'd feel obliged to do something to patch things up.

David set aside his reading glasses and gazed up at her. "You'll be seeing him again soon, won't you?"

Living in Orchard Valley made that very likely. It

was the reason she'd chosen to study in Europe three years earlier. "Naturally I'll be seeing him."

David nodded, appeased. "Good."

"I think I'll go up to my room and read. Good night, Dad."

"Night, Princess."

On her way up, Steffie met Norah at the top of the stairs. Her younger sister glanced in her direction and did an automatic double take. "What's wrong?"

"What makes you think anything's wrong?"

"You mean other than the fact that you look like you're waiting to get to your room before you cry?"

Her sister knew her too well. Steffie felt terrible—discouraged, disheartened, depressed. But in her present mood, she didn't have the patience to explain what had happened between her and Charles.

"What could possibly be wrong?" Steffie asked instead, feigning a lightness she didn't feel.

"Funny you should say that," Norah said, tucking her arm through Steffie's and leading the way to her bedroom. "Valerie asked me nearly the same thing not long ago. What could possibly be wrong? Well, I'd have to say it's probably trouble with a man."

"Very astute of you."

"Obviously it's Charles." Norah didn't react to Steffie's mild sarcasm.

"Obviously." She was tired, weary right down to her bones and desperately craving a long, hot soak in the tub. Some of her best thinking was accomplished while lazing in a bathtub filled with scented water.

She'd avoided bubble baths since the time she'd spent hours in one waiting for Charles.

"Did you two have a spat?"

"Listen, Norah, I appreciate your concern—really, I do… I don't mean to sound ungrateful, but I'm tired and I want to go to bed."

"Bed? Good grief, it's only seven."

"It's been a long day."

Norah eyed her suspiciously. "It must have been."

"Besides, I have a lot to do on Monday."

Norah's interest was piqued. "What's happening then?"

"I'm going to Portland to see about my application at the university and to find an apartment."

For a moment Norah said nothing. Her mouth fell open and she wore a stunned look. "But I thought you told Dad you were going to wait on that."

"I was…"

"But now you aren't? Even after you promised Dad?"

Steffie glanced away, not wanting her sister to see how deeply hurt she was. How betrayed she felt that Charles would believe she was deceitful enough to trick him into marriage. It seemed that whenever Charles Tomaselli was involved, she invariably ended up in pain.

"I feel better than I have in years." David greeted Steffie cheerfully early the next morning. He was sitting at the kitchen table, drinking a cup of coffee and studying the Portland Sunday paper. He welcomed her with a warm smile, apparently not noticing his daughter's lackluster mood. "Beautiful morning," David added.

"Beautiful," Steffie mumbled as she poured herself a cup of coffee and staggered to the table. Her eyes burned from lack of sleep, and she felt as though she was walking around in a nightmare.

She'd spent the entire night arguing with herself about the lies she'd told Charles. In the end, she'd managed to convince herself that she'd done the right thing. Charles *wanted* to believe every word. He'd seized every one of her sarcastic remarks, all too ready to consider them truth.

"What time will Charles be by?" her father asked conversationally.

"Charles?" She repeated his name as though she'd never heard it before.

"I thought the two of you were going horseback riding this afternoon."

"Uh… I'm not sure Charles will be able to come, after all." The date had probably slipped his mind, the way it had hers. Even if he did remember, Steffie sincerely doubted he'd show up. As far as she was concerned, whatever had been between them was now over. In fact, the more she reviewed their last discussion, the angrier she became. If he honestly believed the things she'd suggested—and he certainly seemed to—then there was no hope for them. None.

"I'll get dressed for church," Steffie said bleakly.

"You've got plenty of time yet."

"Norah has to get there early." Her sister sang in

the choir. Generally Norah left the house before the others, but Steffie thought she'd ride with Norah this morning, if for no other reason than to escape her father's questions. From the looks David was giving her, he was about to subject her to a full-scale inquisition.

Attending church was an uplifting experience for Steffie. During that hour, she was able to forget her troubles and absorb the atmosphere of peace and serenity. Whatever solace she found, however, vanished the minute she and Norah drove into the yard shortly after noon.

Charles's car was parked out front.

Steffie tensed and released a long, slow sigh.

"Problems?" Norah asked.

"I don't know."

"Do you want to talk to him?"

"No, I don't." But at the same time, she wasn't about to back down, either. She wouldn't allow Charles to chase her from her own home. He was on her turf now, and she didn't run easily.

Steffie parked behind Charles's sports car and willed herself to remain calm and collected. Her father must have heard them because he stepped outside the house, his welcoming smile in place. He still moved slowly but with increasing confidence. It was sometimes hard to remember that he was recovering from major surgery.

"Steffie, Charles is here."

"So I see," she said with a distinct lack of enthusiasm.

"He's in the stable, waiting for you."

She nodded and, with her heart racing, walked up the steps and past her father.

"Aren't you going to talk to him?"

"I need to change my clothes first."

"To talk? But…" He hesitated, then reluctantly nodded.

By the time Steffie was in her bedroom, she was trembling. Her emotions were so confused that she wasn't sure if she was shaking with anger or with nervousness. But she did know she wasn't ready to face him, wasn't ready to deal with his accusations or his reproach. For several minutes she sat on her bed, trying to decide what to do.

"Steffie." Norah stood in the doorway, watching her. "Are you okay?"

"Of course, I—no, I'm not," she said. "I'm not ready to talk to Charles yet."

"Nothing says you have to talk to him if you don't want to. I'll make up some excuse and send him packing."

"No." For pride's sake, she didn't want him to know how badly she'd been hurt by their latest confrontation.

"You look like you're about to burst into tears."

Steffie squared her shoulders and met her sister's worried eyes. "I'm not going to give him the satisfaction."

"Attagirl," Norah said approvingly.

Changing into jeans and a sweatshirt, Steffie went down the back stairs into the kitchen. She didn't expect to find Charles sitting at the table chatting with her father. What unsettled her most was that he gave no outward sign of their quarrel. Steffie slowed her pace as she entered the room.

Charles stopped talking and his eyes narrowed briefly. "Hello, Stephanie."

"I'll leave you two alone," her father said before Steffie could answer Charles's greeting. He rose, a bit stiffly, and made his way to the door. "I guess you've got plenty to discuss."

Steffie wanted to argue, but knew there wasn't any point. She merely shrugged and remained where she was, standing a few steps from the back stairs. She didn't look at Charles. The silence between them lengthened, until she couldn't endure it any longer.

"I didn't expect you to come," she said in a harsh voice. "It certainly wasn't necessary."

"I'm aware of that."

"I'm not in the mood to go riding and I don't imagine you are, either." In other words, she wasn't in the mood to go riding with *him*.

"I'm not here to ride."

"Then why are you here?"

Apparently Charles didn't have the answer because he got to his feet and walked over to the window. Whatever he saw must have fascinated him because he stood there for several minutes without speaking.

"Why are you here?" she asked a second time, on the verge of requesting him to leave.

He finally turned around to face her. "I don't know about you, but I couldn't sleep last night."

Steffie refused to admit that she'd fared no better, so she made no response.

"I kept going over the things your father said and the things you told me," Charles went on.

"Did you come to any conclusions?" Pride demanded that she not look at him, or reveal how much his answer meant to her.

"One."

Steffie tensed. "What's that?" She had to look at him now.

His eyes finally met hers. Although nearly the entire kitchen separated them, Steffie felt as though he was close enough to touch.

"It seems to me," he began, "that since your father's so anxious to marry you off, and you seem to be just as eager, then fine."

"Fine?" she repeated, wondering if this was some joke and she'd missed the punch line.

"In other words," Charles returned shortly, "I'm willing to take you off his hands."

Ten

"What? Take me off Dad's hands?" Steffie echoed. Surely he wasn't serious. No woman in her right mind would accept such an insulting proposal.

"You heard me."

"Tell me you're kidding."

Charles shook his head. "I've never been more serious in my life. You want to marry me, then so be it. I'm willing to go along with this, provided we understand each other...."

"In that case I withdraw the offer—not that I ever *made* an offer."

"You can't do that," Charles argued, looking surprised. "Your father thinks we should get married and, after giving it some thought, I agree with him."

"That's too bad, since I'm not interested."

Charles laughed softly. "We both know that's not true. You've been crazy about me for years."

Steffie whirled around and crossed her arms, as

though to fend off his words. "I can't marry you, Charles."

"Why not? I know you love me. You said so yourself before you left for Italy, and I know that hasn't changed."

"Don't be so sure."

"Ah, but I am. And recently you showed me again."

"When?" she demanded, trying to recall the conversations they'd had since her return to Orchard Valley.

"The afternoon we met at Del's."

Steffie cast her mind back to that day. They'd met by accident as they'd gone in to pay for their gas. Steffie remembered how glad she'd been to see him, how eager to set things straight. But she couldn't remember saying one thing that would lead Charles to believe she still loved him.

"I didn't say anything."

"Not in so many words, true, but with everything you did. The same holds true for the night I dropped off the azalea and you asked me to dinner. Remember?"

"Yes, but what's that got to do with anything?"

"A whole lot, as a matter of fact. You were continually making excuses for us to be together."

Steffie's face flooded with color. "What's that got to do with anything?" she asked again.

He ignored her question. "We had fun that night, touring Orchard Valley. Didn't we?"

Steffie nodded. She wasn't likely to forget that evening. For the first time in her relationship with Charles, she'd felt a stirring of real promise. Not the kind of hope she'd fabricated earlier, but one based on genuine companionship. Charles had enjoyed her company and they'd laughed and talked as though they'd been friends for years.

"You told me that when you lived in Italy you were too busy with your studies to date much," Charles reminded her.

"So?"

"So that led me to conclude that you hadn't fallen in love with anyone else while you were away."

"I hadn't."

"Your father came right out and told me on several occasions that he was concerned about you because you didn't seem to be dating anyone seriously."

Steffie glared at him, feeling trapped. "I still don't understand what this has to do with anything."

"Plenty. You loved me then, and you love me now."

"You've got some nerve, Charles Tomaselli." She glowered fiercely, hoping he'd back off. "What makes you so sure I'm in love with you now?"

"I know you better than you realize."

"What nonsense!" She managed a light laugh. "You don't know me at all, otherwise you—" She stopped abruptly.

"Otherwise what?"

"Nothing." *Otherwise he wouldn't have believed the things she'd told him.*

"Don't you think it's time we stopped playing games with each other?" he suggested.

"What games?" she snapped. "I gave those up years ago."

Charles frowned as though he wasn't sure he should believe her.

Hurt and angry, Steffie raised her hand and pointed at him. "*That's* the reason I refuse to marry you," she cried. Restraining the emotion was next to impossible and her voice quavered with the force of it. "I suppose I should be flattered that you're *willing* to take me off Dad's hands," she said sarcastically. "Every woman dreams of hearing such romantic words. But I want far more in a husband, Charles Tomaselli, than you'd ever be capable of giving me!"

"What do you mean by that?" Before she had a chance to reply he muttered, "Oh, I get it. You're afraid I'm going to be financially strapped with the newspaper, aren't you? You think I won't be able to afford you."

Steffie was stunned by his remark. Stunned and insulted. "You know me so well, don't you?" she asked him, her voice heavy with scorn. "There's just no pulling the wool over your eyes, is there?" She drew in a deep breath. "I think it would be best if you left." She walked across the kitchen and held open the back door. "Right now."

Charles shook his head. "Sorry," he said. "I don't want to leave." He pulled out a chair and threw himself down. "We're going to talk this out, once and for all," he told her.

"You're too stubborn."

"So are you."

"We'd make a terrible couple."

"We make a good team."

Steffie didn't know why she was fighting him so hard—especially when he was saying all the things she'd always dreamed of hearing.

"I realize I've made some mistakes with this," he said slowly. "It might have sounded callous, offering to marry you the way I did."

"I'll admit that *taking me off Dad's hands* does lack a certain romantic flair," she agreed wryly. She crossed over to the counter for a coffee mug, filling it from the pot next to the stove. If they were going to talk seriously, without hurling accusations at each other, she was going to need it.

"I was angry."

"Then why'd you come here?" she asked, claiming the chair across from him.

"Because," he answered in a tight, angry voice, "I was afraid I'd lose you again."

"Lose me?" That made no sense to Steffie.

"You heard me," he growled. "I was afraid you'd return to Italy or take off on a safari, or go someplace equally inaccessible."

"Portland. I'm moving to Portland, but it isn't because of what happened with you. I intended to do that from the moment I got home." She folded her hands around the hot mug. "Why should you care where I go?"

"Because I didn't want you leaving again."

"Why do you want me to stay, especially if you believe the things I told you yesterday?"

His eyes held hers. "I don't believe them."

"You gave a good impression of it earlier," she reminded him. A fresh wave of pain assaulted her and she looked away.

"That's because I was furious."

"That hasn't changed."

"No, it hasn't," he agreed, "but the simple fact is I don't want you to leave again."

"Unfortunately you don't have any say in what I do."

Charles frowned. "Now *you're* angry."

"You're right about that! Did you really think I was so desperate for a husband I'd accept your insulting offer? Is that what you think of me, Charles?"

"No!" he shouted. "I'm in love with you, dammit! I have been for years. I had to do something to keep you here. I don't want to wait another three years for you to come to your senses."

His words were followed by silence. Steffie stared down into her coffee, and to her chagrin felt tears well up in her eyes. "I'm afraid I don't believe you."

Charles stood abruptly and walked to the window again. Hands clasped behind his back, he gazed outside. "It's true."

"It couldn't be." She wiped the tears from her face. "You were so...so..."

"Cruel," he supplied. "You'll never understand how hard it was not to make love to you that first time in the stable. I've never been more tempted by any woman."

"I...tempted you?" Her voice was low and incredulous.

He turned around and smiled, but it was a sad smile,

one full of doubts and regrets. "I remember when you started hanging around the newspaper office. I was flattered by the attention. Soon I found myself looking forward to the times you came by. You were witty and generous and you always had an intelligent comment about something in the paper. I quickly discovered you were much more than a pretty face."

"I never worked harder in my life to impress anyone," she murmured with self-deprecating humor.

But it didn't take Steffie long to get back to the point. "If that was how you felt, then why did you ask me not to come around anymore?"

"I had to say something before I gave in and threw caution to the wind. You'd recently lost your mother and you were young, naive and terribly vulnerable. I struggled with my conscience for weeks, trying to decide what I should do about you. In case you haven't noticed, I'm six years older than you. That made a big difference."

"The gap in our ages hasn't narrowed."

"True enough, but you're not a girl anymore."

"I was twenty-two," she argued. "At least by the time I left."

"Perhaps, but you'd been pretty sheltered. And you were still dealing with your grief. Your entire life had been jolted, and I couldn't be sure if what you felt for me was love or adolescent infatuation."

Steffie closed her eyes and let the warmth of his words revive her. "It was love," she told him. A love that had matured, grown more intense, in the years that separated them.

"It probably doesn't mean much to you now, but I want you to know how hard it was for me the night I came home and found you in my bathtub."

"But you were so angry."

"It was either that or take you into my room and make love to you."

Steffie still felt confused. "You laughed at me when I told you how I felt that day in the stable...."

"I know," he said simply. Steffie heard the pain and remorse in his voice. "I've never had to do anything that's cost me more. But I never dreamed you'd leave Orchard Valley."

"What did you expect me to do? I couldn't stay— that would've been impossible. So I did the only thing I could. I left."

Charles's hand reached for hers, twining their fingers together. "I'll never forget the day I learned you'd gone to Europe. I felt as if I'd been hit by a bulldozer."

"I had to go," she repeated unnecessarily. "It was too painful to stay."

His fingers tightened around hers. "I know." Slowly he raised her hand to his lips. "I've waited three long years to tell you how sorry I was to hurt you. Three years to tell you I was in love with you, too."

Steffie attempted with little success to blink back the tears.

"If it had been at any other time in your life, if I could've been sure you weren't just trying to replace your mother's love with mine—then everything would've been different. But you were so young, so innocent. I couldn't trust myself around you, feeling the way I did."

"And you couldn't trust me."

He nodded his agreement. "I'm sorry, Stephanie, for rejecting you. But it was as painful for me as it was for you. Perhaps more so, because I knew the whole truth."

"You never wrote—not once in all that time. Not so much as a postcard. Not even an email."

"I couldn't. I wanted to, but I didn't dare give in to the impulse."

"So you waited."

"Not patiently. I expected you to come home at least once in three years, you know."

"I dreaded seeing you again. I was thousands of miles away from you and yet I still loved you, I still dreamed about you. It didn't seem to get any better. Even after three years."

"A few weeks ago, you'd finished your classes and you were in the process of deciding if you were going to stay on in Italy."

"How'd you know that?"

"Your father. He was the only way I had of getting information about you, and I used him shamelessly."

"He told me you started coming by for visits shortly after I left."

"I'm surprised he didn't figure out how I felt about you. I don't think I could have been any more obvious if I'd tried."

"Dad didn't have a clue until recently and then only

because of the—" She stopped when she realized what she was about to tell him.

"Of what?" Charles prodded.

"I…it would be best if you let Dad explain that part."

"All right, I will." He looked away from her momentarily. "Although you never seriously dated anyone, there *was* someone in Italy, wasn't there? A man you cared about?"

"Who?" Steffie frowned in bewilderment.

"A man named Mario?"

"Mario…a man?" He was five now, and the delight of her heart while she'd lived in Italy.

"He caused me several sleepless nights. Your father only mentioned him once. Said you 'adored' him. I went through agonies trying to be subtle about getting information on this guy, but your father never brought him up again."

"Mario," Steffie repeated, smiling broadly. "Yes, I did adore him."

Charles scowled. "What happened?"

Still smiling, Steffie said, "There was a slight discrepancy in our ages. I'm more than twenty years older."

"He's a kid."

"But what a kid. My landlady's son. I was crazy about him." Spending time with a loving, open child like Mario had helped her through a difficult period in her life.

"I see." A slow, easy smile slipped into place. "So you like children."

"Oh, yes, I always have."

"I hope that young man appreciates everything he put me through."

"I'm sure he doesn't, but I certainly do. I know what it's like to love someone and have that someone not love you."

Charles considered her words for a moment. "I've always loved you, Stephanie, but I didn't dare let you know. I couldn't trust what we felt for each other then—but I can now."

She avoided his gaze. She had to ask, although she was afraid to. "If that's true, why were you so angry when Dad suggested we get married?"

Charles sighed. "Frustration, I guess. I'd intended to propose the night we went for dinner. I had everything planned, down to the last detail."

"But why didn't you?"

"I couldn't, not when the past still came between us. You made it clear you didn't want to discuss our misunderstandings. So my hands were tied. I hate to admit it, but I was nervous—even if you didn't seem to notice."

"I made it one of my wishes—I didn't want to talk about the past," she recalled, experiencing an instant twinge of regret.

"And I had to go along with it," he said.

"That still doesn't explain why you were so offended when Dad suggested we marry." His reaction was a mystery in light of the things he was telling her now.

"A man prefers to propose himself," Charles offered

as a simple explanation. "I don't think I could've made my intentions any plainer if I'd hired a skywriter. Then to have first your father and then you—"

"Me?"

"Yesterday I suddenly felt so afraid that you *weren't* lying about why you'd stopped by the house. To deliver the finishing blow, to get me to admit I loved you and then laugh at me…"

"I—I made that part up! I was so mad—"

"*You* were mad?"

"I know, I know. It's just that I had to say something. I didn't think you'd believe all those ridiculous lies, and then you seemed to and that made everything a thousand times worse. I was just beginning to hope we might have a future together."

"I was, too. That's why it hit me so hard."

"I could never intentionally hurt you, Charles. Not without hurting myself."

His eyes held hers, and everything around Steffie faded into insignificance. She was on the verge of disclosing her love when there was a knock at the kitchen door, followed by her father poking his head inside. "Is it safe yet? You two looked like time bombs about to explode twenty minutes ago."

"It's safe," Charles answered, smiling at Steffie.

"I hope you've got everything worked out because I'm tired of waiting. The way I figure it, you should be married by the end of the summer. Your oldest—"

"Dad," Steffie cut in. "I don't think Charles is interested in discussing it right now. Why don't you leave all of that to us?"

"Our oldest?" Charles asked, frowning.

"Child, of course. A girl, then a son and then another daughter. Sweethearts, all three of them. The boy will be the spitting image of you, Charles—same dark brown eyes, same facial features."

Charles glanced at Steffie as though he was questioning her father's sanity.

"I think you'd better tell Charles about the dream, Dad."

"You mean you haven't?" He sounded surprised.

"No, I didn't want to frighten him out of marrying into the family."

"What's going on here?" Charles's eyes roved from Steffie to her father and back.

"You may have trouble accepting this," David said, pulling out a chair and settling himself. He grinned, happy as Steffie could ever remember seeing him. "But I got a glimpse of the future. It was a gift from Grace. She wanted to be sure I had a reason to live and so she—"

"But isn't Grace—"

"She's in heaven, but then so was I, briefly. It was what they call a near-death experience. You can ask Colby if you want."

"Colby?" Charles repeated.

"I'm not convinced he believes me one hundred percent, but time will prove me right. Look at what's happened with Valerie and Colby, just like I said it would. And with you two. You're going to marry this little girl of mine, aren't you?"

"In a heartbeat," Charles confirmed.

Her father's grin practically split his face. "That's what I was counting on. You love him, don't you, Princess?"

Steffie nodded. "More than I thought possible," she said in a hushed voice.

David smiled knowingly and stood up from his chair. "In that case, I'll leave you two to discuss the details of your wedding. I'd like to suggest midsummer, but as I said, I'll leave that up to you." He sauntered out of the room.

"Midsummer?" Steffie shrugged.

"Sounds good to me. Does that give you enough time?"

She laughed. "Sure, and I'll be able to register for my courses, according to plan—if that's okay with you?" At his enthusiastic agreement, she added, "Uh… what do you think about Dad's dream?"

"A boy and two girls, he says."

Steffie nodded shyly.

"How do *you* feel about that?" he asked.

"Good, very good."

Charles reached for her then, taking her in his arms with the strength of a man who'd been too long without love. He buried his face in the curve of her neck and breathed deeply. "I nearly lost you for the second time."

"You'd never have lost me, Charles. I've loved you for so long, I don't know how not to love you."

"I love you, too, Stephanie. Give me a chance to prove it."

In her eyes, he'd proved it when he hadn't laughed

at her father's dream. She knew what he was thinking, perhaps because she was thinking the same thing herself. They were in love and had already decided to marry, so it didn't matter what her father had predicted after his supposed sojourn in the afterlife. It was the course they'd willingly set for themselves.

He kissed her then, and her heart seemed to overflow with love, just as her eyes overflowed with tears.

"Stephanie," Charles whispered, his lips against hers. "We have a lot of time to make up for."

"It'll take at least fifty years, won't it?"

"At the very least," he murmured, kissing her again with a need that left her breathless.

David Bloomfield relaxed in his rocker on the front porch, his smile one of utter contentment. It was all coming to pass, just as he'd known it would. Just as Grace had told him. First Valerie, and now Steffie. His grin widened.

My goodness, he thought. *Norah's in for one heck of a surprise.*

* * * * *

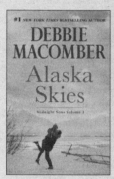 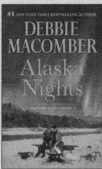 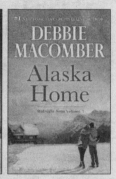

New York Times **bestselling author**

DEBBIE MACOMBER

National Bestselling Author

SHEILA ROBERTS

**Discover two heartwarming tales
in one stunning collection!**

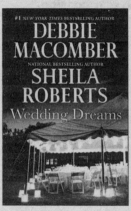

First Comes Marriage
by Debbie Macomber

Janine loves her grandfather but balks at his plan to choose her a husband. Zach, the intended groom, has recently merged his business with the family firm, and Grandfather insists it would be a perfect match. Zach and Janine agree on one thing—that Gramps is a stubborn, meddling old man. But… what if he's right?

Sweet Dreams on Center Street
by Sheila Roberts

Sweet Dreams Chocolate Company has been in the Sterling family for generations, but now it looks as if they're about to lose it to the bank. Unfortunately, the fate of Sweet Dreams is in the hands of Samantha's archenemy, Blake, the bank manager with the football-hero good looks. It's enough to drive her to chocolate.

Available now, wherever books are sold!

Be sure to connect with us at:
Harlequin.com/Newsletters
Facebook.com/HarlequinBooks
Twitter.com/HarlequinBooks

www.MIRABooks.com

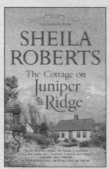

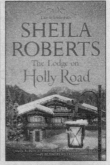
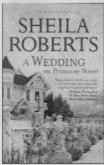
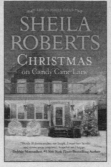
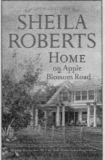

Turn your love of reading into rewards you'll love with

Harlequin My Rewards

**Join for FREE today at
www.HarlequinMyRewards.com**

Earn **FREE BOOKS** of your choice.

Experience **EXCLUSIVE OFFERS** and contests.

Enjoy **BOOK RECOMMENDATIONS**
selected just for you.

PLUS! Sign up now
and get **500** points
right away!

Earn **FREE REWARDS** Join Today! HarlequinMyRewards.com

MYR16R

Get 2 Free Books,
Plus 2 Free Gifts -
just for trying the Reader Service!

STRS17

DEBBIE MACOMBER

33019	ALASKA HOME	__ $7.99 U.S.	__ $9.99 CAN.
33018	ALASKA NIGHTS	__ $7.99 U.S.	__ $9.99 CAN.
33017	ALASKA SKIES	__ $7.99 U.S.	__ $9.99 CAN.
32988	OUT OF THE RAIN	__ $7.99 U.S.	__ $9.99 CAN.
32918	AN ENGAGEMENT IN SEATTLE	__ $7.99 U.S.	__ $9.99 CAN.
32798	ORCHARD VALLEY GROOMS	__ $7.99 U.S.	__ $9.99 CAN.
31894	ALWAYS DAKOTA	__ $7.99 U.S.	__ $9.99 CAN.
31888	DAKOTA HOME	__ $7.99 U.S.	__ $9.99 CAN.
31883	DAKOTA BORN	__ $7.99 U.S.	__ $9.99 CAN.
31838	THE MANNING SISTERS	__ $7.99 U.S.	__ $9.99 CAN.
31678	HOME IN SEATTLE	__ $7.99 U.S.	__ $8.99 CAN.
31645	TO LOVE AND PROTECT	__ $7.99 U.S.	__ $8.99 CAN.
31624	ON A CLEAR DAY	__ $7.99 U.S.	__ $8.99 CAN.
31598	NORTH TO ALASKA	__ $7.99 U.S.	__ $8.99 CAN.
31587	A MAN'S HEART	__ $7.99 U.S.	__ $8.99 CAN.
31580	MARRIAGE BETWEEN FRIENDS	__ $7.99 U.S.	__ $8.99 CAN.
31551	A REAL PRINCE	__ $7.99 U.S.	__ $8.99 CAN.
31457	HEART OF TEXAS VOLUME 3	__ $7.99 U.S.	__ $8.99 CAN.
31441	HEART OF TEXAS VOLUME 2	__ $7.99 U.S.	__ $8.99 CAN.
31426	HEART OF TEXAS VOLUME 1	__ $7.99 U.S.	__ $8.99 CAN.
31413	LOVE IN PLAIN SIGHT	__ $7.99 U.S.	__ $9.99 CAN.
31395	GLAD TIDINGS	__ $7.99 U.S.	__ $9.99 CAN.
31357	I LEFT MY HEART	__ $7.99 U.S.	__ $9.99 CAN.
31325	A TURN IN THE ROAD	__ $7.99 U.S.	__ $9.99 CAN.

(limited quantities available)

TOTAL AMOUNT	$ _____
POSTAGE & HANDLING	$ _____
($1.00 for 1 book, 50¢ for each additional)	
APPLICABLE TAXES*	$ _____
TOTAL PAYABLE	$ _____

(check or money order—please do not send cash)

To order, complete this form and send it, along with a check or money order for the total above, payable to MIRA Books, to: **In the U.S.:** 3010 Walden Avenue, P.O. Box 9077, Buffalo, NY 14269-9077; **In Canada:** P.O. Box 636, Fort Erie, Ontario, L2A 5X3.

Name: _____
Address: _____ City: _____
State/Prov.: _____ Zip/Postal Code: _____
Account Number (if applicable): _____
075 CSAS

*New York residents remit applicable sales taxes.
*Canadian residents remit applicable GST and provincial taxes.

MIRA®

MDM0517BL